OF SMOKE AND BETRAYAL

CURSED REALMS

BOOK TWO

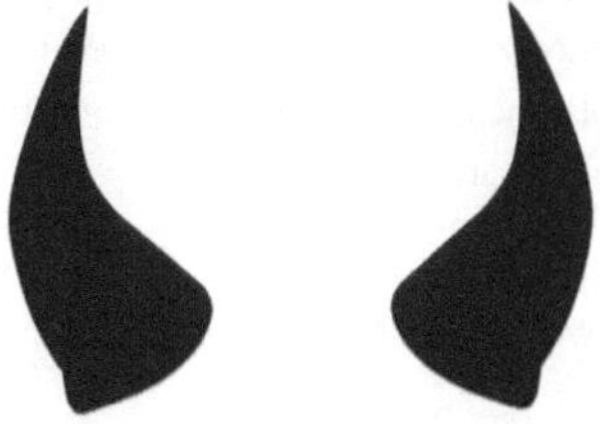

WHITNEY L. SPRADLING

Midnight Tide
PUBLISHING

First Edition

ISBN 978-1-958673-24-9 (paperback)

Published by Midnight Tide Publishing | Midnight Tide Publishing

Edited by Meg Dailey | The Dailey Editor

Cover by Etheric Designs | https://etherictales.com

CONTENT WARNING

This book contains adult themes that may not be appropriate for all audiences. These themes include: graphic on page sex and sexual content, language, the mention and discussion of suicide, mental health issues, possession, blood, death, and violence.

Suicide and Crisis Lifeline

If you or someone you know needs help, please call the Suicide and Crisis Lifeline at 988.

You are not alone. Help is available.

For those scrappy girls who find themselves being beaten down over and over.

This one is for you.

LAINEY

THE LIBRARY WAS THANKFULLY EMPTY AS LAINEY pushed through the massive wooden doors leading to the maze of shelves. In the ten months she'd been queen, this room had become her sanctuary. The domed ceiling two stories above shone with ethereal light and cast the balcony that wrapped around the upper level in a warm glow. While the first floor was cold and uninviting, the second floor beckoned, like a witch waving an enticing treat to an unsuspecting princess.

Lainey had explored every inch of the library in the ten months following the breaking of the curse over Faerie. She knew where the history section was, the political and science books, and the tomes on religion. She knew where the cranky librarian—whom she secretly enjoyed pestering—would hide in the shadowed corners to avoid her. At the top and to the right of the winding staircase, she knew there was a cushioned nook that was bathed in the golden light from the sun above—the perfect reading spot.

She also knew where the tiny selection of romance books was shelved. High up and out of reach—out of sight, out of mind. Those stories were her lifeline, the one thing keeping her afloat in the chaos of her life. Being Queen of the Unseelie Court was not all fun and games. She hadn't expected it to be, but she also hadn't expected it to be quite this awful.

Phoenix was always busy. He had meetings all day, every day. He stayed up into the night, well past the time Lainey would finally give up and go to sleep. In the morning, she would wake, and his side of the bed would already be empty. She took breakfast and lunch in solitude in her room. Dinner was the only time she saw Phoenix, and usually he was too distracted talking strategy with his councilors to notice her.

It hurt more than she was willing to admit. A physical ache in her chest at the thought of her mate forgetting her.

Lainey quickly walked through the library, double checking that it was really empty. After ensuring she was alone, she headed for the middle of the room. She spotted her quarry at the top, nowhere near where she could reach. This was why she had to ensure the library was empty. Lifting her skirts, Lainey placed a slippered foot on the shelf, stretching up with her arms to grab as high as she could reach.

As quickly as she could, she scaled the bookcase. It wasn't easy wearing a dress and slippers. She could have asked for a ladder, or found one herself, but this was more fun. A bit of rebellion in her now structured life. An adventure to get her heart rate up when it seemed to have flatlined. Lainey reached the top and scanned the titles, shuffling down the length of the shelf as she went, cursing silently when her skirts got tangled on the spines of books. *The Pirate's Mistress.* Perfect. Lainey stretched out her arm and snagged the volume.

Before she could descend, a crack echoed through the library.

Lainey froze, heart in her throat, as the shelf beneath her slippers broke and the world lurched. The book fell from her hand in her desperate attempt to find purchase with her fingers, nails scraping against the wood. A scream tore from her lungs, then cut off abruptly as she jerked to a stop. It felt as if her shoulders had been pulled from their sockets, and the pain caused her breath to leave her in a rush. With every ounce of strength she possessed, Lainey held on. Even with her toes pointed, the next ledge was too far, and so she dangled, sweaty fingers slowly slipping against the smooth wood.

A quick glance down, and Lainey swallowed around a startled squeak. Too far. Much too far. It was going to hurt when she fell.

The shelf tipped. The front slid down, sending books hurtling to the floor. They pelted Lainey in a flutter of paper and the thud of leather. Her fingers lost their purchase, and she cried out as she plummeted. She landed painfully on her back, the impact knocking her breath from her. Stars danced and swirled in her vision as she attempted to suck mouthfuls of air into her stunned lungs. Everything ached. Her back and ass throbbed, and she couldn't move. All Lainey could do was lay there in a pile of books with her skirts tangled around her thighs.

"Oh, dear," someone muttered further down the stacks.

Lainey turned her head and would have groaned if she could have gotten oxygen into her lungs. Of course Lady Voras, the biggest gossip in the palace, would walk into the library right at that moment. Her disapproving stare burned through Lainey, but Lainey refused to let her embarrassment show.

Boots thudded on the ground and Ash skidded into view, sword drawn. He regarded Lainey, sprawled in the pile of books with pieces of the broken shelf scattered around her. A slow grin spread across his face. "Are you okay, Your Majesty?" Unmistakable mirth threaded through his voice, a slight tremor where he was attempting to keep his laughter at bay.

Lainey huffed and leveled a stare at her friend. "Unless you plan on fighting the books, I don't think you need your sword." She brushed books out of the way and sat up with a grimace.

Ash was immediately kneeling by her side, sword sheathed at his waist. "Are you okay?" he asked more seriously.

"Fine," she grunted. Lainey pulled her skirts down and avoided looking in Lady Voras' direction.

"What the hell were you doing?" he asked, looking around at the paper and leather carnage.

"Trying to get a book on the top shelf." Damn it. She'd lost the book. After all that, she refused to walk away without her prize. Dignity already damned, Lainey pawed through the pile of books on the floor until she found the one she wanted.

"*The Pirate's Mistress*?" Ash's lips quirked, and his voice quivered as he tried to fight back his laughter once again. "All this for a smut book?"

"Screw you." She pushed Ash's shoulder, and he fell on his ass, laughing so hard, he had to hold onto his side. "Oh no, don't bother trying to help your queen stand. Just sit there and snicker like the useless idiot you are." Despite her harsh words, she had to bite the inside of her cheek to stop her own smile from breaking free. If Lady Voras hadn't been here to witness, she would've probably laughed too.

Ash seemed to recall they weren't alone and stood gracefully before helping Lainey to her feet. He glanced to the end of the aisle and said, "Everything is fine here."

Clearly knowing a dismissal when she heard one, Lady Voras turned on her heel and left the library in a swish of emerald skirts.

Ash watched her retreat with a frown. "Well, I give it ten minutes before everyone knows what happened here."

Lainey groaned. "Fan-fucking-tastic. Just what I need."

The Unseelie Court had been less than welcoming to her. They accepted Phoenix—he was their rightful king, after all. But Lainey, as a Sylph with air magic, belonged in the Seelie Court. Not to mention she was a half-breed. Everyone made sure she was aware of that.

Ash studied the mess on the floor. "Master Corbin will love you even more for this."

Lainey snorted. "It's his fault. I asked him to move these books to a lower shelf. He sniffed at me and walked away. Prude."

"Well, let's get out of here before he finds us and makes us clean it up."

Lainey and Ash walked through the dreary gray halls in silence. She had been warned many times about not saying anything important—politically or personally—outside of her room. People were always listening, always trying to find something to use against her. As a result, Lainey rarely spoke outside of her rooms.

The constant fear and worry were tiring, a weight she carried around daily that made each step ten times harder. She didn't like how paranoid she'd become. Every glance from a royal, every snicker or whispered word, brought a fresh wave of dread, the cold sweat making her clothes clingy and uncomfortable. She went to bed every night utterly exhausted. It was beyond her comprehension how someone could be so tired after a day of saying nothing, doing nothing, being alone.

She lived for the training sessions with Ash. Besides her maid, Cerise, Ash was one of the few people she talked to. Originally Phoenix's best friend, he had quickly become one of Lainey's as well. He was the only person she trusted with her life—besides Nix—which was why she'd made him captain of the queen's guard. Ash took his job seriously. Their daily training sessions to work on her self-defense skills, as well as her magic, were grueling, but she still enjoyed them.

The heavy wooden door to her rooms creaked on its ancient hinges as Ash pushed it open, holding it for Lainey to slip inside. She placed the book on the low table in front of the fireplace. Glancing around the room, she grimaced. This suite had originally belonged to Princess Azura, Queen Esmeray's sister. It was so dreary. The receiving room, as she was told it was called, was all dark stone and dark furniture. Shiny black floors and rough black rock walls surrounded her. The tables were dark brown wood, and scratchy gray fabric covered the couch and chairs in front of the fireplace.

She had grand dreams of fixing the place up, and not just her own rooms. The entire palace needed a facelift. Esmeray's reign had been dark and dreadful, and Lainey didn't think anyone needed a reminder of what transpired in the past. Color and light, that's what the palace needed. She just didn't know where to begin or who to talk to about it. Of course, she could always ask Phoenix, but she would have to find him first.

Ash plopped down on a chair and froze as it groaned alarmingly under his weight. "One of these days, this ancient thing is going to collapse under me."

Lainey placed her hands on her hips and studied the room once more. A black wooden door in the far left corner led to her and Phoenix's bedchamber, the only room she liked in this whole godsforsaken palace. Everything else needed a change. Feeling determined—and bored—Lainey looked at Ash. "What time is it?"

Ash huffed a breath, scrubbing a hand down his face. He'd tried countless times to teach her how to tell the time by the position of the sun, but even he lost his never-ending patience with her when she failed to grasp the concept. "We have about," he peered out of the window and pursed his lips, "four hours until dinner. Why?"

"Let's go." She grabbed a cloak, then a floppy hat from the hook by the door which she shoved on her head. It was a poor disguise, but worth the attempt anyway.

They wound their way through the palace, Ash's boots echoing off the stone walls, until they reached the main doors. Lainey was envious of his boots, and so were her feet. The damn slippers Cerise always insisted she wear provided no support. She'd lost track of how many rocks and sticks she'd stepped on in the village. It wasn't an uncommon sight to see her hopping up and down on one leg, cursing and rubbing her aching foot.

"Mind telling me where we're going?" Ash asked, pushing the large wooden door open for her. "Do I need to get a guard, or will we be okay with just the two of us?"

"Ugh." Lainey looked back at him over her shoulder and rolled her eyes. "Your serious side is *dreadfully boring*," she drawled in a fake English accent. Bounding down the stone steps and over the drawbridge, she waited until their feet were on the path to the village to explain. "I'm sick of how dreary my room is. It needs some color. And new furniture. We're going shopping."

"Do you have money for this grand scheme of yours?"

"I'm the queen, Ash. Of course I have money."

He snorted. "That's not quite how it works. I know your dad has been explaining all of this to you."

"Yes, along with 'you're wearing skirts, Lainey, keep your legs closed' and 'quit yawning, it's not queenly.' But between all the government and social hierarchy shit, my mind is mush. I don't remember anything he says. Besides, I wasn't good with money in the human realm, why would it be any different here?"

Ash chuckled and ruefully shook his head. "Oh, Lainey. I'm not sure Faerie is going to know what to do with you."

"THIS IS ALREADY SO MUCH BETTER," she declared.

She and Ash had spent the entire afternoon shopping. Despite the negative effect the curse had had on the village and its many shops, the fae were trying their hardest to get back to normal. The villagers she encountered were more than happy to supply their queen with their hard work. At least they accepted her. The fae of the court, on the other hand, were an entirely different beast.

A beautiful woven rug now cushioned the floor in front of the fireplace. The deep purple and blue, offset with the palest green, added the pop of color Lainey had been desiring. Four brightly colored paintings hung on the walls, all depicting various locations throughout Faerie. Small glass and wooden knickknacks decorated various surfaces, adding charm and character to an otherwise drab atmosphere.

"Once the furniture is delivered, it will be a completely different room," she said.

"Don't forget that monstrous light fixture." Ash leaned against the door, shaking his head at Lainey's purchases.

"Oh, yeah! That will bring it all together!"

The young carpenter, a fae whose dark, rough skin reminded Lainey of tree bark, had been all too happy to provide his queen all-new furnishings. Sturdier, more comfortable, and covered in a soft white fabric that would bring more light to the room. Then she'd walked past a shop selling blown glass ornaments, and an idea popped into her head. She couldn't resist asking the older shopkeeper if he could make a chandelier. A giant one. With glass stars and moons. He jumped at the opportunity, thankful for her support and how it would help get his shop back up and running, and he promised it would be done.

She couldn't wait to show Phoenix.

"Cerise should be here soon to help you get ready for dinner. We're hosting another noble family who defected after Esmeray's demise," Ash said, pushing off of the doorframe. "I'm going to go get ready too, so I can do a walkthrough of the dining room before you get there to make sure everything looks secure. Another guard will escort you." He turned to the hallway, muttering, "Damn, I really wish I had cameras to monitor everything."

Lainey rolled her eyes at him again, but secretly, she was grateful to have Ash in her corner. She didn't doubt there were fae in Unseelie who would try to hurt her. Especially in the courts. Having Ash by her side gave her the confidence she needed to do this job.

About half of the noble families in the court had defected, refusing to swear fealty to her and Phoenix as the new king and queen of the Unseelie court. They'd all stated their reasons were because they didn't want a king and queen who were not born and bred Unseelie. The truth, however, was they had benefited from Esmeray's rule. She'd made sure they had whatever they needed as long as they supported her. Phoenix had been meeting with them, trying his best to bring them back to court to reduce the risk of them bringing more tension and war to Unseelie's doorstep.

A knock on the door drew Lainey from her thoughts, and Cerise pushed into her room with a smile on her pixie-like face. "My lady," Cerise said as she bowed low in her black skirts, her short blond hair falling into her brown eyes. "It's time to get you ready."

Lainey sighed, headed for her bathroom, and prepared for an hour of torture filled with lace, tulle, curling wands, and cosmetics.

LAINEY

"You look beautiful, your majesty."

Lainey studied herself in the mirror and frowned. Her maid wasn't wrong. She looked beautiful, she just didn't look like herself. Didn't feel like herself. Instead of her usual black leggings, band tee, leather jacket, and chucks, Lainey wore an evening gown. An incredibly fancy evening gown. Her braided hair wound around her head like a coronet, and a small diamond tiara perched in front of the braid.

Giving the dark green satin skirts a swish, Lainey shifted back and forth in her velvet slippers. Everything about the ensemble was impractical. The skirts were heavy and kept getting tangled in her legs. The slippers were uncomfortable, doing nothing to cushion her feet from the hard surface of the marble floor. And the knife she was used to wearing at her waist clashed horribly with the dress—not that she cared about matching, but the nobles of the Unseelie court frowned upon her arming herself. What need did a fae queen have of physical weapons when she had magic to defend herself? If only Lainey were more proficient with her magic.

Instinct was a hard habit to break, and Lainey still didn't feel safe in the fae realm. She couldn't help but think of the worst-case scenario. What if she had to run? What if she had to defend herself or someone she loved? The dress and slippers and lack of weapons hindered her and threw her off balance.

Ignoring Cerise's baffled expression, Lainey kicked off the slippers, leaving them lying in the corner of the room. She dug through her closet until she found her favorite leggings—a memento from her time in the human realm—and slipped them on under her dress. At least if she had to run, she could cut the skirts and still be decent. Next, she pulled out her worn chucks and sighed as she slipped them on.

"That's much better." She grinned at her reflection.

Her maid cleared her throat, stared at Lainey with wide eyes, and said, "Yes, well. If you don't need anything else?"

Cerise barely waited for Lainey to dismiss her before hurrying out of the room. She was just as uncomfortable with Lainey as Lainey was with the whole maid situation, although she did enjoy having someone else to talk to, even if it was usually awkward and uncomfortable.

The door to the sitting room opened, and Lainey hurried from her dressing room to see who had entered. She stopped abruptly as her eyes met Phoenix's across the room. Goosebumps broke out over her skin as those copper eyes traveled over her. A smile tugged up his lip, revealing his slightly pointed teeth, and her heart fluttered in her chest. She hadn't seen enough of that smile in the past few months. Unsure what to say to him, she just stared. He was as handsome as ever. It didn't matter what he wore —leather coat and jeans or tunic and pants—Phoenix could pull off any look.

His smile faltered when Lainey hesitated. As if a heavy weight had settled on his shoulders, he sagged, swallowing thickly. "Lainey," he breathed. The yearning in his eyes was a knife to her heart.

She bit her lip before taking a step toward him. Before she knew it, his arms were wrapped around her, pulling her in close. His familiar scent of smoke and fire and the warmth of his magic surrounded her and she shuddered. A sob crawled up her throat, but she swallowed it down. God, she'd missed this. She'd missed him. Her eyes burned, and she squeezed them shut to keep the tears from falling.

Phoenix pulled back and took her face between his palms, his touch burning deliciously. He searched her face, seeing the emotions swimming in the depths of her eyes. "I'm sorry," he said and shook his head. "I haven't been here."

Not knowing what to say, she said nothing. She couldn't—wouldn't—tell him it was okay. It wasn't okay. It was so far from okay, but she didn't know what to do about it. When she'd agreed to this crazy plan of becoming queen of the Unseelie Court, she knew things would change. She just hadn't expected to lose her mate—her best friend—in the process.

Rather than trying to find the words Phoenix wanted to hear, Lainey stood on her toes, and Phoenix met her halfway. It was the first kiss they'd shared in months. She'd almost forgotten what he felt like, tasted like. Desire shot through her, turning her blood to fire inside her veins as their bond flared to life. She needed this. They both needed this.

Phoenix seemed to know what she was thinking. He pulled her closer and deepened the kiss. It still wasn't enough. Lainey needed all of him. Sliding her hands under his tunic, she ran her fingers over the heated skin of his abdomen. He growled against her mouth, the sound settling low in her gut, and he moved his hands to her back, branding her through the fabric of her dress.

The first button popped open, followed by the second and third. Phoenix ran a finger down the exposed skin of her back, and she bit his lower lip before sucking it into her mouth. The fourth button came undone, and the chill in the air teased her skin where Phoenix's heat warmed it.

"Phoenix, please," she begged. "No teasing. Not this time." It had been way too long for teasing, and they had dinner to attend in a few minutes.

Determined to make this happen, Lainey unbuttoned

Phoenix's pants, then lifted up her skirt. Phoenix chuckled but went with it. He moved his hands to the front of his pants, where his erection was fighting to escape.

Before he could move any further, a knock sounded at the door. Lainey froze and closed her eyes. She lowered her skirts, her heart dropping with them.

"Go away," Phoenix growled. "We'll be down shortly."

He reached for her, but Lainey pulled away. She knew how this was going to end.

"My king." The guard on the other side of the door knocked again. "You're needed immediately in the study."

"It can wait." Phoenix reached for Lainey again.

"I'm sorry, Your Majesty." The guard's voice quivered, as if he were scared to interrupt his king. "This can't wait."

The sound of more voices on the other side of the door sealed the deal. Lainey pulled the pieces of her heart back together. She steeled her spine and tried to smile, but she failed. Phoenix's face crumpled at the sight of her pain. He opened his mouth to speak, but Lainey interrupted him.

"Go," she whispered, eyes burning with unshed tears. "You're needed." She couldn't tell him she was the one who needed him most.

A muscle ticked in his jaw, and he sighed. He quickly fixed his pants and buttoned the four buttons on the back of her dress. Each one closing made her dress feel too tight. Turning on his heel, Phoenix strode from the room without a backward glance at Lainey, and the tears that finally spilled from her eyes.

She tried. She tried so hard to hold herself together. To ignore the pressure building in her chest. Her heart shattering and crumbling to dust. Once again, she failed. She sucked in a breath, but her chest was too tight. The air couldn't make it all the way to her lungs. Her reflection in the mirror shocked her. It wasn't just the dress that made her not look like herself. The empty, glazed eyes were new. Even after her mom and sister's deaths, she hadn't felt this hollow.

All she wanted was the person she'd fallen in love with. The man who had somehow broken down her walls and taken up residence in her heart. She had left everything behind for Phoenix. Okay, that was a bit of an exaggeration. She hadn't had much to leave behind. But she had left the only home she had ever known to start a new life in Faerie.

The first two months had been great. They'd done everything together, and Phoenix had rarely let her out of his sight. He'd always had a hand on her, either gentle strokes on her skin or twirling her hair around his finger. She had felt so loved and cherished. They had laughed together, learned together, and lived together. But after a couple of months, it all changed. Soon, Lainey saw less and less of the man she had married. She hadn't realized she could miss someone so much. Even losing her sister hadn't hurt this badly.

Lainey tore the tiara from her head, scalp stinging as strands of black hair pulled free from the braid, falling to frame her face. The tiara clanged against the marble floor as she let it fall from her fingers. She had to get out of here. Out of this empty room that reminded her of everything she was missing.

The hallways were dark and dreary as Lainey ran through them, skirts gathered in her fists, and the soles of her chucks thudded softly on the floor, the sound echoing in the silence. She stayed in the shadows, desperate to avoid anyone seeing her and wondering why she wasn't at dinner. She just couldn't paste another fake smile onto her face and make it believable.

The door Lainey was headed for appeared ahead. Plain wooden with a brass handle and set into the gray stone wall in a shadowed nook. The first time she saw it, she'd almost walked right past it. It had immediately piqued her curiosity, and she'd followed the stairs behind the door, up and up and up.

She did that again tonight, the burn in her legs welcome compared to the ache in her chest. The dark spiral staircase seemed to go on forever, but it ended at a small landing. The door to the circular room beyond had been destroyed—either by violence or decay—but the furniture inside the room remained.

The first time Lainey visited, she had kicked up so much dust, she'd been sneezing for days afterward. Since then, she had taken time each visit to clean and organize. Something about this room calmed her. Whether it was the windows that circled the entire space providing an unparalleled view of the land beyond, or the monstrous, cylindrical instrument sitting on a tripod in the middle, one end pointing to a wooden hatch in the ceiling. Or maybe it was the fact that no one seemed to know this room existed, and when she came up here, she could be herself without the eyes of the court upon her. Judging and weighing.

Lainey walked to the wall and pulled on the lever attached to the gray bricks. She grunted as it slowly moved, her muscles straining to pull harder. The groan of rusty hinges grated against her ears, and she grimaced. Palms aching, Lainey looked up and smiled. A chill wind swept in from the open hatch in the ceiling, making goosebumps raise on her arms. The night sky beyond was bright, and without the light pollution from a city, millions of stars twinkled in the vast darkness.

She ran her hand over the instrument in the middle of the room. It was some kind of ancient telescope. Every time she came here, she tried to make it work, but it was well and truly broken. In the end, she'd end up lying on the floor on a blanket she'd drug up here one visit.

For a time, she could lose herself in the burning lights of the stars and the silver moon glinting off the few clouds scuttling by. It hadn't taken her long to realize the constellations here differed from the ones in the human realm. She spent these nights creating her own and challenging herself to find them again during the next visit. Forcing her mind away from the thoughts that only caused her pain.

Footsteps sounded on the stairs, and Lainey sat up, muscles tensing. No one had ever found her up here. She searched for something to use to defend herself, while her magic swirled in her veins. Maybe it wasn't such a smart idea to come up here alone. Anything could happen, and no one would ever know.

The footsteps grew louder, and each one sent her heart racing faster. Ash's lessons rushed to the front of her mind, and she stood, situating her feet in a fighting stance. Taking a deep breath, she wiped her palms on the skirts of her dress and readied her magic. It wasn't until the soft scent of freshly cut grass hit her nose that she relaxed. A second later, Ash appeared in the broken doorway. He'd combed back his shaggy blond hair for the evening, and he'd dressed almost as finely as Phoenix. His grin was all Ash though, and something in her chest eased at the sight.

"I should have known you would find some place to hide and leave me alone down there." He scanned the room, eyes widening when they landed on the telescope. "Damn, that thing is old. Does it work?" He leaned down to peer into the eyepiece.

"It's broken," Lainey answered quietly.

Ash hummed as his hands moved over the metal. "I don't think it would be hard to fix," he said, almost too quietly to hear. He caught himself and looked at Lainey again. "What are you doing up here?"

"How did you find me?" She sat back down, arranging her ridiculous skirts around her.

"Please," Ash snorted. "It's my job to know where you are."

Lainey rolled her eyes and threw herself backward on the blanket, releasing an indignant huff.

"Should have thought about that before you assigned me as captain of the queen's guard." He sat next to her and glanced at the sky. "You definitely can't beat the night sky in Faerie."

Lainey said nothing, and they sat in silence for a few minutes, watching the stars slowly move across the inky backdrop.

"You didn't answer my question," Ash prodded.

"What question?"

He elbowed her. "Don't play dumb. It doesn't become you."

Her voice was quiet when she finally answered, almost inaudible in the circular room. "I can't do it anymore." She saw him tense beside her, but she continued, "I can't take another night pretending to be something I'm not. Watching the distance between Phoenix and me grow bigger and bigger." She cleared her throat at the roughness that gathered at her words. "I can't fake another smile and pretend everything is okay. It's not okay, Ash. Nothing is okay." Her voice cracked on the last word, and tears blurred the stars above her.

"Shit, Lainey." Ash grabbed her hand and squeezed. His callouses scraped against the ones she had built with the training they did together. "I knew you were having a hard time adjusting. I didn't realize it was that bad."

"Hard time adjusting," she mumbled, then forced a harsh laugh. "That's an understatement. I'm not a queen, Ash. The court knows it and they don't accept me. They never will."

"You need to keep trying. You need to be seen around doing things. The people have had no chance to get to know you. You always hole yourself up in your room."

"I go to the orphanage almost every day," she retorted.

"That's a start, but it's not enough." He squeezed her hand again. "I know your dad has been trying to help you. Why won't you let him?"

"We were supposed to do this together. As a team." She wasn't talking about her dad, and Ash knew it. Lainey blinked rapidly to clear the tears from her eyes. "But that's not what's happening. He's leaving me behind. He's choosing his crown over me."

"Lainey." Ash gently grabbed her chin and made her meet his stare. "You need to talk to him. Really talk to him. Tell him how you feel. Tell him what you need and what you want. That is the only way he can fix this."

She didn't want to ask, tried to keep her mouth closed, but the question escaped anyway. A whisper in the silence. "Did he even realize I wasn't at the dinner?"

Ash opened his mouth, then closed it again, pressing his lips in a tight line. His bright green eyes shone with pity.

His silence stretched, as did the bond in her chest. Was her tether to Nix growing more taut? Or was the strain of that bond just her imagination? Unable to handle Ash's stare and what his silence meant, Lainey stood. "I need to be alone," she gasped. Not waiting for Ash's response, she left through the broken door. He would follow her at a distance, and she didn't care. As long as he didn't talk to her. She headed for her room, and another night of fighting tears and sleeping alone in her bed.

LAINEY

THE OTHER SIDE OF THE BED WAS, OF COURSE, EMPTY when Lainey woke the next morning. The sheets were cold, and she couldn't tell if he had made his side of the bed or if he hadn't even slept there in the first place. She stared at the ceiling, at the beautifully carved phases of the moon above her head. The gold paint shimmered in the early morning light filtering through the window. She was almost tired of seeing it, despite how pretty it was. What she wanted to see upon waking up was her mate.

The weight of missing him pressed down on her, compressing the hollowness in her chest that grew every day. Her heart struggled to beat against the weight. It was slow and sluggish, a physical manifestation of their bond stretched to the breaking point.

"Fuck!" Lainey yelled and slammed her fists into the soft mattress. Her little outburst opened a door inside her. This had been happening more often. Whenever her anger took over, it was like it opened a gateway, allowing something dark to slither through her.

At first, she thought she was imagining things. But the more it happened, the harder it was to pretend it was nothing. That darkness would invade her mind, and for a moment, she would revel in the idea of destroying everything around her. If Phoenix was going to break her, then everyone else should have to suffer along with her. The sinister thoughts would give her pause, and that would be enough for the darkness to dissipate, taking her anger with it and leaving her mind once again soaked in sorrow.

Forcing herself to her feet, Lainey quickly dressed in a simple gown and braided her hair over her shoulder. When she stepped in front of the mirror, she grimaced. She would've killed for her old wardrobe.

Deciding she looked decent enough, she hurried out of her chambers before Cerise made an appearance. Lainey didn't want to do the fussy shit today. She was barely hanging on as it was. If she had to deal with fancy skirts and slippers, she would probably crack.

Ash wasn't waiting for her in the hallway. While she knew he couldn't spend every waking moment with her, she was always disappointed when he wasn't there. He was one of the few bright spots in her lonely days. Instead, this morning, she found Warren. Ash had picked him to be his lieutenant, deeming him trustworthy and skilled enough to keep Lainey safe. Usually, it was one of the two of them at her side during the day.

Warren dipped his head in acknowledgement. "Good morning, My Queen."

"Morning, Warren."

A flush spread across his cheeks at Lainey's use of his name. These fae were all so used to the formality Queen Esmeray had required. Lainey couldn't stand that. Treating someone as inferior to her made her skin crawl. Luckily, Warren was loosening up the more he guarded her.

Lainey made her way toward the dining hall for breakfast, something she only did once a week to meet with her dad. They used this time to get to know each other after having spent Lainey's entire life apart. Every Monday morning and Thursday evening they met in the library for lessons. Her dad wasn't royal by any stretch, but his knowledge of the inner workings of how the courts worked was helpful. He was doing his best to impart his knowledge to his daughter.

Not for the first time, Lainey wished Phoenix's dad had returned to Faerie after they broke the curse. He'd spent time as the king of Unseelie after he married Queen Esmeray in a plot to overthrow her. Unfortunately, many fae did not look highly upon him because of his past, so he'd remained in the human realm. His knowledge would have been invaluable, however.

Lainey spotted her dad as soon as she entered the dining hall. A buffet along the far wall offered breakfast foods from porridges and pastries to fruits and casseroles. The scents, usually comforting and mouthwatering, had made her stomach churn more often than not lately. Long wooden tables filled the large space with benches for sitting. Only a quarter of the tables were filled this early in the morning, and Lainey was grateful. Fewer eyes to weigh and judge her.

She quickly filled her plate at the buffet and took a seat across from her father. She studiously ignored the looks and whispers that followed her wherever she went. This time, she definitely heard the word 'library' uttered throughout the space. So, Lady Voras had indeed spread the tale of Lainey climbing and falling off a bookshelf for a smut book. Wonderful.

"Morning," Lainey muttered as she dropped her plate to the scarred table with a clang. She followed the plate, plopping gracelessly onto the bench. Decorum be damned. If they were going to talk about her, she might as well give them something good to gossip about.

Her dad squinted at her, a crease forming between his brows. "Is everything okay?"

She snorted. "Yeah, just peachy."

Zephyr resembled Lainey's sister so much, it was almost painful to look at him. His hair was the same color as Emma's when she hadn't dyed it blond. His blue eyes were identical to Emma's and Lainey's—the one trait she shared with them both. It was the smile that killed Lainey, though. When her dad smiled, all

Lainey could see was Emma, and it made her heart thump painfully behind her ribs every time, knowing she would never get another smile from her sister.

"What's the matter, Elena? I can tell something is wrong. Talk to me about it." Desperation colored his voice as he leaned in closer, hands twitching against the table as if to reach for her.

He wanted so badly for them to have a real father-daughter relationship. She just wasn't sure it was possible. She had gone her whole life thinking he'd abandoned them. For twenty-six years, Lainey had hated the very idea of her dad. The man who had caused her family so much pain and heartbreak.

It wasn't until she came to Faerie that she found him, alive and trapped by the same curse she had been about to be sacrificed for, just like Emma had been. She'd tried to open up to him in the six months she had known him. It was hard for her, though. The thought of allowing this man in, giving him a place in her heart, was utterly terrifying. She was a grown woman and had no idea how to act like a daughter in the first place, let alone to a complete stranger. Not to mention everyone who had ever been part of her life, everyone she had ever trusted, had left her. Her mom had committed suicide, her sister had been murdered.

And then she met her mate, and she let him in. She let herself fall, hard and fast, and she trusted him to catch her.

He had. But then he'd dropped her. He'd left her too. Maybe not literally, but it sure as hell seemed like he had. It was like the mate bond was some giant cosmic joke, and somewhere, whoever made these decisions was laughing their ass off. Even her mate had broken her. It was no wonder she couldn't let her dad in.

There was so much she had to work through, but it seemed like things just kept piling on top of her, slowly drowning her in emotions and feelings she didn't know how to handle. So instead of dealing with them, she brushed them under the rug to be pulled out and examined at a later date. She really was a mess. She wasn't even sure a therapist would be able to help her unpack her trauma.

Tears burned her eyes and clumped on her lashes, and Lainey squeezed her lids shut tight. *Not here, not now.* She begged them not to fall. Of course they didn't listen. One escaped and slid down her cheek. She wiped it away hurriedly, but not quick enough.

"Elena, please talk to me," her dad said, his voice soft and loving. "I want to help you, but I can't if you don't let me in."

It was too much. She couldn't breathe. The tears were seconds from spilling down her cheeks. And the weight of every noble's gaze pushed down on her, curving her shoulders inward. She stood from the table, not having touched a bite of food, and said, "I can't ... I ... I'm sorry ..."

Lainey fled the dining hall, the stares of her subjects like a fiery brand on her back. She practically ran down the hall to the front entrance and pulled the heavy wooden doors open with a grunt. As soon as she stepped foot outside, the tears fell. She collapsed onto the top step and drew her knees to her chest. Burying her face in the folds of her skirt, she let it all out in ragged sobs that wracked her chest, making the ache of longing for something just out of reach that much more painful.

Behind her, Warren's presence was like a warm ray of sunshine on her back, and she took some comfort in knowing she wasn't alone at the moment, even if he was witnessing his queen fall to pieces in public.

She really didn't know how much more she could take. All her life, she had felt alone. Sure, she'd had Emma, but she had been more of a mother figure than a sister. After she had let Phoenix in, she'd gotten used to having somebody she could rely on, someone to care for her and keep her safe. How quickly she let herself get sucked into those feelings. Now, it was as if someone had ripped the rug out from under her, sending her tumbling backward into that solitary lifestyle, and it made her question how she'd survived so long before meeting Phoenix. It was so fucking lonely.

Lainey sucked in a breath and squared her shoulders. With

shaking fingers, she brushed away the tears. This was not the time for her to lose it. Warren appeared in front of her and reached a hand down to help her to her feet, and she took it with a small, embarrassed smile pulling at the corners of her lips.

"I think you're doing a great job, considering it was only a few months ago that you didn't know this world even existed." Warren's voice was deep and quiet, speaking only for her to hear. "You should allow yourself some grace to get comfortable in this world and this new role."

Lainey studied him. His brown eyes were kind in his sharp, angled face. His nose, slightly crooked, had clearly been broken at least once. Black hair fell just below his shoulders in a smooth curtain. With thighs as thick as tree trunks and arms heavily corded with muscle, he had the form of someone used to physical activity. A guard's body.

She could understand why Ash had chosen him to be lieutenant. He was kind and caring but capable of protecting her if the need arose. Lainey smiled at him. It didn't reach her eyes, but none of her smiles did anymore. "Thank you, Warren."

He smiled back before he turned away. "Where are we headed, Your Majesty? The orphanage, I presume?"

"Yes, the orphanage."

Lainey had stumbled upon the orphanage by pure luck. She'd been walking through the village one morning and heard a baby crying. The sound had come from an alley that was dark and damp, and it hadn't stopped. When she investigated, she'd found a baby no older than one month, wrapped in a ratty blanket, lying in a broken wooden crate.

There was no one around, and Lainey knew she couldn't leave the baby, so she took it and asked the owner of the closest shop if they knew anything. They didn't but said it wasn't uncommon for that to happen. They directed Lainey to the orphanage, and she'd been visiting daily ever since.

The village was small, and the farms on the outskirts typically provided enough produce for the village and palace. As Lainey walked down the winding dirt streets, she took in the sights, sounds, and smells like she always did.

The curse had hit all of Faerie hard. The buildings were so rundown, it looked like a stiff breeze might knock them over. Vines and moss covered many of them, giving off creepy witch-like vibes. Most shops didn't even have signs over their doors announcing what they sold—you had to look inside the broken windows to know what was on the shelves. The once prosperous realm had suffered, and the evidence was still visible ten months later.

Lainey suspected the Unseelie Court had never been as prosperous as the Seelie Court, but she hoped that would change under her and Phoenix's rule.

The fae in the streets varied from human-looking to creatures not resembling anything she could have made up in her mind. Scales, feathers, and fur were common to see in place of skin. Wings sprouted from many fae, and claws tipped the hands of others. The streets were a rainbow of color, not one fae looking like another. Lainey enjoyed getting out and seeing all the inhabitants of Faerie. Because many of them were half-breeds as well, they had been more welcoming toward her than the pure-blooded nobles of court.

The orphanage was at the opposite edge of the town, butting up against an open, grassy field where the children often played. The building was a sprawling two-story that boasted many rambling additions, and the mismatched facade always made Lainey smile. It was one of the few structures that didn't have vines crawling all over it. Instead, the gray, brown, and white stones were visible for all to see.

There was no need for her to knock. Her daily visits were welcomed and enjoyed by the children, so Lainey stepped up to the simple wooden door and pushed it open, leaving Warren outside to guard the entrance. Immediately, the scent of baking bread and the sound of children laughing greeted her. A woman's voice filtered through the noise, singing a soft melody. Calm settled over her shoulders, and the tension she always seemed to be holding in them drained away as it did every time she visited.

From the first moment Lainey had stepped foot through the front door, she'd been drawn in. Everything about this place spoke to her. Growing up basically an orphan with just her sister to raise her, Lainey felt a connection with each child who lived here. And the respect she had for the women who ran the orphanage grew every day.

"Oh! Your Majesty. It's good to see you." Mira, the fae who'd been singing, widened her glittering opalescent eyes in joy. Her dark green scales shone in the early morning light streaming in through the window. Teetering a little, thrown off balance by the baby in her arms, Mira swept into an unsteady curtsy, her vibrant purple hair falling over her shoulder.

"Good morning, Mira. And please, call me Lainey," she said for what felt like the hundredth time, a repeated plea uttered every time she visited. It had yet to stick.

Mira just smiled, stepping lightly around an abandoned pile of blocks on the floor, and asked, "Would you like to hold little Dela?"

Lainey held out her arms. "I'd love to." Mira placed the little faerie in her arms, and Lainey smiled for real. "You've grown so much, little Dela," Lainey cooed to the baby. She'd been so small when Lainey found her three months ago, her iridescent green wings had been bigger than the rest of her.

Lainey ran a finger down Dela's pert little nose. The baby opened her shimmering green eyes, the same color as her wings, and blinked sleepily at Lainey before reaching a chubby fist out to grab the braid snaking over Lainey's shoulder. Lainey walked to the window and sat in a rocking chair, holding the baby close to her chest.

She'd never imagined herself having children—she'd been too busy trying to survive. But after meeting Phoenix, the thought had crossed her mind. What would it be like to start a family with him? She'd spent many nights imagining him as a dad, smiling with pride and love at a child they had created. Those dreams had quickly vanished along with her mate, it seemed.

"My Queen, is everything okay?" Mira tentatively knelt next to the chair.

Lainey hadn't even realized her eyes had closed, and that she had ceased rocking back and forth. She hastily brushed a tear off her cheek and forced a smile to her lips.

Before she could tell Mira the lie sitting on her tongue, Mira cleared her throat. "I hope this isn't too forward of me, but I want you to know you can talk to me if you ever need someone to talk to." She smiled shyly and ducked her head. "I know this is definitely too forward, but I've seen a change in you over the past couple of months. There is a sadness in your eyes that grows each time I see you. I can't imagine being thrust into the position you have been with no training and no friends. I imagine it gets lonely," Mira mumbled. Then she drew in a breath and lifted her head to meet Lainey's gaze, then said in a tone that was all kindness, "Just know that you aren't alone."

There was no pity or judgment in her shimmering eyes, just understanding and sincerity. Compassion. Lainey swallowed the lump in her throat. Her chest tightened, and she couldn't draw in a deep enough breath to fill her lungs. Mira saw right through the fake smile. *I imagine it gets lonely.* She had no idea how lonely Lainey was.

"Thank you," Lainey whispered, hoping her trembling lips weren't that noticeable.

Before Mira could say more, a sound like stampeding elephants echoed throughout the orphanage. Mira popped to her feet and placed her hands on her hips, facing the doorway leading to the main hall. The door burst open, and Mira held up a hand, halting the stampede of children in their tracks.

"Not another move," she threatened. "Queen Lainey is holding baby Dela. You will wait until she hands the baby over to me."

Once satisfied the children would not charge into the room,

Mira turned around and snagged the baby from Lainey's arms. Lainey quickly stood and prepared herself. Between one blink and the next, screaming, giggling children attacked her. She let them tackle her to the floor and laughed as they smothered her with hugs.

Twelve children lived in this orphanage, ranging in age from Dela's four months to Avo's fourteen years. In the three months she'd been visiting, Lainey had gotten to know them all. They each had a story that tugged at her heartstrings, but it was Avo's that spoke to her the most.

The young fae was leaning against the wall with his arms crossed over his chest. He had small black horns hidden in his snow-white curly hair. He was possibly the most beautiful fae she had ever seen, with dark skin and beautiful bright purple eyes that reminded Lainey of her own. The sadness that dwelled in his gaze was too similar.

When she'd first talked with Avo, he had refused to say anything personal. But the more comfortable he became, the more he opened up. His story was remarkably similar to Lainey's. Both of his parents died while he was young, and he didn't remember either of them. His older sister raised him until she died of illness when he was only seven years old. He ended up at the orphanage, where he had spent the past seven years.

The older he got, the more he helped around the orphanage. But Lainey had had an idea. Avo was frequently covered in dirt— it was caked under his nails, and the knees of his trousers were permanently stained. The garden was Avo's favorite place to spend his free time.

Lainey disentangled herself from the pile of children and ignored their pleas for a story. "I have a question for you, Avo," she said with a soft smile.

Motioning for him to follow, Lainey made her way down the hallway, the squeals and laughter of the other children fading behind her. The sitting room she ushered Avo into was mostly unused and contained a green velvet loveseat and a pair of mismatched armchairs. A bookshelf in the corner displayed paintings of past children who'd lived at the orphanage, and Lainey's heart always dropped when she saw them. How many more would be added in her lifetime? Avo waited for Lainey to take a seat on the couch before he perched on the edge of a chair.

"I was wondering," she began, "if you could do anything with your life, what would you want to do?"

His brow furrowed, and the chair creaked as leaned back. "What do you mean, Your Majesty?"

"Please, call me Lainey, Avo. I mean, when you're older, what do you want to do? You won't stay here forever, right?"

Avo swallowed and thought for a minute. "I really enjoy working in the garden out back. I like to see the things I plant and care for take root and grow. But I don't think being a gardener is something I'd be able to do. I don't have any money."

"What about a farmer? They plant food and harvest it for the town and palace to use. Would that be something you'd be interested in?"

"Yeah, I think I would enjoy that. Being able to provide for people would be nice."

Lainey smiled. "Would you want to visit a farm with me? I know of a farmer who is looking for some extra work, and he said he's willing to pay you."

Avo's eyes lit up. "Really? He would pay me to work on his farm?"

Lainey nodded. "You could continue to live at the orphanage and work on his farm during the day. He would teach you everything you need to know about farming, and if you save your money, one day you'll be able to have your own."

Tears glistened in Avo's purple eyes. "I don't know what to say," he whispered.

"Say yes. Farmer Kellen said you could start tomorrow."

The joy and excitement on his face shone as bright as the sun. "Yes!" He bounded out of the chair and threw himself into Lainey's arms. "Thank you so much."

LAINEY

LAINEY RETURNED TO THE PALACE FEELING LIGHTER than when she left. She had been making small talk with Farmer Kellen a few days ago in the market, and when he'd mentioned he needed an extra set of hands to help around the farm, she'd immediately thought of Avo and his dirt-covered pants. That thought had blossomed into a full-fledged idea.

These children would have nowhere to go once they grew up. They would have no place to live, no money to their name, and no skills to earn a job. Lainey had talked her idea over with Mira, and together, they came up with a plan. As the children got older, they'd each be paired with someone in the town who would help teach them a skill and pay them for their work.

Mira would work with them on learning how to manage their money, so they would hopefully have savings built up by the time they left. They would be prepared to find a place to live, buy food and clothing, and find a job using the skills they'd learned. Essentially, they were completing an internship.

Avo's excitement at the possibility of a future, and the thought that the other children would also have that opportunity, gave Lainey the extra boost she needed to return to the palace.

Her good mood didn't last long. As soon as she crossed the

drawbridge, Lainey spotted her dad and Ash standing in front of the main doors, waiting for her. Her steps faltered, and she only kept going because Warren's hand on her lower back propelled her forward—a silent way of communicating she wasn't alone.

Ash gave her a grim smile as she climbed the steps, his usually vibrant green eyes duller than usual. "We need to chat."

Lainey's stomach dropped to her feet. "About what?"

"In the study," her dad said with a pointed look around. It was never safe to talk in the open.

Lainey followed them into the study. She'd been silently hoping Phoenix would be there, but all that greeted her were empty chairs. A large window provided plenty of natural light, but even that couldn't brighten the overly dark atmosphere. As with the rest of the palace, black floors and walls made up the study. Dark wooden furniture only added to the bleakness. The only bright spot was the bookshelf, with spines of every color providing a pop of brilliance.

Lainey sat in a chair, and her dad took the chair behind the desk. Ash dismissed Warren and took up residence against the edge of the desk with his arms crossed.

"Phoenix has been in talks with his advisors about sending a delegation to the Seelie court," her dad said, expression carefully blank. "Your last visit there did not end well, and Queen Orabelle had been under Esmeray's thrall. We all believe it would be best to send someone to ensure Queen Orabelle is aware we mean no harm to her or her court."

Lainey closed her eyes. She could already guess where this conversation was going.

Ash took over the explanation, speaking gently. "Most of the councilors agreed you would be the best choice. You are half Sylph, so it only seems logical for you to be the one to go."

Lainey swallowed. "But, I can't do that. I don't know what to do. I'd probably just mess everything up." The thought of being a delegate to the Seelie Court made her stomach churn. What a horrible idea, sending the inexperienced one to deal with a queen.

"That's not true, Lainey," Ash said firmly. "You can do more than you think you can. However, I agree you shouldn't be the one to go. You're a queen, not a delegate. It's bullshit," he spat.

"Ash," her father warned. "The decision has been made. You won't be traveling alone. I will go with you, as I am familiar with the Seelie Court. Ash, of course, will be your guard, along with a few trusted others."

Lainey didn't hear the last part of her dad's statement. She got hung up on the fact it had already been decided. "Who made the decision?" she asked Ash, stomach dropping even more.

He turned away, refusing to meet her gaze. "It doesn't matter," he hedged.

Lainey laughed bitterly. "He's sending me away, even though we barely see each other to begin with. Is he that eager to get rid of me?"

"Lainey, that's not it at all, and you know it," Ash replied, trying to make her see reason. "He is doing the best he can, and listening to his advisors is what he is comfortable with at the moment. They recommended you be the one to go."

"But he made the final decision," she said flatly, her voice devoid of emotion. "He's the king, Ash. He can do whatever the hell he wants, and he's choosing to send me away."

"It's only for a few weeks," Ash placated. "You'll be back before you know it."

Lainey snorted and shook her head. "When do I leave?"

LAINEY WATCHED her maid bustle out of the bedroom. Everything was packed and had already been sent to the carriages. All that was left was her. She stood in the center of her room, holding her breath, waiting, wishing against all hope for that *one* person to stop by. She stood there until Ash popped his head past the door.

"It's time, Lainey."

Lainey nodded and swallowed. She followed Ash out the door and through the halls. A bubble of hope grew in her chest as she approached the main entrance. She tried not to let it get too big, but that was the problem with hope. Once it was there, you couldn't get rid of it. It just kept growing and growing, expanding with each breath you took. Until the bubble popped, and you were left disappointed.

The entryway was empty. A few servants scurried around, making sure everything was set for their departure, but that was it.

The bubble didn't pop.

Even after she walked through the front doors and saw only more servants, more guards, more unfamiliar faces.

It still didn't pop.

She stood next to the carriage and looked behind her, seeing the empty doorway. No one in the halls behind it.

Pop.

He hadn't even said goodbye.

She'd thought she knew what pain was. The constant throbbing ache that made every part of your body hurt. How the cold constantly crept under your skin, making you unable to find a single kernel of warmth to heat your aching joints. The heaviness that settled into every limb, making even the simplest of tasks impossible. How each heartbeat thudded sluggishly behind your ribs, reminding you with each thump of what you had lost. She thought she had experienced the worst of it with the loss of her family. She thought nothing could beat the pain of learning she had just lost everything that had ever mattered to her.

She'd been wrong. So very, very wrong.

This pain topped it all.

Her mate, the person who had been gifted to her by the stars, had sent her away and hadn't even bothered saying goodbye. Her chest hurt—and not just her chest, but her heart. The very bond that connected them felt pulled taut, stretched to the point of breaking, and it was crippling. Lainey pressed her hand to the organ beating behind her ribs. How could it still be beating when it felt like it was being torn in two?

"Lainey?"

Ash's gentle hand on her shoulder propelled her to turn back to the carriage. Accepting his help, she climbed inside, with Ash following behind. The door closing seemed so final. Like a chapter of her life had just ended and a new one was being ushered in. A chapter she wasn't ready to start and knew she wasn't going to enjoy. Lainey couldn't bring herself to look out the window facing the palace. She didn't think she could handle seeing that empty doorway again. Instead, she turned to the other window, although she didn't really see the landscape spreading before her. Everything was blurry, as if she were underwater with open eyes.

"Hey, are you okay?" Ash asked quietly from his position on the bench opposite her.

She turned to face him. "What did I do wrong?"

Ash's brow furrowed. "What do you mean? You've done nothing wrong."

"He didn't even say *goodbye*." Her voice broke on the last word, but the tears building on her lashes wouldn't fall.

Ash's expression dropped. He pressed his lips together and exhaled through his nose before switching seats to sit next to her. The smell of a forest after rain surrounded her at the same time his arms did. She leaned into the embrace and rested her head on his shoulder. When was the last time someone had held her?

"You've done nothing wrong, Lainey," he said quietly but firmly. "Don't blame yourself for what's happening. Phoenix has a lot to figure out. I think he just needs time to do that. Never doubt what he feels for you, though."

"How could I not doubt it?" she asked with a humorless laugh. "He sent me away, Ash. He made that decision and then he couldn't even be bothered to say goodbye." A sob caught in her throat, and she swallowed it down. "I can't even tell you the last time we had an actual conversation. I left my world to be with him. We agreed to do this together, and he is doing the exact opposite. I've never felt so alone in my life, and you know how alone I was before I met you guys." Her voice shook with each word spoken, the sobs climbing higher up her throat, threatening to sweep her away.

Ash's arms tightened around her, and he rested his chin on the top of her head. "You're not alone, Lainey. Phoenix may be doing everything wrong. But you're not alone. You will always have me. I'll be here, guarding your back, no matter what happens."

His words unlocked the gates, and the tears burning her eyes finally spilled over. Ash was true to his word, and he held her as she silently cried. The carriage carried her farther and farther away from the palace and the man she had fallen in love with. With each turn of the wheel, the tears slowed until they stopped. Her body was too exhausted, too worn down to cry anymore. For now, at least.

Lainey sat up and wiped her face. "Thank you," she said quietly.

She turned her head to the window again. The landscape passed by, but she still didn't take any of it in. She hurt too much, and she couldn't focus on anything but the pain in her chest. Her thoughts kept drifting to Phoenix and how much she missed him. How much longer could she do this? How much more could she take, physically and mentally? She was worn ragged by her constant heartache. Her body was on the verge of giving up. No matter how much she wanted to go on, the fight was quickly leaving her. At some point, she would break, and she feared that time was coming soon.

Desperate to give her mind something else to think about, she turned her attention to Ash. "Why is Faerie so ... primitive ... compared to the human realm? I mean, they have access to everything the human realm offers. Why do they still use carriages? Why no electricity?"

"A lot of the technology in the human realm doesn't work in

Faerie," Ash answered. "Electricity in particular. Something about the magic in the atmosphere interacts with electromagnetic signals or something. I don't know. I'm not a scientist." He shrugged and tossed a grin at her. "Also, Faerie has been cut off from the human realm for twenty-five years. Think of how much technology has changed in the human realm in that time. Faerie hasn't had the opportunity to keep up."

"Oh," Lainey said. "That makes sense, I guess."

They fell silent, and Lainey returned her attention to the landscape. She was used to watching things pass by in a blur as she rode in cars. In a carriage, everything moved slowly. Waving green grasses and wildflowers attempted to cheer her up, but they failed to bring her joy. Mountains stretched off in the distance, their peaks craggy and snow covered. It was beautiful, and usually it took Lainey's breath away. Today, it all appeared a little dimmer. Some of the luster and magic of Faerie was missing.

The carriage jostled her on the bench. Being so wrapped up in her pain, she hadn't realized how uncomfortable it was. The cushions weren't very soft, more like flat pancakes that provided absolutely no barrier to the hard wooden bench beneath. She shifted around, trying to get comfortable, but it was futile. It was like they hadn't been replaced in all the years they had been there and were now permanently flattened and useless.

"How long will it take to get to the Seelie Court?" she asked Ash.

"Two days. We should arrive early tomorrow evening."

Lainey groaned. Two days stuck in an uncomfortable carriage with nothing to entertain her except Ash and her depressing thoughts. She should have brought *The Pirate's Mistress* for a distraction. "This will be the longest two days of my life."

"PLEASE, Ash. I'm going crazy in here!"

"It's not safe. My job is to protect you. Let me do that.

Besides, it's only been six hours." He gave her a look, like a parent would give a child on a long road trip.

"I can't sit in here any longer. My mind won't stop circling back to Phoenix. I'm spiraling. I need a distraction. And my ass hurts." Lainey gave him her best wide-eyed pouty-lipped look. "Please, Ash. I'm begging you."

Ash turned his gaze to the ceiling of the carriage and sighed heavily. "Fine, but you have to listen to me out there. If I say get back in the carriage, you do it without question. Got it?"

Lainey quickly agreed, and Ash banged his fist on the ceiling. The jostling slowed as the carriage came to a stop, and Lainey let Ash climb out first. When he popped his head back in to say it was all clear, he helped Lainey down. She took a deep breath of the fresh magical air, letting it fill up the empty places inside her.

"What's going on?" her dad asked as he trotted back to the carriage on his horse.

"I want to ride. The carriage is uncomfortable and stuffy." She raised her hands above her head and stretched, the bones in her back popping delightfully.

"Is that a good idea?" he asked Ash, who shook his head and rolled his eyes.

"There is no talking sense into her," Ash grumbled. "I've learned it's best to not argue and just let her get her way."

"Screw you, Ash," Lainey mumbled.

Ash chuckled and slung an arm around her shoulders, turning her toward a guard who was bringing a horse their way. "You know I'm just kidding. I don't want you sitting in that carriage thinking of nothing but Nix. If riding for a while helps, then we'll make it work."

"Thanks."

He squeezed her once before taking the reins of the horse. Lainey grabbed the pommel and swung up into the saddle before reaching down for the reins. She refused to ride side saddle—she'd probably fall flat on her face if she tried—so her skirts rode up, exposing her legs. Luckily, she was wearing her leggings, but she still adjusted her dress, covering herself as much as she could. No point in giving people more to talk about.

Another horse was brought for Ash, and he rode next to Lainey as the party set off again. She made herself take in the sights, sounds, and smells. She forced herself to think of anything other than Phoenix. However, no matter how hard she tried, thoughts of him kept creeping in.

The dirt road they traveled on wound through the landscape, rising over hills and dropping into valleys. It meandered around trees and over streams, through tall grasses and colorful wildflowers. The colors were brighter than in the human realm, and there was an imperceptible shimmer in the air that made everything sparkle.

Birds sang in the trees with sounds she had never heard before. Would Nix know their names? Her chest ached at the reminder, and she pushed the thought aside. The air was fresh and smelled of something sweet she couldn't quite name. Maybe Nix could ...

Being out of the carriage was helping. Yep. Totally helping.

She rode the rest of the day. Ash remained by her side, and to her surprise, Warren did as well. She hadn't even been aware he was joining them until he rode up on the other side of her. The time passed in a blur of conversation she tried to pay attention to and the constant ache of missing her mate.

When Ash announced they were going to stop and camp for the night, Lainey stood to the side as her tent was set up. She was still getting used to having people do things for her. Inside her tent, she had a collapsible bed, a small table and chair, and her trunk filled with clothing.

Ash popped his head into the tent after Cerise had helped her get ready for the night. "Is this okay?" he asked, motioning to the inside of the tent.

"It's fine. I don't need anything fancy. I'm not ..." She stopped herself before she could say she wasn't really a queen. If she had a quarter for every time she said or thought that, she'd be able to fund the reconstruction of the village. "It's fine," she muttered.

"I'd stay with you, but that wouldn't be proper, so you'll have the tent to yourself."

She nodded. She had figured as much, but she still wished Ash could stay with her. The more time she had to herself, the more she could dig herself further and further into her depressing thoughts.

She ate a small dinner at the table, not really hungry but forcing herself to swallow each bite, then curled up in the extremely uncomfortable bed. It took her hours to fall asleep, but when she did, she wished she hadn't. Dreams plagued her all night. Dreams of Phoenix. Of him leaving her. Cheating on her. Hurting her. She tossed and turned until the sun rose the next morning.

LAINEY

LAINEY'S LEG BOUNCED UNCONTROLLABLY, CAUSING the whole carriage to rock. She couldn't seem to get her fingers to stop tapping a rhythmless beat on her thighs, and her lip was sore from how much she'd chewed on it.

"Relax, Lainey," Ash said, seated across from her. His arms were spread along the back of the carriage seat, looking for all the world like he didn't have a single worry.

"Easy for you to say," she snipped. "You don't have to meet a queen while acting like a queen, something I have no idea how to do." Sighing, she let her head thump against the back of the bench. "Sorry. I didn't mean to bite your head off. I'm just..." She stalled out. Too many words vied for attention, and she didn't know which one to pick. Scared? Exhausted? Unsure? Heartbroken? Take your pick.

"I know," Ash said softly. "But you can do this. You have been doing it for months now. I have complete faith in you."

"Well, you're either crazy or stupid for having that much faith in me." She looked out the window and muttered, "Probably both, knowing you."

Ash snorted and opened the carriage door. Once he hopped out, he reached back to help her down. The Seelie Court palace was much nicer in appearance than the Unseelie palace. Neatly manicured vines climbed the facade of the white stone structure. Three tall turrets soared high into the sky, each capped with a golden roof.

There were no steps leading to the front entrance, but massive stone pillars held up an overhang that created a porch-like appearance. Intricately carved dark wooden doors opened, and a fae woman dressed in a pale gray dress stepped out and waited for them to approach.

Hopefully, the hospitality had improved from her last visit, where she'd been unconscious when she arrived and thrown into a cell. Her death had hung over her head the entire time as the Seelie queen tortured and prepared to kill Lainey to keep the curse from being broken.

"Are you sure this is a good idea?" she asked Ash quietly as they approached the front doors.

"Not at all," he replied through a tight smile that looked forced. "But I'll be here, and I won't leave your side. Warren will also be with us the entire time, so we're doublemint baby."

"Doublemint?" Her brows furrowed and she looked at Ash in confusion.

"Yeah. Double the flavor, double the fun." He grinned at her. "Doublemint gum. You'll have double the protection with me and Warren."

She groaned at the almost-dad-joke quality to his statement, but a smile pulled her lips up. Leave it to Ash to calm some of her nerves with an old gum commercial. Still, as she came to a stop in front of the grand doors, she surreptitiously wiped her hands on her skirts and swallowed.

"Welcome, Your Majesty," the fae in gray said as she bowed low. "I am Rose, the head of staff for the palace. It would please me greatly if I could show you to your rooms. Queen Orabelle has dinner planned for this evening to welcome you to the Seelie Court."

"Thank you," Lainey replied with a nod of her head. She was

pulling from every movie she'd ever seen in the human realm that depicted royalty of any kind. If she hadn't been so terrified, she'd probably have laughed at how much she felt like Mia from *The Princess Diaries*. Never in her life had she ever felt so connected to a fictional character. Hopefully, no one saw how nervous she really was. It took all of her self-control to keep her hands still and not fist them in the fabric of her skirts.

"Your help will be taken care of in the staff quarters, and your guards may stay in the barracks." She gave Lainey a small, polite smile and tilted her head to the open doorway. "Everyone else may follow me."

Lainey, her dad, Ash, and Warren followed Rose through the palace. Lainey recognized little from her last visit here. Granted, she had been a prisoner, destined to be murdered, thought the man she was falling in love with had betrayed her, and had just found out her father was still alive, so she'd had other things on her mind.

The pale marble floors were veined with gold, and colorful paintings and tapestries hung on the white stone walls. In every nook and cranny, there was a sculpture or carving resting on a marble plinth. It was the exact opposite of the Unseelie palace. Day versus night. Light versus dark. Good versus evil.

Rose led them up a grand curving staircase to the second floor and down another similarly decorated hallway. She stopped in front of a door and motioned with a graceful wave. "This is your suite, your majesty. Your companions may stay in the room down the hall. Dinner is served just after sundown. Please ring the bell if you need anything."

With a small curtsy, Rose departed and left Lainey standing in the hallway. Was that what was supposed to happen? Was she being slighted? No one appeared concerned, and Rose had been friendly enough, but she couldn't shake her insecurities. She wished she knew more about the rules of royalty. Despite her dad having taught her everything she needed to know, in the moment, all of it seemed to have flown right out of her head. *This is why I'm not cut out to be a queen.*

Ash opened the door and stepped into the room. He signaled to Lainey to wait while he checked for any danger. When he was sure it was clear, he motioned her inside. The setup was similar to her rooms at the Unseelie palace: a receiving room with a bedroom and bath off to the left. The difference was the light and airy atmosphere, and decorations of silver and green. She itched to run her fingers along the smooth fabrics and scrunch her bare feet into the soft rug. It was a beautiful suite, and it was more welcoming than her own back in Unseelie.

"See, this is the kind of room I could live in," Lainey said.

Ash snorted and sat in a chair by the fireplace.

"So, what now?" Lainey asked as everyone settled in around her room.

"We wait until dinner," her dad replied.

Lainey's dad took the time to give her a crash course on the Seelie Court and the way things were run. It was a lot of repeated information, but Lainey listened to it all, thankful for the refresher and the distraction from the constant ache of her crumbling heart. She also used the time to prepare herself mentally for meeting Queen Orabelle again.

"What happens if things go badly?" she reluctantly asked.

"Warren and I will get you out however we can while your dad creates a distraction," Ash answered. "You need to make sure your magic is ready to go. Have a shield primed, as well as a weapon. You do really well with freezing someone in place, so that plus a couple throwing daggers, and you'll be good."

"I really don't think it will be necessary," her dad added. "Queen Orabelle has always been a kind and just ruler. Her actions during the curse were because of the influence Esmeray had over her. But, like Ash said, it's better to be safe than sorry."

"Don't let—" A soft knock on the door followed by Cerise poking her head in cut off whatever Ash was going to say.

"It's time to get ready, Your Majesty," Cerise said with an

awkward curtsy as she juggled the bags and garments in her hands. "I have something I think you will like," she continued, with an excited sparkle in her dark brown eyes, after everyone filed out of the room. "I had a dress made for you a month ago, and if you like it, the seamstress said she could make more."

Lainey groaned inwardly. She could only imagine what Cerise had asked the seamstress to make, but it wouldn't surprise her if it included more tulle and lots of glitter. Lainey stripped out of her traveling dress—a simple dark blue garment with a matching jacket—and raised her arms to let Cerise drop the new dress over her head.

When the fabric settled, Lainey gasped. "Cerise! I can't wear something like this. It's way too revealing."

Lainey approached the floor-length mirror and stared at her reflection. The dress—if it could be called that—was dark green. The bodice was tight with sheer long sleeves that came to points on the tops of her hands. Delicate gold beading adorned the bodice and sleeves in whirls and swirls.

The problem was the bottom half. It almost reminded Lainey of a wrap dress in the human realm. The skirt was completely open in the front, attached to the bodice with golden thread.

Lainey turned from the mirror to find Cerise standing with a smile on her face as she held up a pair of black leather leggings. "These go under it, Your Majesty."

Lainey grinned as she snagged the leggings from her maid and tugged them on. When she turned back to the mirror, she laughed. "I love this, Cerise. It's perfect." They weren't as stretchy or comfortable as her leggings from the human realm, but they were better than nothing. She would be able to move freely in the skirts, making it easy to run, fight, and reach for her weapons if needed.

Cerise handed her a pair of black leather boots. "I thought you may like it. I noticed you usually wear those old leggings under your dresses. Along with those shoes. These boots may look better."

Lainey wanted to hug her. She refrained, though, and pulled the boots on, lacing them to just under her knees. Cerise quickly brushed her hair and curled it, leaving it in loose, shiny waves over her shoulders.

As she stared at herself in the mirror, with black kohl thickly lining her lashes, in her new boots and leggings, Lainey felt more like herself than she had in months. Despite her cheeks and collarbones looking more pronounced from weight loss, it was enough to bring tears to her eyes. "I can't thank you enough for this, Cerise," Lainey whispered as she fanned her face to keep her tears from falling.

"Would you like me to have more dresses made like this?"

"Yes, please!"

Cerise nodded and bobbed a curtsy just as there was a knock on the door. Her maid rushed forward and answered it, admitting Ash.

He stopped in the middle of the room as his gaze landed on Lainey. His mouth dropped open before a slow smile lifted the corners of his lips.

Lainey twirled and said, "Looks good, right?"

"You look like a badass," he laughed. "That is the perfect dress for the Unseelie queen."

"You think?"

"Absolutely. I can see you starting a new trend within the court."

Lainey grinned, but the smile faded quickly. What would Phoenix think of her new look? It was darker and edgier, both things Nix would have loved just a few months ago. Now, he probably wouldn't even mention it, if he even looked at her to begin with. She closed her eyes, took a deep breath, and squared her shoulders. It wasn't time to think of her mate. She needed to be in the moment for this dinner with Queen Orabelle. Thoughts of Phoenix would have to wait.

Dinner was held in the queen's private dining room. A large glass table took up most of the space, with a small raised dais in the right corner where a musician played soft music on some kind of string instrument Lainey had never seen before. Potted green plants with large yellow blooming flowers lined the white marble walls, and a chandelier of hundreds of candles hung from the ceiling.

A few of the noble court members had been invited and were already seated at the table when Lainey entered. The women all wore flowing dresses in the palest of pastels, while the men wore pale gray trousers and white shirts that buttoned to the neck. They all stood and bowed or curtsied as Lainey entered, which only made her nausea grow.

Seated near the head of the table, to right of where Queen Orabelle would sit, Lainey nervously fidgeted with the edge of her skirt under the table. She wished her dad had been able to attend, but he hadn't been invited. At least Ash was standing guard behind her chair. His presence and the scent of green things comforted her. And knowing Warren remained outside the dining room to guard the entrance gave Lainey an extra boost of comfort.

The door opened and Queen Orabelle swept into the room, followed by two guards. Her dress was pale blue and made of the most flowy fabric Lainey had ever seen. The skirts seemed to swirl around the queen on a phantom breeze. Then again, they probably were. Queen Orabelle was an earth elemental, and one of the ways earth elementals and sylphs overlapped was the ability to harness wind.

Everyone stood as the queen approached the table. The men bowed low at the waist, and the women curtsied. Lainey dipped her chin as her dad had directed her to do. A queen greeting a queen. Equals.

"You may take a seat," Orabelle said in a melodic voice.

Lainey shivered as she sat. The last time she heard that voice, it had been threatening to torture her. She swallowed thickly and kept her attention on the porcelain plate before her.

"Queen Elena, it is a pleasure to have you visit," Orabelle said.

Lainey jumped at the use of her title, still not used to hearing "queen" before her name, even after ten months. She wasn't sure she would ever get used to that. "Thank you, Your Majesty. I'm looking forward to my visit."

Lainey watched Queen Orabelle closely for any signs of anger. Her black hair was curled and piled on top of her head. A silver crown, designed to look like crashing waves, perched in front of the curls. The queen's beautiful purple eyes were bright against her skin, despite the shadows dancing in their depths, but there were no signs of anger on her face.

The queen signaled with the lift of one finger, and servants entered carrying silver trays laden with food. They dished out the meal and disappeared in a routine that appeared almost like a dance. Lainey had the briefest mental picture of *Beauty and the Beast*, with the singing and dancing silverware and china. She shook her head to clear it of that image and tuned into the tail end of the queen's toast.

"To many years of happiness."

"To happiness," everyone said together and raised their glasses.

The food on her plate looked delicious—some kind of roasted meat in a creamy sauce with the brightest vegetables Lainey had ever seen—but her stomach rolled and tumbled. She feared she'd be sick, throwing up anything she managed to eat, even though she knew she had lost too much weight recently.

Lainey picked at the food, moving it around the plate to make it look like she had eaten more than she had. The servants kept her wine glass filled, but she only took a few small sips. She needed to keep her head clear. Conversation flowed freely between the nobles and the queen. They had the appearance of a group of people who spent a lot of time together and were comfortable with each other. She paid attention to the conversation, but they kept it light and free of any topic that would cause drama—talk of their children, of the latest fashions and newest plays showing at the theater.

Lainey tried to ignore the awkwardness that made it seem like she was watching everything happen through a foggy window. With each deep breath she took, she tried to wipe away the condensation, but it just kept spreading, blocking her view and keeping her separated from everyone else. It was nothing new for her, but it made her uncomfortable. If they had sent anyone else to be a delegate, they would probably have been engaging in conversation and asking questions.

Lainey was too unsure of herself to do that. She didn't know what was appropriate to talk about and what wasn't. She lacked the experiences these people had in the Faerie realm. Were the plays they mentioned similar to the ones in the human realm? She couldn't bring herself to ask for fear it would alienate her even more. Instead, she kept her mouth closed and counted down the minutes until she could return to her room.

When the queen finally stood from her chair, Lainey exhaled in relief. She stood with the rest of the dinner guests and dipped her head once again as the queen left. Lainey sat for a few more minutes before Ash subtly tapped her back. With another sigh of relief, she stood from her chair and nodded at the nobles, who also stood and bowed to her, before leaving the room.

Back in her chambers, Lainey collapsed in the chair by the fireplace with her arm across her eyes. "That was absolutely awful," she muttered as she peeled off her boots with her free hand.

"It wasn't that bad," Ash said and sat next to her. "You could have talked a bit more, but I get it."

"You didn't say much?" her dad asked.

"She didn't say anything." Ash pulled her feet into his lap and dug his thumbs into her arch.

Her dad gave her a look, one of those an exasperated father gives his misbehaving child, which she ignored. Whatever. She was doing the best she could.

"As a visiting royal, you will get an invitation to talk with Orabelle tomorrow. Until that happens, a guide will provide you a tour of the palace." Her dad walked to the door as he talked, ushering Warren in front of him.

His tone grated on her, like he was chastising her before she even did anything wrong. And he wondered why she was struggling to let him in. She wasn't used to having a father figure in her life, let alone one who imposed his authority over her.

He paused at the threshold, looking back at her with hope lighting his bright blue eyes. "I can also send word to some family. You can meet with them sometime this week, should you wish."

"That would be nice," she said honestly. It would be nice—but at the same time, it made her itch under her skin. More people she had to put on a fake smile for. More people she had to impress when she couldn't even impress her own court. The constant back and forth of her emotions was exhausting. It was like she was on a roller coaster and she couldn't just feel one thing. Excitement, confusion, hope, fear, loss, betrayal. It was too much, and she was just so, so tired.

"It will be done, then. Get some rest, Lainey. Tomorrow is an important day."

Lainey nodded as her dad and Warren left. Ash and Warren would be taking turns staying in Lainey's sitting room. It wasn't protocol—they should stay in the hallway—but Ash was more comfortable with someone in the chambers. Lainey was too.

Ash stood, depositing her feet on the couch cushions. "Your dad's right," he said gently, dropping a kiss to the top of her head. "Get some sleep. Tomorrow is a big day."

Lainey nodded and headed toward the bedchamber. Before she could close the door behind her, Ash spoke up again.

"And, Lainey? I'm proud of you."

She nodded her head, but tears blurred her vision as she stripped for bed and climbed under the covers. When was the last time somebody had said they were proud of her?

ASH

ASH'S EYES WATERED AS HE YAWNED FOR THE hundredth time. He knew he should be paying attention, but he was bored out of his mind. History had always been his least favorite subject in school, and this tour of the Seelie palace was the epitome of boring history. Even though the information was interesting, and a part of his life he'd never been able to experience, he just couldn't listen to another word the old fae was droning on about.

The fae in question was quite possibly the oldest fae Ash had ever seen. His skin was paper-thin and so wrinkly, he looked like a Shar Pei. Wisps of white hair framed his face, but the top of his head was completely bald. Ash wasn't sure he had ever seen a fae so old that they had lost their hair.

His voice was dry and monotone as he recited the history of the Seelie Court like he was reading from a textbook. This dude had probably been alive at the creation of Faerie and lived through everything he was explaining.

Ash was thankful Warren was with them because he at least appeared alert while he scanned their surroundings. Someone could have snuck up on Ash and he wouldn't even notice. He shook himself, trying to physically wake himself up. Lainey's safety was his top priority, and he would not fail her.

He watched Lainey as she attempted to pay attention to the history lesson. She kept shuffling her feet, and she'd had to hide multiple yawns behind her hand. Her usually bright blue eyes were dull, but he knew it wasn't because of boredom. Watching her slowly unravel was becoming more and more alarming, and he knew if things didn't change, he would have to step in.

This little half-breed had wormed her way into his heart, and he would do anything he had to for her. As soon as he'd met Lainey, he knew there was something special about her. It had been so easy to befriend her, and his instincts as a fae male had awoken at the idea of having someone to care for. Someone to protect. He'd done that, and he would keep doing that.

Phoenix had always been his closest friend, the one person he could rely on through thick and thin. But right now, Ash wanted to tear into him for what he was doing to Lainey. She'd lived through hell in the human realm. She'd left the only world she knew to rule a world she knew nothing about. Despite everything she had been through—all the loss and heartache, all the surprises and discoveries—she had remained strong.

But she was finally breaking.

Ash didn't know what to do. He'd tried to talk to Nix, but the man had brushed him off, saying something about his relationship with Lainey being none of Ash's business. Bullshit. Lainey had become almost as good a friend as Nix was. It was one hundred percent his business if Nix was hurting her.

"Why are you staring at me?" Lainey whispered. She'd scooted closer to Ash but was still nodding and pretending to be interested in what their guide was saying.

"You have something on your face," he murmured.

Lainey's eyes widened, and she wiped her face with her hand before seeing the smirk pulling up the corners of Ash's lips. She discreetly elbowed him. "Asshole."

Ash chuckled and slung his arm around her shoulders. Fuck

propriety. "I was just thinking how grateful I am to have you as a friend." He kept his voice low, but the guide was so immersed in his lesson, he wouldn't have noticed an asteroid hitting the palace.

Lainey's shoulders lifted as she took a deep breath, then leaned into him. "I don't think I've ever thanked you for everything you've done for me. I can't put into words how much your friendship means to me."

"No thanks needed, little half-breed."

She huffed a laugh at the use of his nickname for her. Neither of them moved as the guide wandered off around the corner, oblivious to the fact he had lost his audience.

Warren cleared his throat. "The guide has moved on."

Ash grinned at Lainey. "What do you say we blow this popsicle stand?"

"Blow this popsicle stand?" Warren muttered with a furrowed brow.

Lainey laughed, but the smile quickly faded. "I can't. We should catch up."

She slipped out from under his arm and hurried around the corner. Warren followed quickly, while Ash lingered a second longer.

He had to do something. He couldn't watch Lainey break any more than she already had.

They endured another thirty minutes of mind-numbing history before a servant came and informed them Queen Orabelle was ready to meet with Lainey. Ash was relieved to end the tour, while Lainey looked utterly terrified.

"You'll do great," Ash whispered in her ear as they followed the servant through the halls. "Just be honest with her. Tell her what happened and that you have no plans to hurt her court. And I'll be with you the entire time."

Lainey nodded and swallowed. He looked behind him and raised a questioning brow at Warren, who also nodded. They were both ready to protect Lainey at all costs.

The servant led them through the halls, and Ash took in the

scenery while monitoring their surroundings. The Seelie Court was much nicer than the Unseelie Court. Maybe Lainey was right about sprucing up their new home. The atmosphere in the Seelie palace was lighter, not as oppressive. Tapestries and gilded paintings depicting the flora and fauna of Faerie hung on the walls, while statues of past Seelie queens stood watch in the corners. It was vastly different from the dark and brooding hallways of the Unseelie palace.

They stopped in front of a light-colored wooden door, and the servant knocked twice before opening and ushering Lainey and Ash through the doorway. Warren remained in the hall, once again guarding against any threats from the outside. Inside the Seelie queen's personal audience chamber, Ash took up position against the wall, while Lainey stood nervously, waiting for Orabelle's greeting.

Bright light filtered through large floor-to-ceiling windows that took up the entire length of the back wall. Beautiful gardens with a myriad of colorful flowers beckoned from the other side, and Ash itched to walk the paths between the blooms and let his magic free. Two pale pink chaises faced each other across a low table spread with trays of delicious-looking desserts and a porcelain tea set.

Queen Orabelle relaxed in one chaise, with a guard silently posted behind her. When Lainey entered, she stood and offered a dip of her chin. Her flowing, light purple gown swirled around her and accentuated her violet eyes.

"Please, sit." Orabelle nodded her head to the chaise across from her as she perched on the edge of her own.

Lainey quickly sat, arranging her split skirts to cover her legging-clad legs. If she noticed Orabelle's look of distaste as she eyed her dress, she didn't show it.

Orabelle waved an arm toward the low table between the chaises, and bracelets jingled on her slim wrist. "Help yourself to some tea and pastries."

The pot of tea trembled slightly as Lainey poured herself a

cup. She took no pastries, and Ash could almost hear her thoughts about dropping crumbs on herself in front of another queen, although he would've been more worried about spilling the tea.

"I am glad you could visit," Queen Orabelle said as she set her cup on a delicate-looking saucer.

He listened closely but could hear nothing negative in Orabelle's voice. She was polite, and possibly even genuine.

"There is much for us to discuss. But first, I would like to apologize for my actions the last time you visited." A shadow passed over Orabelle's eyes as she spoke. "As you are aware, I was under Esmeray's thrall. I would never have agreed to keep the curse in place had I been in my right mind. My people and my lands are my number one priority. It pains me greatly to see the shape they are in and know I was the cause of it."

Lainey said nothing. She raised her cup to her lips, and Ash watched as she tried—and failed—to hide her grimace. He had to bite his cheek to keep from laughing. Lainey hated tea. Coffee with a healthy dose of whiskey was her go-to.

Luckily, Orabelle was too lost in the past to notice. "My thoughts were not my own," she continued, "and I regret the pain I may have caused you. I hope in the future, you will be able to forgive me."

Ash's eyebrows jerked toward his hairline, and his jaw wanted to fall to the floor, but he hid his shock behind a forced bland expression. Not that he had ever met a queen before, but he'd never pictured one to be so humble. It impressed him that she had admitted her fault and asked for forgiveness.

Lainey set her teacup on the table and folded her hands in her lap. "I understand, and I do not blame you for your actions."

A relieved breath rushed out of Orabelle. "I suppose before I jump to hoping for a friendship, I should ask about your plans for the Unseelie Court."

Friendship? Lainey looked slightly taken aback but quickly recovered.

"My ... mate ... and I hope to restore Unseelie to its former glory." Ash's heart broke at the way she hesitated on the word "mate." "We have no nefarious plans for you or your court. In fact, I would like to talk about opening the borders between the courts for trade."

This time, it was Ash who was taken aback, jerking so suddenly, he bumped the wall behind him. He blinked, then blinked again as he processed Lainey's words. This was not part of their plan—although it was a good idea. Lainey was just supposed to assure Queen Orabelle of their good intentions.

Trade between the courts had ceased during Esmeray's reign. Both courts had suffered greatly for it. The Seelie Court had always been more carefree and was known for their art and music. Unseelie had always had to work a little harder for their well-being and were known for their scientific discoveries. With no trade between the courts, Unseelie had lost a tremendous amount of income, not being able to sell their discoveries to the Seelie court. Not to mention the impact the lack of arts had on the people.

Lainey sighed and shook her head. "Look, I'm just going to be real with you."

A bemused expression crossed Orabelle's face, and Ash smiled. Lainey was over pretending to be something she wasn't. He was sure this was going to get interesting.

"I'm sure you realize I know nothing about being a queen. I barely know anything about Faerie. My dad told me what it used to be like, and that is what I want. I want to bring Faerie back to what it used to be. He told me that when Esmeray was on the throne, all travel between the courts stopped. I would love for that change. I would love for our people to travel freely and get to know each other. I would love for Seelie to bring everything you offer to Unseelie and vice versa. I just feel like there is so much we could do together." Lainey stopped her rushing words with a click of her teeth. She squeezed her hands tightly in her lap and waited for Orabelle's response.

The queen smiled. "That is a noble goal, and one I can get

behind. I agree. A lot of harm came from Esmeray's reign, and trade between the courts needs to be reinstated. I would love to be part of bringing Faerie back to life."

Lainey exhaled. "Good, because I don't think I could do it alone."

Orabelle studied Lainey for a second. "You know, being a queen isn't easy. Being a queen in a land you know nothing of is even harder. I think you are doing a great job, and I would love to help you as well. We can all use friends now and then, wouldn't you agree?"

Lainey was silent for a moment, probably debating the best course of action. Ash wanted to tell her to take the queen up on her offer. From everything he had heard about Queen Orabelle, she was an honest person. Lainey seemed to come to the same conclusion.

"I would really appreciate that," she said quietly.

Queen Orabelle smiled. "Good." She clapped her hands together once and sat up on her chaise. "I heard you have some family in Seelie you would like to visit. Take today to do that. Tomorrow night, I'm organizing the first ball since everything happened, and I'd love for you to be our guest of honor."

Ash watched pain flash across Lainey's face before she schooled her expression into something resembling excitement. If he had to guess, he would have said the first thought to cross her mind was attending a ball without Phoenix. Her first ball, to be exact. He clenched his jaw tightly at the anger he felt toward his best friend. The temptation to beat sense into Nix was so strong, he had to take a cleansing breath. How the idiot couldn't see what he was doing to his mate was a mystery to Ash. When they got back to Unseelie, he would have to talk to Nix again. And use any means necessary to make him see sense.

"I would love that," Lainey replied. "I've never been to a ball."

"It will be lovely," Queen Orabelle said as she stood from her chaise. "Maybe we can talk more tomorrow. Informally, of course." She offered Lainey a kind smile.

"Thank you. You're right. It would be nice to have a friend."

Ash opened the door for Lainey, and she passed by him into the hallway. He nodded his head toward Queen Orabelle before following Lainey out.

"Opening the borders for trade, huh?" he asked as he fell in next to Lainey.

She shrugged. "Seemed like the right thing to do."

Ash grinned. He raised his hand to ruffle the hair on top of her head. "I'm so pwoud of you, my wittle baby queen," he said mockingly.

"Stop it!" She knocked his arm away and set about straightening her hair.

"But seriously, I am proud of you. You're going to do great."

Lainey made a noncommittal noise in the back of her throat as they rounded a corner and ran into her dad, pacing the length of the hall.

"How did your meeting go?" he asked. The nervous energy he put off was impossible to ignore, and his brown hair was mussed like he'd run his hands through it multiple times.

"It went pretty well, actually," Lainey said almost defensively. "She mentioned something about a ball tomorrow night, and I didn't bring anything to wear to a ball."

"Maie will be able to figure something out," he answered. "Speaking of, a bunch of our family has gathered at the bakery. Would you like to meet them?"

Lainey swallowed then nodded. "Yeah, I think I would."

LAINEY

A DELICIOUS ASSORTMENT OF BAKED GOODS, AS WELL as various flavors of tea, sat upon the quaint tables throughout Glaze and Honey, Maie's bakery. Lainey wanted to enjoy them, but her nerves were getting the better of her. She picked at a raspberry torte, but it tasted like ash on her tongue. So many members of her family had shown up—aunts, uncles, cousins, and even her grandmother—and Lainey was drowning.

"You're doing great." Aunt Maie smiled kindly and laid her hand on top of Lainey's.

Everyone kept saying that, but she was having a hard time seeing what they were seeing. How could they possibly think she was doing great? She was barely holding it together. If they could have gotten a glimpse inside of her, they'd run away screaming. She was an absolute mess.

Her family attempted to engage Lainey in conversation, and she replied politely with short, succinct answers. *How do you like living in Faerie?* It's different, but fine. *Do you miss the human realm?* A little bit. *What do you like most about Faerie?* The landscape and the colorful flowers.

Everything she said fell short and seemed to bring every conversation to a screeching halt, but she didn't know what else to do. They didn't understand her or her situation. They had no clue what she had gone through before she came to Faerie, or what she was going through now. And they didn't truly try to get to know her—not that she wanted them to. Sharing her life story was not something she wanted to do.

The awkwardness was getting to her, crawling under her skin like millions of tiny spiders, making her twitchy. She was self-conscious and unsure of everything, and she didn't know if she should act like herself or the queen. Should she ask questions or just listen politely? She second guessed every answer she gave. Just in case they thought she was fidgety or eager to leave, she tried not to move too much. The anxiety of it all was unbearable.

Lainey had never been self-conscious before, but she'd never had so many eyes on her at one time either. Everyone was studying her. They were trying to figure out who she was, this long-lost daughter of Zephyr. She had returned to them, but she hadn't returned as just a normal fae. She was a queen. And a queen of the Unseelie Court to boot.

Conversation rolled around her, and she heard her name being mentioned, but the sounds were all blurring together. She couldn't pick out individual words, and even as she tried to decipher what was being said, it became harder and harder. Sweat rolled down her back and between her breasts. It wasn't a warm day, but Lainey felt as if she were sitting in a sauna. It was hard to draw in breaths, and the more she focused on her breathing, the more difficult it became, until her vision faded and blackened at the edges.

A heavy hand on her shoulder startled her. "Let's go for a walk," Ash whispered in her ear.

His voice was like a light at the end of the tunnel. It was a tether she could grab onto to pull herself from the depths of her panic. Lainey stood in a daze and let Ash guide her through the front door.

Outside, without the multitude of eyes on her and surrounded by fresh air, Lainey took a deep breath.

"Better?" Ash asked with a comforting hand on her back.

She shook her head. "Physically? Yes. Mentally? Emotionally? Not even close." Her voice broke on the last word. She pressed her trembling lips together in the hope that she could keep herself from crying.

Ash peered around before tugging her down the alley next to the bakery. It opened onto a small grassy area that was thankfully empty of people and out of sight of anyone walking through the town. He sat on the grass and pulled her down next to him.

"It's okay to cry, Lainey. It doesn't mean you're weak or unfit to be queen." He wrapped an arm around her shoulders and pulled her close. His heart beat steadily in his chest, and his familiar and comforting scent of nature flooded her senses. "You're only human ... well, fae ... but you get what I'm saying."

"I shouldn't be here," she whispered. "I shouldn't be doing this. I don't belong in Faerie, Ash. This was a mistake. *All* of it was a mistake. I never should have agreed to becoming queen." Her words poured out of her, no breaths between as she rushed to voice them. She had to get them out. She had to make *someone* see the truth. "I could do this with him. I'd be strong enough to handle all of this if he was with me." Tears built along her lashes and fell down her cheeks, each one a representation of her pain, heartbreak, fear, anxiety, and self-doubt.

"Don't say that, Lainey," Ash gently reprimanded her. "You don't need anyone to do this. You're strong enough and smart enough on your own. You don't need Phoenix—that fucker," he muttered before continuing. "He doesn't make you someone else. You are still you, with or without him."

"I'm not so sure I am. I mean, I know I don't know much about being fae, but I can feel him." She placed her hand over her heart. "I can feel the bond between us. It gets thinner and weaker every day, Ash. What happens if it disappears? Can that happen? Does anyone know? Because I'm not so sure who I would become if that day ever occurred."

"That day won't ever occur. I promise you, I will do

everything in my power to make sure that never happens." He pulled away and placed his hands on her shoulders, turning her to look at him. "And if it does, you will still be Lainey. You will still be the same scrappy girl from New York City who survived so much—lost so much—and still came out on the other side swinging."

Lainey shook her head and wiped away her tears. She didn't know how to tell Ash that she didn't think he was right. Each passing day, the bond between her and Phoenix shriveled a little more. Each bit of shriveled bond exposed more and more of her soul, and it was different than it used to be. The darkness brewing inside of her was very slowly eating away at the light inside of her.

And what scared her the most was that she wasn't scared of that darkness.

Some small part of her wanted to welcome it. She wanted to give in to it. Let it fill her, consume her, and utterly destroy her. It was a terrifying and exciting thought.

Lainey squeezed her eyes shut and inhaled a huge breath, filling her lungs to bursting. When she released it, the darkness rising inside of her slowly ebbed away. It would be back, though. It always came back.

"Do you want to head back to the palace?" Ash asked as he watched her closely.

She nodded. "Yeah. I don't think I can handle much more today."

"Do you want to say goodbye to your family?"

"I know I should, but I just … I can't." She looked at him, eyes wide and begging him to understand.

Ash motioned to Warren, who had been guarding the alley, and he jogged toward them. "Can you tell Zephyr we're heading back? Lainey's tapped out."

Warren's brows scrunched. "Tapped out?"

"She's exhausted and can't handle much more," Ash clarified for the fae.

His expression cleared, and Warren nodded before heading back to the bakery.

"Can we walk? Please?" Lainey asked Ash. Her lungs constricted just thinking of the confining space of the carriage.

Ash grabbed her hand in response and led her through the streets. She tried to distract herself with the sights and sounds of Seelie. It was so different from Unseelie, and it broke her heart. It didn't seem fair there was such a difference between the two.

While Seelie was run-down from the curse, you could still see the beauty hiding under the layers of grime and overgrown gardens. The once quaint structures lining the main street were grayed and dilapidated, but they were slowly being updated. Fresh coats of paint covered many of the shops, and fae were actively working on replacing crumbled stone and rotted wood. Children pulled weeds and planted new flowers under the watchful eyes of their elders.

It differed vastly from Unseelie, where one could tell the state of the town had already declined prior to the curse. Buildings were falling down and being overtaken by vines. Any color had long since faded away, and gardens were nothing but dead weeds. It was rare to see a window still intact. Walking through Unseelie gave Lainey the distinct impression of walking through an old-school New York City ghetto.

As she walked, she made plans in her head. It helped her take her mind off her own pain. There needed to be a committee that was devoted to fixing, and eventually the upkeep, of the Unseelie Court. She would have to talk to the treasurer, or whatever he was called in this realm, to determine a budget. And Mira would be a good person to ask about villagers who'd be interested in helping.

Before she knew it, Lainey had arrived back at the palace and had to once again put on a fake smile. It was late enough that she didn't run into many people on the way to her room, but the few she did see stared at her for her unconventional dress. This, at least, she was used to. It almost brought her comfort, this subtle but familiar rebellion against the norm. She'd never been one for conventional clothing in school. Black had always been her favorite color, and her clothing was proof of that. Leggings or skinny jeans, sweatshirts, band tees, and the occasional leather jacket had been her staples.

They reached Lainey's rooms, and Ash took the first watch outside her door. She quickly changed into a nightgown—which was still super weird to her—and threw her hair into a messy bun on top of her head before climbing into bed. The soft mattress practically swallowed her as she settled in.

Phoenix would have hated this mattress. He preferred a slightly harder surface to sleep on. She shrieked into the silence, banging her fists uselessly against the soft padding, and mentally kicked herself for thinking of him. When was the last time she'd fallen asleep with him? Five months? More? She really needed to sit down with him and talk about things. The problem was getting him to stay still long enough to listen to her. She couldn't believe how much it hurt to think about him. It wasn't the typical pain one felt from losing someone, whether to death or a break-up.

This pain was physical. It felt as if something inside her chest was being torn into pieces. If she had to guess what a heart attack felt like, she would have said this was similar. She didn't think it was her heart that was hurting though. It was the bond. The ribbon that tied her and Phoenix together. The connection that had grown every day after she had given him her blood to heal him.

She had felt that ribbon grow into existence and become more and more prominent as they spent time together the first few months after they took up their crowns. But lately, that ribbon was shredding to pieces. Becoming thinner and thinner the more time they spent away from each other.

Lainey had cried so much lately she didn't think she had any more tears. Instead, she lay in bed, alone, feeling each shredded piece of ribbon waving in her chest, while her eyes remained dry. She supposed she was reaching her breaking point. The point where she had no feelings left to feel. Just empty and numb. Like after Emma's death. Phoenix had been the one to bring her out of that numbness. Now he was pushing her back into it. It scared her to think about what would happen when she stopped caring altogether.

LAINEY LEFT Queen Orabelle's personal receiving chamber covered in sweat. They had talked for almost two hours, and Lainey had never once relaxed during their conversation. Orabelle did her best to make Lainey feel comfortable. She'd been wearing a casual dress and no crown, but there was no forgetting who she was.

Lainey second-guessed everything she said to Queen Orabelle, just like she had with her family. She worried over each movement of her body. She dissected every word out of Orabelle's mouth, searching for some kind of hidden meaning. For all Lainey could tell, Orabelle was being honest. She was truly looking for a friendship. The thought, while comforting, was utterly terrifying.

Lainey had never had friends. Growing up, Emma was her only friend. At least now she could consider Ash a friend, but it was different with him. Natural. Easy. Trying to befriend a queen was another beast entirely.

In her chambers, Lainey collapsed face-first onto the couch with a huff, one leg on the cushions, the other hanging off the edge. Her dad looked up from the book he was reading with a raised brow.

Ash smirked from his chair and sat back with his legs spread casually. "That rough, huh?"

"I was on guard the entire time," Lainey replied, words muffled from the couch cushion. "It was exhausting. I have no idea how to even be a friend."

Ash made a noise in the back of his throat. "Not true. You just have to be yourself. Believe it or not, you're a very likable person, Lainey. You just have to let people see the real you."

Lainey shook her head. Letting people in was the hard part. It always backfired. So far, the only person in her life who meant something to her that hadn't hurt her was Ash.

Her dad inspected his hands resting in his lap. Lainey knew he blamed himself for the pain she had felt growing up. And in a way, she blamed him too. It wasn't fair to him, but some part of her couldn't let it go.

He cleared his throat and looked up, sadness swimming in his blue eyes. "Maie and Nin will be here shortly to help you get ready for the ball," he said, changing the subject.

Lainey groaned. The ball. Two words she never imagined she'd say outside of sports. Because honestly, who even held balls anymore? The closest thing she'd ever encountered was prom, and she hadn't even attended that. For one, she hadn't been able to afford a dress. For another, it wasn't really her scene. Now she'd have to attend one and face it and all of its strangeness without Nix, without her mate, surrounded by people she didn't know. Thinking about it exhausted her further.

"Anything I need to know about ball etiquette?" she asked flatly, sitting up with a huff.

Her dad took a breath and drew himself up for another long lecture on manners while they waited for Maie and Nin to arrive. He explained everything she needed to know about attending a ball. She tried to memorize it all, but there were so many nuances she knew she would forget something.

As the visiting royal, they would announce her just before Queen Orabelle. When Orabelle entered, Lainey was expected to greet the Seelie queen with a nod and a kiss to either cheek. Throughout the ball, drinks and hors d'oeuvres would circulate, and Lainey could only accept them from a servant wearing a special crest on their shoulder. She wasn't allowed to drink more than three glasses of wine or eat more than two hors d'oeuvres.

There were more rules, but already her brain was slowly pushing out the excess information.

Lainey ran through the rules over and over in her head until there was a knock on her door. Warren opened it from the outside and let Maie and Nin enter. Various types and colors of fabrics overflowed from Aunt Maie's arms, and Nin carried a basket filled with what Lainey assumed was makeup and hair products.

Maie smiled warmly at Lainey. "I brought you some options." She hefted her arms and grinned at the dismay on Lainey's face. "I'm sure we will find something you approve of."

"I'll see you later tonight, Lainey," Ash said before he left her room with her dad.

Lainey took a fortifying breath before facing her aunt. "I will not wear anything pink or purple."

Maie laughed. "I had a feeling. I brought only darker colored dresses. Seemed more fitting for the Unseelie queen. And I told your maid we'd help you get ready. I hope that was okay?"

Lainey nodded and watched as Maie laid the dresses out on the back of the couch. There were four altogether. Two red—one dark, the other bright and vibrant—a deep purple, and a navy blue. The dark red dress was something she'd never have chosen for herself, with a deep neckline and curve-hugging design. But ... Phoenix would have loved it.

The second one that caught her eye was the deep purple dress. She'd told Maie no purple, but this garment was such a dark purple, it was almost black in certain lighting. Criss-crossing layers of tulle made up the bodice with a sweetheart neckline. Clear crystal beads adorned it in diagonal lines that reminded Lainey of shooting stars. Sheer billowing sleeves hung off the shoulders and cuffed at the wrists. Layers of tulle flared out from the waist to form a full skirt.

Lainey ran her fingers over the tulle. "This one."

Maie and Nin helped her dress. It was weird. It felt like something she would have done on a prom night with her mom and sister. A rite of passage she never got to experience. If she thought too hard about it, her eyes would blur with tears, so she focused her thoughts on the movements her body made rather than the deeper meaning behind them.

"Where did you get these dresses?" she asked Maie. "They're all exquisite."

"Your cousin, Avella—whom you haven't met yet—is a seamstress," Maie said as she adjusted and fluffed the skirts. "She works for a lot of the ladies in the court. These dresses were all ordered but never picked up after the curse began. They have been lying in her shop collecting dust, and I thought they were all about the right size for you."

"And of course, she was right," Nin added. "This dress fits like it was made for you."

Lainey brushed her hands down her belly, smoothing out the material. Nin grabbed her hands and led her to a chair, where she began curling and pinning Lainey's hair while Maie started on her makeup. They chattered away while they worked, and Lainey attempted to join in. She just felt too out of place. No matter how welcoming they were to her, she felt as if she didn't belong.

She wasn't sure where she did belong.

Maie and Nin stepped back to admire their work. Maie clasped a hand to her mouth, and Lainey could have sworn she saw unshed tears shimmer in her aunt's eyes.

"You look just like your grandmother when she was younger. If you had blond hair, you could be her twin."

A punch to the gut she wasn't expecting knocked the breath from her lungs. She immediately pictured Emma wearing this dress. With her blond hair and blue eyes, looking so much like their dad, Emma would have been exactly what Maie was imagining.

Not for the first time, Lainey wondered what Emma would have made of all of this. She wouldn't have had any trouble adjusting to Faerie, and she would have just jumped in, guns blazing, and been right at home here. She wouldn't have second guessed her every word, every move, every breath. Emma should have been the one. Not Lainey.

"Hey," Maie said quietly. "Why the sad face?"

"I was just thinking about my sister. This is something she would have loved doing."

"I am so sorry, Lainey." Maie took her hands in her own and squeezed them gently. "It is never easy to lose a sibling."

Shadows crossed Maie's face, and Lainey remembered she had also lost a sibling. Aldric had died helping rescue Phoenix.

"It's all my fault," Lainey whispered.

"I don't want to hear that from you, Lainey." Maie crossed her arms and fixed her stare on Lainey. "He knew what he was risking when he agreed to help. I'm glad you could get your mate out of the dungeon."

Lainey couldn't stop the flinch. Her mate. Phoenix. The one who was actively breaking her heart.

"Lainey?" Aunt Maie asked. "Is everything okay?"

"Is it possible for mate bonds to be broken?" Lainey whispered, then immediately clamped her mouth shut. She had not intended to say that out loud.

Maie's eyes widened, and Nin's mouth popped open. When Lainey's gaze traveled to her, she snapped it shut with a click of her teeth.

"Why are you asking?" Maie queried.

Lainey wrapped her arms around her middle and curved her shoulders inward. Damn her internal filter for not catching that before she spoke.

Maie sat on the couch and pulled Lainey down next to her. "You know, you can talk to me about anything."

Lainey bit her lip and swallowed down her words. She had already made the mistake of saying something she shouldn't. Instead, she fidgeted with the skirts of her gown and wished she could take her question back.

"Are you second-guessing the bond?" Maie asked. "It's okay if you are. You've been through a lot lately."

Lainey shook her head. "It's Phoenix. We've hardly talked to each other in the past few months. He didn't even say goodbye when I left." She placed her hand over her heart. "I feel like … I feel like the bond is breaking. I'm scared it will disappear."

"A mate bond can only be broken by choice. There is an entire process you have to go through for that to happen, and both parties have to be involved." She narrowed her eyes at Lainey. "It is odd you feel like it is weakening. Even if you were to both ignore each other for years, the bond would still be there."

Lainey chewed on her cheek. It definitely felt as if the bond was slowly disintegrating. She felt further from Phoenix than she ever had. Even the blood bond had been less of a pull the last time she had been in his presence.

Shaking her head, Lainey forced a smile to her face. "I'm sure it will all be okay."

A knock at the door and Warren popping his head in the room drew their attention. "Ready, My Queen?"

"Yes, thank you." Lainey took a deep breath and stood, squaring her shoulders.

Maie stood and brushed her blond hair over her shoulder. "Lainey—"

"Thank you for helping me get ready," Lainey interrupted. One look at the concern in Maie's eyes had Lainey hurrying toward the door, eager to avoid any kind of heartfelt discussion. "Let's get this over with," she muttered as she passed Warren and entered the hall.

ASH

He was running late. Ash hurried through the hallways of the Seelie palace and mentally berated himself. *Stupid, stupid Ash. You had one job, jackass.* He had been talking to Lainey's dad and lost track of time. They were both concerned about her, about her weight loss and depression, but neither of them knew what to do. He was planning on talking to Phoenix when they returned to Unseelie, but he wasn't sure how Nix would respond.

Lainey wasn't the only person who had noticed a change in him. Ash hadn't seen Phoenix any more than Lainey had, but the few times he *had* seen his friend, he hadn't been the same person Ash grew up with. Phoenix had always been reserved and drawn apart from others, but he had never been distant from the people he cared about.

Phoenix was the epitome of a fire elemental. He burned hot for his loved ones. He was a protector, someone you could always count on to have your back, and he would do absolutely anything to make you happy. But since he'd taken up the crown? It was like he'd become someone else entirely. There was no more friendly banter. No more hanging out just for shits and giggles. There was no more checking in, making sure everything was okay. Nothing. It was all gone.

The closer Ash got to the ballroom, the more fae he saw in the hallways. He slowed his steps so he didn't draw too much attention to himself. Slipping into the ballroom, he stood against the wall and scanned the room. The Seelie queen had spared no expense for the first ball since the curse.

Magical twinkling lights floated near the ceiling and cast a soft glow over the marble dance floor. Pale green fabric wrapped around the pillars and shimmered with an inner light. Vines climbed the walls, and massive white flowers bloomed on them. Ash ran a finger over one of the soft petals, and his magic hummed in response, a soft vibration under his skin.

A band played in the corner of the ballroom, sending haunting and ethereal music floating over the heads of the fae on the dance floor. He spotted Warren along the opposite wall, and he followed his line of sight until he saw Lainey chatting with a group of fae.

Fuck. Nix should have been here to see his mate. She looked beautiful in the dark purple dress, with her black hair curled softly and falling over her shoulders. Her smile would fool the people who didn't know her, but it didn't fool Ash. Despite the small curve to her lips, her eyes were unfathomably sad. She hadn't even looked that sad after her sister's death.

Guilt rose within him, mixing with the despair that choked him every time he saw Lainey break a little more. Had he been doing enough to make sure Lainey was okay? Was there more he could do? When they got back to Unseelie, Ash would make sure Nix took his head out of his ass. There was no other option.

He made his way along the wall until he stood next to Warren. "Everything going okay?"

"As well as can be expected," Warren replied. "She seems to be doing okay. At least most people appear to be falling for the act."

It didn't surprise him that Warren was aware of Lainey's

unhappiness. He was incredibly perceptive, which was one reason he was such a great guard.

After a few more minutes watching Lainey, Ash told Warren he would be in the solarium just down the hall and he excused himself. It seemed safe enough, and he knew Warren would protect Lainey. He didn't want her to see him and latch onto him. As much as he loved her company, and as much as he was glad he could be an anchor for her, she needed to stand on her own. He didn't want to go far, though.

He wandered through the indoor garden for over an hour. He loved gardens. Being in one was like a recharge of his magic. Gardens, and nature in general, were comforting places to him. He always felt at home in nature. Inhaling the humid, earthy air, Ash's shoulders lost their tension for the first time in months. As he walked on the meandering stone path, he let his fingers trail over leaves and petals, giving each plant a little jolt of magic.

His parents had ensured their children knew as much of their heritage as possible. Ash had studied the books his dad brought from Faerie whenever he'd had a chance, and Faerie horticulture had quickly become his favorite subject. So much so, his dad had to frequently make trips back to Faerie to get new books.

It was on one of these trips that the curse locked the gates and separated his dad from the family. The guilt he experienced after that had been crippling, and Nix had been the only one who could get through to him. When they broke the curse, Ash had spent the first two months searching for his dad. He hadn't found him, and he tried to not let himself think about it too much. Hopefully it meant his dad had returned to the human realm as soon as possible.

Ash plucked a flower from a bush and sat on a bench in the middle of the garden, twirling the flower between his fingers. The petals were velvety soft. The color was the palest blue he had ever seen. It kind of reminded him of a mix between a lily and daisy, with long petals like a lily but the number and shape of petals like a daisy. It wasn't a flower found in the human realm. Was it an ameredium? No, that wasn't it. A meadow bell? No, those were yellow. A—

A shout ripped him from his thoughts. The flower slipped from his fingers to be trod under his boot as he took off at a run back toward the ballroom. Fae were streaming from the room, some crying, some screaming, some quiet but afraid. His heart stopped in his chest as a patrol of guards with weapons drawn pushed their way through the crowd and past the double doors.

Ash took off after them, elbowing fae out of the way and ignoring their angry glares. He had only one thought in his head: Lainey.

Ash craned his neck to see over the crowd, still trying to evacuate. His heart stopped again when he saw a body prone on the floor and a circle of guards around it. It didn't resume beating until he realized the dress was pink and not dark purple. His gaze traveled the perimeter of the ballroom, and he breathed a sigh of relief.

She was okay. Lainey was standing behind Warren, peeking around his larger frame. She was shaken, if her wide eyes and white-knuckled grip on his arm were any indication. Ash worked his way through the last remaining fae.

"Are you okay?" he asked.

Lainey nodded her head, her black hair falling over her shoulders, and she reached for Ash. He wrapped her in a tight embrace, anxiety draining from him. Lainey was okay.

"What happened?" He peered over his shoulder at the girl laying on the ground.

She wasn't moving. The guards made way for a healer, who approached and knelt next to the body. Ash didn't need any magic to know the girl was dead. He could tell her chest wasn't moving, and her skin was already turning a sickly shade of gray. Her outstretched arm appeared to be reaching for pieces of a shattered glass. The pale green stem the only piece still intact.

Zephyr's lessons came back to him. Only the royals drank out of glasses with pale green stems, served by special servers. What was this girl doing with one of those glasses? Ash watched as the healer reached a finger out to one of the broken pieces, and a soft light flared from her hand. She recoiled and held her hand tight to her chest.

"Poison." The softly spoken word echoed through the mostly empty ballroom.

Queen Orabelle, surrounded by a force of guards, shifted on her feet. "How did she get one of those glasses?" the queen asked.

Lainey took a deep breath and stepped away from Ash. "She got it from me," she whispered. "I forgot about the three drink rule after I'd already grabbed the glass. I gave it to her. I ... I didn't even think about it."

The blood in Ash's veins froze, and he glanced at Lainey. "That glass was meant for you," he said. "Someone tried to poison you."

ASH HANDED Lainey a glass of water. She took it but looked at it skeptically.

"It's okay. I collected it myself," he reassured her. He sat next to her on the couch in her sitting room and glanced at Zephyr. "What now?"

They had filled Zephyr in on the attempted poisoning. Lainey sat quietly through the entire conversation, her eyes slightly glazed as if lost in thought. If Ash knew her at all—and he did—he would've bet she was contemplating this whole queen thing again. He frowned as he watched her. One day, he would have to show Lainey how capable she was at this gig. Now wasn't that time, however.

"We leave at first light," Zephyr said, voice and hands shaking. He hadn't taken his eyes off Lainey since they had told him someone tried to kill her. "Because we don't know who did this or how many more there may be, we need to get her home as quickly as possible."

"I agree." Ash bit his lip as he thought through what happened tonight. "Lainey was clearly the target. She only accepted food and drink from certain servants, so it had to have been a targeted attack."

"I was thinking the same thing, but I can't figure out why someone in the Seelie Court would want to hurt Lainey." Zephyr's brows drew down, deepening the laugh lines around his eyes. "She poses no threat to Seelie. In fact, she has helped Seelie by removing Esmeray and breaking the curse. It makes no sense." He shook his head, bewildered.

"Esmeray had to have supporters here," Ash replied slowly. "That is the only thing I can think of. She would have had people here watching Queen Orabelle. Maybe they thought to get revenge?"

"Maybe," Zephyr murmured. "But to me, something isn't adding up."

Ash tensed as someone knocked on the door. Lainey scooted closer to him, closing the little distance between them. He gave her a reassuring squeeze on the arm as Warren stood to answer the door.

Queen Orabelle entered and quickly waved a hand when they all attempted to stand and bow. "No need for that," she said kindly.

Zephyr stood and nodded his head, motioning to his now empty chair for Queen Orabelle to sit. She smiled and took his seat, arranging the skirts of her ball gown restlessly.

"I am terribly sorry for tonight, Queen Elena. I assure you, I did not know that was going to happen. My guards began searching and questioning immediately, and I believe we found the person behind it. The only thing is ..." She trailed off, studying Lainey intently. "This person claims his orders came from someone in the Unseelie Court. We tried to get more information out of him, but he grabbed a knife from a guard and took his own life before they could stop him. We are currently questioning more servers to ensure he was the only one."

Ash's blood froze in his veins. Someone from Unseelie ordered this? Who would have done that? It was no secret that many of the nobility didn't like Lainey, but to go so far as to have her poisoned? "Thank you for this information," he said to Queen Orabelle. Lainey was in no position to respond. She trembled next to Ash, so much that the water in her glass sloshed over the side. "Unfortunately, we feel the safest course of action is to leave in the morning." Although it appeared Unseelie wouldn't be any safer.

"I understand," she replied. "Is there anything I can get for you in the meantime?"

"Thank you," Ash said, "but I think we're okay."

Queen Orabelle stood and headed for the door. "If you think of anything, please ring the bell." With those last words, Queen Orabelle swept out of the room.

They fell into silence after Orablle left. No one said anything, too stunned to even comprehend Orabell's words. Eventually, Warren stepped outside to guard the door while Zephyr and Ash remained outside the sleeping chamber after Lainey settled in for bed.

Ash couldn't help but second guess everything. What the hell had they gotten themselves into? There had always been a risk of danger when they came to Faerie. And Lainey had had her fair share of near-death experiences, but something about this one hit him hard. If she had drunk that poison, there would have been nothing he could have done to save her. He would have lost her, just like it seemed he'd lost Phoenix. He wasn't sure he could handle losing Lainey too.

There hadn't been many times in his life that he'd been afraid. But this was definitely one of those times. Terror swept through him so fast, so powerfully, it made his legs weak. He'd always taken his job of protecting Lainey seriously, but now the stakes had been raised. And for the first time, he wondered if they were doing the right thing by remaining in Faerie.

LAINEY

She had been back in Unseelie for two days. She remembered little of the journey home, mainly because she'd slept most of the way to stave off boredom. Ash hadn't let her ride, insisting it was safest for her to remain in the carriage. She didn't blame him, but damn, she had almost gone crazy in the cramped space.

Phoenix hadn't come to see her when she got back. It didn't surprise her, but it still hurt, like an open wound that had been rubbed until it was bloody and raw. Ash had told him about her being targeted and almost poisoned, as well as their suspicion about where the order had come from. And even though Ash tried to phrase Phoenix's response nicely, she had gotten the gist: He didn't care. Lainey was positive he wasn't even sleeping in the same room anymore. Every morning, his side of the bed hadn't been touched. His smell no longer lingered on their sheets. She was about at her breaking point.

And the darkness growing inside her kept whispering things that were driving her closer to that point. *It was Phoenix. He ordered the poisoning.* The more she heard it, the more she believed it.

All of her free time the past two days had been spent at the orphanage. It was her safe space. Somewhere she belonged—the only place in Unseelie she had a place. Her plans for the internships took a lot of her focus, as did finding villagers who wanted to be part of the rebuilding committee. She was grateful she had those two things to fall back on to keep herself busy and her mind occupied.

But in those silent moments, she was drowning.

"Your Majesty?"

Lainey shook herself out of her thoughts. Cerise stood in front of Lainey's open wardrobe with a raised brow and her head tilted to the side.

"I'm sorry," Lainey sighed, running her hands through her hair. "What did you ask?"

"Which dress did you want to wear tonight?"

"Did you have any more of the dresses with leggings made?" If she had to suffer through a political dinner, she at least could feel somewhat like herself.

Cerise smiled broadly. "Yes, I did." She pulled two dresses down and held them up for Lainey's inspection.

They were the same style as the first dress, with split skirts and leggings, only with different colors and decorations. One was dark blue and seemed more casual, with fewer embellishments. The other was black, with swirling gold stitching and beading. The phases of the moon traveled up both sheer sleeves, and glittering stars adorned the bodice and split skirts.

Lainey fingered the black dress. "This is beautiful," she murmured in awe.

"The perfect dress for the Unseelie queen," Cerise said quietly.

"Then this one it is," Lainey said, then untied her robe.

Cerise quickly helped Lainey into the dress and leggings and began working on her hair and makeup. Lainey sat in silence, contemplating everything. She could just leave. Travel to the gate tree and go back to New York. No one would have to know, although she was sure her dad and Ash would figure it out pretty quickly. She had nothing there, but it seemed like she had nothing here either, besides heartbreak and the possibility of death.

Ash's friendship was the only thing preventing her at the moment. That and the orphanage. She felt a duty to them to stick it out and help those children. The problem was, she didn't feel she had a duty to the rest of Unseelie. The citizens of Unseelie were accepting enough. The higher class made it blatantly clear they did not want her. Part of her stubborn streak wanted to stay just to piss them off.

But how much longer could she stay and feel the bond with her mate disappearing? How much longer could she handle the pain and loneliness that surged forth when she thought of Nix being so close but so, so far away?

"Your Majesty?"

Lainey blinked and pulled her hand away from where it had been rubbing her chest. When she forced her thoughts away and refocused, she found Cerise standing in front of her with a small frown on her pixie-like face.

"If I may be so bold, is everything okay?" she asked tentatively.

Lainey forced a smile. "Yes, everything is fine. Just a lot on my mind." She looked in the mirror and gasped.

Cerise had done a fantastic job at making Lainey look like herself yet regal like a queen. Her eye makeup was dark, with black wings and thick lashes. The lipstick was a red so dark, it bordered the line between red and black. Her black hair fell in a smooth, straight sheet down her back. A simple golden band perched on her brow and sparkled in the candlelight.

Lainey stood and took in her entire appearance in the mirror. She looked like the queen of the underworld—badass, beautiful, and intimidating.

Ash popped his head inside her rooms. "Ready?"

"Yes." Lainey turned toward the door, and Ash's jaw dropped. He whistled. "You look amazing, Lainey."

"Thanks." *Maybe Phoenix will notice me tonight. Not that I need to look a certain way for a man to notice me.* She hated that that was the first thought to pop into her head.

Ash walked with Lainey down the halls of the palace. "Our guests tonight are pretty high priority," he said. "Lord and Lady Davers, two of Esmeray's fiercest supporters when she was on the throne. Nix's goal is to figure out where they stand now and decide how true their words are."

Lainey swallowed. "Is there any risk?" She forced her hands to unknot from the skirts of her dress as she remembered the girl drinking from her glass and falling dead to the floor.

"No major risk, no." Ash shook his head, but his eyes continued scanning their surroundings. "Someone will test your food before it's delivered, and you are to only eat and drink food served by Leif."

Leif, another guard and Warren's significant other, had proven trustworthy rather quickly. He was young but capable, with broad shoulders that looked like they could carry the weight of the world.

"I will be within arm's length of you at all times. Warren and your dad will also be there, along with the rest of your guard."

He wasn't taking any chances tonight, and that eased some of her anxiety. At least the anxiety she felt about her own safety. She was more nervous about seeing Phoenix after not having spent any time together in weeks.

Before they entered the grand dining room, Ash pulled Lainey to a stop. He turned her to face him and placed his hands on her upper arms. "Just ... Just stay strong tonight, Lainey," he said with a gentle squeeze. "You look beautiful and you are an amazing person. Don't forget that."

Her nerves fluttered harder in stomach. If Ash was giving her a pep talk, he must have thought things would go poorly. She nodded and reluctantly pushed open the dining room doors.

The room was beautiful, one of the few in the palace that was decorated nicely with furniture that wasn't dreary and falling apart. The black walls and floors shone in the candlelight. Golden candelabras and chandeliers provided ample light even in the nighttime hours. The glass table took up much of the room, and the massive arrangements of white and red roses sitting on top of the glass perfumed the air.

Members of the court filled the table, and not a single one stood to pay their respects to the queen. Not that she cared too much. Having all that attention on her would have been unnerving, but it grated on her knowing they disliked her that much. Even the Seelie court members had stood when she entered the dining room, and she wasn't their queen.

She had eyes only for her mate, though, as she walked around the table. Phoenix was seated at the middle, as was customary in the Unseelie Court. The closer to the center of the table, the higher your status. Lainey's steps faltered briefly when her gaze landed on him. She would never not think he was handsome. The slight point of his ear was visible through his brown hair that caught the light of the candles. The red in the strands burned to life under the flames. She silently begged him to look her way. She wanted to see those swirling copper eyes.

He was too engrossed in conversation with the couple sitting across the table to notice Lainey taking the seat next to him. Or he was just ignoring her completely. Lainey settled into the chair and paid no mind to the stare from the lady across from her, who could only be Lady Davers. The disgust in her dark brown eyes almost choked Lainey.

Lady Davers was beautiful. She had faint lines at the corners of her eyes, which told Lainey she was fairly old. Fae didn't show their age until they were at least three hundred years old. Her dark blond hair was piled high on her head in loose curls. She wore a dress in the typical Unseelie fashion—dark colors, tight bodice with a deep V neckline, full skirts, and elbow-length gloves.

Her husband, Lord Davers, had similar creases at the corners of his blue eyes. His brown hair was cut short, revealing slightly pointed ears. Lord Davers also wore typical Unseelie fashion for the men. High-collared jacket buttoned all the way to the top, the jacket flared out at the waist over tight breeches tucked into boots.

Neither glanced in Lainey's direction, except to give her dirty looks. She peered at Phoenix from the corner of her eye, then quickly averted her gaze. She couldn't handle it. He reminded her of a rogue king, with the golden crown perched lopsided on his head and his jacket and white shirt unbuttoned to display a fair amount of his tan chest.

She tried to tune in to their conversation, but the servants entered and filled the plates, quickly distracting her. Besides Lord and Lady Davers, the rest of the table was also filled. More nobles vying for attention, either trying to get into Phoenix's good graces legitimately or attempting to trick him into letting them in.

Leif served Lainey a meat and rice dish and filled her glass with red wine. A burst of uncertainty swept through her when she eyed the wine glass. Leif gave her a reassuring nod and stepped away. Before anyone could begin eating, Phoenix stood from his chair, the legs scraping loudly against the black marble floor.

"Thank you all for attending tonight," he began. "It is indeed a momentous night that I get to announce the appointment of Lord Davers as head of my council. I hope you all will join us in celebrating."

Lainey barely swallowed a startled gasp. As the crowd at the table politely clapped and congratulated Lord Davers, she cast her gaze to her dad standing in the shadows by the door. He met her gaze with confusion and a subtle shake of his head.

What was going on? Lord Davers had been in Esmeray's pocket. Why would Nix appoint him as head of his council? Even the way he was talking didn't sound like Nix. Too formal and stuffy. Uncertainty wormed through Lainey. A pit formed in her stomach, settling like a lead ball, and she had to force herself to sit still, although her hands under the table knotted in the fabric of her skirt.

Once Nix had returned to his seat, everyone at the table began eating. Even if Lainey hadn't feared poison, she'd completely lost her appetite. This wasn't the Nix she'd fallen in love with. That guy was long gone, replaced by some foreign stranger. Lainey pushed the food around her plate and attempted to listen to the conversation flowing around her, but it was too hard. All she could hear was her heart pounding in her ears and a dull ringing that was steadily growing louder.

Listening to Phoenix's voice created a deep longing inside of her. It seemed like forever since she'd heard him speak. She hung on every word he said, although she didn't process any of them. She just listened, letting his voice flow through her, and attempted to soothe the jagged edges of her heart.

Lainey froze in place, her fingers tightening on her fork, when Phoenix reached his hand across the table. Not toward her but toward the pretty fae sitting on the other side of Lord Davers. She had golden-blond hair cascading over her shoulders in loose waves. Her brown eyes were the same shape and color as Lady Davers'. Her pale complexion was the twin to Lord Davers'. It could only have been Seraphina, the Lord and Lady's eligible daughter.

Phoenix grasped her hand. A hand devoid of the glove so common in the Unseelie Court. His thumb stroked back and forth across her pale skin. He leaned forward, and Lainey felt the knife in her heart as Nix smiled at Seraphina. The girl giggled and batted her eyelashes, but her other ungloved hand clasped the top of Phoenix's.

Lainey couldn't hear their conversation over the roaring of blood in her ears. She watched them smile and tease each other, their gazes roving over exposed skin. Nix licked his bottom lip before tugging it into his mouth with one of his elongated canines.

He was ... he was *flirting* with her. While Lainey sat right there, Nix was *flirting* with Seraphina Davers! Shame burned her cheeks at the same time devastation swept through her. A weight settled on her chest, making it impossible to draw breath. Her skin prickled, flushing hot then cold. Saliva pooled in her mouth as bile climbed up her throat. She was going to be sick.

Pushing back her chair, Lainey rose as gracefully as she could and made her way to the door. The eyes of the court burned into her back, but she didn't care. Every second, she was closer to losing the contents of her stomach. Her dad had the door already open for her, and she stumbled into the hallway with her hands clamped over her mouth.

Lainey's boots slipped on the smooth marble floor as she rushed around the corner, nearly sending her crashing into the opposite wall. She wasn't going to make it to her rooms, so she shouldered her way inside the closest broom closet. As soon as the door closed behind her, she bent over and heaved, choking and gagging as she threw up. Tears sprang to the corners of her eyes, and they quickly built until she was sobbing. The door opening ushered in cool air that attempted to dry the stickiness on her skin and provided light she wished would go away.

Ash placed his hand on her back, and another wave of nausea rose. She heaved again, this time spitting up only bile—she hadn't been eating much lately. Ash's large hands held her hair back until the nausea passed. She straightened but couldn't make herself face Ash. Shame continued to warm her cheeks, even as her tears slid down her overheated skin.

Ash was having none of that. He turned her to face him and wrapped his arms around her. "I'm so sorry, Lainey," he whispered. "I don't know what's happening, but I swear, I'm going to fix this. He won't keep hurting you like this, or I'll rip his fucking balls off and choke him with them." He pressed his hand to the back of her head, pushing her harder against his chest. "This isn't Nix. You know this isn't something he would ever do."

She wanted to ask him why he thought that. Bite, spit, and rage that clearly he was wrong. He was wrong about everything. Because Phoenix would do it—*had* done it. They'd all seen it. But her tongue was heavy in her mouth, thick and coated in the sourness of bile, and she couldn't bring herself to move. So she let Ash hold her up as she all but crumpled to the floor.

And she finally broke.

LAINEY

NUMB. EVERYTHING WAS NUMB. EXACTLY LIKE WHEN she'd found out Emma was murdered.

Ash walked her back to her room, and when he tried to follow her inside, she stopped him. "I need to be alone," she choked out around the lump in her throat.

Ash frowned. "Lainey, I—"

She stepped into her room and closed the door in his face. Nothing he said would make this situation any better, and she couldn't bear to listen to his attempts to cheer her up.

Walking to the mirror, Lainey stood and stared at her reflection. When had she gotten so thin? And her eyes. There was nothing in her eyes. No life. No joy. They were vacant and empty. A small part of her mind rebelled, banged tiny fists against her skull and screamed. She was stronger than this. She shouldn't let a relationship define her. She shouldn't let a broken heart break her.

But this was different. This wasn't a typical relationship. She had formed a bond with Nix—a physical, emotional, magical bond. It went deeper than the average earthbound relationship. The betrayal of that bond, the *breaking* of that bond, was not so easy for her to overcome.

She ripped off the dress and hurled it into the corner. She was a fraud—an adult playing dress-up, playing at being a queen. Tulle and silk puddled on the floor, layers of soft fabric floating down gently. In the wardrobe, Lainey dug through the dresses to the very back. She pulled out the T-shirt she had worn when she first arrived in Faerie. It was mostly intact, with only a few tears. She pulled it over her head and returned to the mirror.

The leggings were perfect. All she needed were her chucks. She pulled out the bag she had brought from Earth and peered inside. It was empty except for her wallet with her ID and a few dollars. She had left her bank card at Phoenix's penthouse when they left. She quickly threw more leggings into the bag, along with a couple of shawls. The dresses were useless. When she returned to the mirror, she ripped the crown from her brow and chucked it into the bag. Maybe she could sell it.

She'd just finished braiding her hair when the door to her room slammed open. It hit the wall with a crack and rebounded. Lainey jumped, then gasped at the sight of Phoenix in the doorway. His light brown eyes fixed on her in a hard look, brows pulled down to crease in the middle. A shiver worked down her spine. He hadn't looked at her in so long, but now her discomfort grew under that stare. It was cold. Almost blank. The fire was missing from his irises.

He took a step forward, and Lainey reflexively took a step back. Phoenix noticed, and a small smile curled the corners of his lips. It wasn't a pleasant smile. It was cruel and cold. Phoenix closed the door behind him, but not before Lainey saw the body of a guard lying unmoving on the ground. Her blood froze in her veins. She wasn't okay with this. Something was off.

Phoenix backed her against the wall. She pressed her palms against the smooth stone. It was cool against her sweat-slicked skin. Her heart was pounding, and the closer he got, the more she could smell him. Each inhale was a knife to the gut. He smelled just like Phoenix. A crackling fire on an autumn night. Tears pooled in her eyes, but she blinked them away.

"You're scared," he stated. His voice was emotionless, and he raised both arms and placed a hand on either side of her head, boxing her in.

She didn't respond, but his eyes dropped to her throat as she swallowed. He lowered his head to her neck, ran his nose up the column of her throat, and her body responded. It recognized Phoenix—her mate—and it craved him. She wanted his touch. She wanted his body on hers. She wanted to taste him, smell him, feel him. The need for him was overwhelming.

But this wasn't right. Her mind balked at his touch and rebelled against her body's reaction. Phoenix pressed her harder into the wall, and the heat from his body and magic surrounded her. Oh, how she'd missed that. She melted a little inside, feeling it again. She wanted to wrap her legs around him and pull him even closer.

Before her body could betray her further, Phoenix claimed her mouth in a rough kiss. It was almost painful, as if he was trying to mold their mouths together. She clamped her lips shut tightly and wedged her palms between them. Placing her hands on his chest, she tried to push him away, but he didn't budge. Instead, he broke the kiss long enough to grab her hands in one of his, pinning them to the wall above her head.

"Phoenix—"

She was cut off when his free hand wrapped around her throat and squeezed. It wasn't enough to cut off her air completely, but it was enough to cause her to gasp in fear. He took that opportunity to claim her mouth again. This time, he slid his tongue inside, and Lainey tried to recoil. The wall at her back prevented her from pulling away, and a whimper worked its way up her throat.

The pressure around her neck increased. She tried to lift her knee to push him away, but his leg wedged between hers prevented it. Hoping to throw him off balance, she bucked her hips, but he stood firm. All she managed to do was turn him on even more. His erection pressed against her hips, and her traitorous body heated at the sensation of his thigh pressed against her core.

Tears leaked from her eyes, and she shut them tightly. Why was he doing this? When her brain grew fuzzy from lack of oxygen, his hand loosened, and he pulled back. She snapped her eyes open.

"Stop ..." she gasped. "Let me go."

He wiped a tear from her cheek with the hand that had just been choking her. For a second, she saw the old Phoenix. His eyes darkened, and a glimmer of fire shone through. She felt his body tense. But then he blinked, and his stare was once again cold and empty.

"Please, Nix," she begged through her tears.

He smiled that cruel smile and trailed his hand over her breast, stopping to pinch her nipple through the fabric of her T-shirt. She flinched, and he laughed. The sound wormed into her bones and made her tremble. It wasn't a human sound.

"I bet this turns you on," he growled.

She tried to shake her head, but Phoenix kicked her legs farther apart and ran his hand down her stomach to the waistband of her leggings. When he curled his fingers around the hem, her heart stuttered, and true fear bubbled inside of her. There was no way she could fight him off, and if he kept moving his hand south, he would indeed find her wet, because her body still wanted him. But it wanted Nix, the man she loved. Not this monster.

Lainey sucked in a breath and screamed. The sound wobbled in her throat, but she hoped it was loud enough for Ash or Warren to hear. One of them should have been near, right? The sound startled Phoenix, and he pulled back. Lainey took that opportunity to push him again. This time, he staggered backward, and when he looked into Lainey's eyes, she saw the swirling copper she loved so much. He shook his head and grimaced. When he closed his eyes, his body relaxed, and pure ice filled his vision when they opened again.

Something was seriously wrong.

The door to her room burst open, and over Phoenix's shoulder, Lainey saw that Ash stood in the doorway with his sword drawn. He hesitated when he saw Phoenix, but as soon as he noticed Lainey huddled against the wall with tears staining her cheeks, he stormed forward.

"What the fuck is going on?" he demanded. He pushed Phoenix aside and grabbed Lainey's hand, tugging her close.

Phoenix shrugged his shoulders. "Spending time with my mate. What does it matter to you?" That voice was so cold. So foreign. It sounded nothing like Nix

Lainey latched on to Ash's bicep with a claw-like grip. "Make him leave, Ash. *Please*," she begged, and her voice broke. She was trembling so hard, she thought she might fall to the floor.

Ash studied Lainey before lifting the sword and pointing it at Phoenix. "Leave. She doesn't want you in here, and frankly, neither do I," he said sharply. "I don't know what the fuck has gotten in to you, but until you figure your shit out, leave Lainey alone."

Phoenix laughed again, and Ash stiffened under her hands. That sound was not natural. "I'll humor you for now," he said darkly, "but just this once. Next time, I'll take what is mine." He shoved his hands into his pockets and sauntered out of the room.

As soon as the door closed, Lainey's legs gave out, and she collapsed to the floor in a shaking puddle of limbs and tears. She didn't know what to make of what had just happened. She felt violated, but at the same time, she was still turned on. Her body wanted Nix so badly, but that hadn't *been* Nix.

Ash sheathed his sword, and the world swooped as he lifted Lainey into his arms and carried her to the bed. The mattress dipped under her weight, and she immediately pulled her legs to her chest and wrapped her arms around them, trying to make herself as small as possible. Staring blankly at the floor, Lainey tried to gather her chaotic thoughts and control her trembling limbs. Ash's boots on the floor as he walked to the bathing room were steady, and Lainey latched on to the rhythmic, predictable sound. When he returned, he handed her a cup of water and draped a cool washcloth around the back of her neck.

"What just happened, Lainey?" Ash asked tightly.

She sniffled and took a drink of water, the cool liquid soothing her burning throat. "I don't know," she whispered brokenly. "He came in here and ... he ... he forced himself on me. I feel so conflicted," she admitted. "I told him no, and he didn't stop. I didn't want it, but at the same time, I did. I'm desperate for him, and it's like I'm willing to take him any way I can. It's pathetic."

"It's not pathetic. That was a very confusing situation. I think anyone would feel the same way you are." He took a breath and turned to face her. "Lainey, did Nix seem weird to you at all? I mean, besides the fact he forced himself on you. I know that wasn't like him."

She nodded. "His eyes. They were ... empty. Like he wasn't in there. And the laugh ..." She shuddered just thinking about it. That sound would haunt her for the rest of her life.

Ash bit his lip and shook his head. "Something isn't right. I have a weird feeling about all of this."

"What are you thinking?" she whispered.

"You need to leave."

ASH'S WORDS echoed in Lainey's head as she hurriedly threw more supplies in her bag, then followed Ash through the palace. They moved quickly, keeping to the shadows to avoid notice. In the stables, Ash saddled two horses, and before she knew it, they were galloping through the night across Faerie to the gate tree. Because they didn't know where the gate tree in Unseelie opened in the human realm, and they were too scared to ask anyone, they chose to use the tree in the Seelie Court.

Her heart thundered as fast as her horse's hooves. This was it. She was really leaving. She'd already planned on leaving, but thinking about it and actually doing it were two different things. Knowing she wasn't betraying Ash helped, but the thought of leaving behind the one person in her life who had been a constant pillar of strength was terrifying.

She tried to keep her mind from wandering to Phoenix, but as always, she failed. What had just happened was a lot to process. Her hands shook as she tightly gripped the reins. Adrenaline coursed through her veins, from both her encounter with Nix and because of what she was doing.

Instead, Lainey focused on her surroundings. She took in the way the moonlight gilded the grass in its silver light. The wildflowers blew in a soft breeze and gave Lainey the impression they were dancing wildly under the moonlight. Stars dotted the deep blue sky, so many, she couldn't imagine how they all fit in the vast expanse above her head. While Faerie was beautiful during the day, at night it transformed into something ethereal, something only seen in fairytales.

Both horses were lathered and panting heavily by the time Ash slowed their pace. Up ahead, the sweeping branches of the gate tree beckoned with fingers trailing in the river around the island. Their horses' hooves seemed loud in the silence as they clopped over the arching stone bridge. The moon was reflected in the still waters like an eerie eye from some kind of river monster, and Lainey shivered as she remembered the monster that had pulled her into the water when they first arrived in Faerie.

In front of the gate tree, Ash stopped and dismounted. He let the reins drop, and his horse wandered a few feet away to graze in the tall grasses of the island. Lainey followed suit, standing quietly in front of the immense trunk. The outline of the door was barely visible in the moonlight.

"Here," Ash said as he handed her a wallet. "It has my credit and bank cards, as well as the key to the penthouse. Everything should be as it was since we never really planned on staying here originally. Nix's dad bought the penthouse for him, and it's been paid off, so there shouldn't be any issue with that."

She took the wallet and stuck it in the front pocket of her bookbag. "Do you think he'll try to find me?" Her voice was emotionless in the dark.

Ash shook his head, his blond hair catching the moonlight and glinting silver. "I have no fucking clue. If it were the old Phoenix, I'd say absolutely. Now? He's too unpredictable, and I have no idea what he'll do."

Lainey swallowed and nodded. Ash took her arm and turned her to face him. His green eyes glowed in the darkness.

"Go to the penthouse and take Nix's bank card. It will be too risky to use his credit card. If he tries to find you, he'll be able to track it. Take the bank card and pull out as much money as you can, then don't use it again. His pin is zero-seven-two-three."

"His birthday," she whispered.

"There is a note in my wallet. Read it when you're safe in New York. I don't want to risk talking about it here. Don't stay in the penthouse longer than a day or two."

"What about Beck?" she asked, fingers grasping the front of Ash's shirt. "We haven't heard from him here. What if he is still in the human realm?"

Ash furrowed his brow in thought. "I can't imagine he's still hunting you. The curse is broken, and there is no more need for a sacrifice. But do whatever you have to do to stay safe."

Lainey nodded, and her eyes welled with tears. This was it. She was leaving her mate. She was leaving her best friend. They hadn't even trusted her dad with their plan, so she was leaving without saying goodbye to him. Even knowing what staying behind meant, she wasn't sure she was ready for this.

Ash grabbed her head and placed a kiss on her forehead before wrapping her up in his strong arms. She loved his hugs.

"You've got this, Lainey. I have complete faith in you." He squeezed her a little tighter. "This isn't goodbye. We're going to make this right."

She didn't know what to say. She didn't even know what was going on. Ash refused to talk about it. Hopefully, whatever was in that note would clear things up. She hugged him tighter and pulled his earthy scent into her lungs, committing his comforting presence to memory.

When Ash pulled back, Lainey almost grabbed him again. She couldn't really be doing this, could she? There was no one for her on the other side. Was she really leaving the only people in her life behind? Her throat closed, and she fought back the sob that was climbing higher in her chest.

Ash took a step away. Then another. Lainey turned to the door again and closed her eyes. She took a deep breath before squaring her shoulders and opening them again. With nervous flutters in her stomach, Lainey walked to the gate tree and placed a shaking hand on the rough bark.

Golden light flared and illuminated the outline of the door. Lainey pushed, and a section of the door shifted, rotating inward. Without a backward glance at the life she was leaving behind, Lainey stepped into the light.

LAINEY

IT WAS SO LOUD. AND GRAY.

After having spent ten months in the fae realm, the bustling streets of New York City overwhelmed her. Even in the late evening hours, cars zipped past and horns blared, sirens wailed and people chattered. Colors appeared muted and monochromatic. There was no imperceptible shimmer of magic in the air like there was in Faerie.

Lainey hurried her steps. Being out in the open made her skin crawl. An itch had started between her shoulder blades as soon as she stepped out of Central Park, and it followed her down the city streets as she made her way to the penthouse. It was too soon for Phoenix to have realized she'd left. And the likelihood Beck knew she was back in New York was slim to none. But she felt like people could tell she was different. She felt as if there were a shimmery layer of magic surrounding her. A remnant of her time in Faerie that made her stand out.

The apartment building loomed in front of her, and a pang of sadness washed through her. The last time she had walked through those doors, she'd been with Phoenix and Ash. Now she was returning alone. She shouldered her way into the lobby and made her way to the elevators. Her heart pounded. She was terrified someone was going to stop her and ask what she was doing there. It had been ten months since they'd walked through this lobby.

She made it to the elevator bank without incident and used Ash's key card to activate the button. The ride to the top floor was quicker than she remembered. Then again, she was dreading stepping foot into that penthouse, and she knew memories were sure to assault her. When the doors slid open, she took a deep breath before slowly approaching the penthouse. It was like she was preparing herself to walk into a war zone.

The lock chirped, and the little light on the card reader flashed green. She paused just inside and let the door swing shut. It smelled like … like *home*. If she really focused, she could still smell Phoenix and Ash in the air. She released a breath, and her eyes burned as memories assaulted her.

She hadn't spent much time in the penthouse, but the time she did had been monumental. She had learned more about herself in those few days than she had her entire life. Ash had been a comforting presence from the very beginning, and her friendship with him had only grown. And Phoenix …

She couldn't think about him.

Lainey sat her bookbag on the counter and pulled out Ash's wallet. Inside, she found a piece of parchment folded into a small square. She opened it and saw Ash's sharp, angled print scrawled across the page.

Lainey,

I have a theory about what is happening to Nix. What I've seen from him reminds me of a story I once heard. I'm not sure how to fix this, so I need you to help.

I think Nix may be possessed by a demon.

Find Madam Elvie. Ask her if she knows anything about possession and the demon realm. She is the only one I can think of who may know how to save Phoenix.

Hurry, though. And be safe. I can't look after you both, so I need you to take care of yourself. Remember everything I've taught you.

I'll see you soon.

-Ash

The parchment dropped from her numb fingers. Demon realm? That was a thing? And Ash thought Nix was possessed by a demon. That would mean everything that had happened hadn't really been him. That damn bubble of hope sparked to life in her chest again. She tried to squash it, but it grew. If they could figure this out, she could get her mate back.

Lainey glanced at the microwave. It was nine in the evening. She couldn't go running to Madam Elvie's this late. With reluctance, Lainey headed to her room in the penthouse. She stopped outside the door and glanced farther down the hall. Nix's room was down there. She had never been in there before. With determination, Lainey continued past her door.

She stopped in front of Ash's room and peeked inside. Clothes were strewn all over the floor and desk. A few dead plants sat in the corner, and a Green Day poster hung above the messy bed. She smiled, even as her heart throbbed in her chest. She already missed him and the chaotic energy he let off. Closing the door, she continued until she reached the last door in the hall. With her hand on the doorknob, she paused to steady herself.

She pushed inside and inhaled. His scent permeated this space. She quickly shut the door, hoping to keep it from escaping. Bonfire, autumn nights, and musk. A scent uniquely Phoenix, and it tore open the wound inside of her even more.

The room was clean. Nothing was out of place, and it brought a smile to Lainey's face. The bed was made and the floor free of the clothing Ash's room had been strewn with. There were no decorations adorning the walls and no plants to brighten the space. It was stark and subdued, just like the man himself.

Lainey approached the bed and pulled down the comforter. She ran her hand over the black cotton sheets before kicking off her chucks and climbing under the covers. Wrapped in his sheets with his scent still clinging to them, with her head resting on the pillow his head once rested on, she felt closer to him than she had in months.

She missed Phoenix so much, her heart hurt. She wanted her mate back. Unable to keep them at bay any longer, Lainey let her tears fall. Alone again in New York city, Lainey cried herself to sleep.

Lainey woke early after a night of tossing and turning. The hot shower was amazing, and she stood under the spray longer than she should have. She imagined herself shedding her old skin and welcoming the new. Ash's letter had set a fire in her veins. No longer would she sit around and let life happen to her. It was time to take control, and lucky for her, she had something to fight. Her mate was in trouble, and there was something she could do to help.

With new determination flooding her system, Lainey left the steamy bathroom and walked down the quiet hallway to her room. It was weird being here alone. At any moment, she expected Ash to pop his head inside with a joke or a teasing insult. In her room, she rooted through her closet for clothing. She found a pair of jeans she'd left behind and pulled them on, but she had no extra shirts.

Crossing the hall into Ash's room, Lainey dug through his closet. A worn black Yellowcard tee fell off a hanger, and Lainey scooped it up with a smile. She pulled it over her head and tied the bottom in a knot at her waist. Wearing one of his shirts, with his earthy scent still lingering on the threads, made him seem closer than he really was. It helped to push back the despair and keep the fire burning. She quickly grabbed more shirts and shoved them into a backpack before heading to the kitchen.

In a drawer, she found Phoenix's wallet, and she dropped it into her bag along with Ash's. Shouldering the bag, she stood in front of the door, knowing it was probably the last time she would set foot inside the penthouse. It was okay, though. She'd cried her final tears last night and woke up with a new bubble of hope growing inside of her. And this bubble she wouldn't let pop. This time, there was no one to rely on but herself, and she was ready to prove that she could do it. She had a plan, and she would get the information needed to save her mate. No more wallowing or self-pity. It was time to step up to the plate.

With a plan in her head and determination in her step, Lainey made her way to an ATM and withdrew as much cash on each card as the machine would allow. As she shoved the money into Nix's wallet, she caught movement out of the corner of her eye. There was nothing out of the ordinary when she glanced around. Shaking off the anxiety burrowing into her gut as paranoia, Lainey stopped at a bakery to get a bagel and coffee before beginning the trek to Madam Elvie's.

She'd charged Nix's phone last night, and she desperately hoped he wouldn't be able to track her while she was using it. She didn't have much of a choice, though, unless she spent some of her cash on a burner phone. Now, she used it to make sure Madam Elvie was still running her little psychic business. According to Google, she was—not that that meant much. Lainey hoped she'd be able to help, or at least point her in the right direction to find help.

The last time Lainey had stood outside this building, it was freezing, and she'd had Ash and Nix at her back. Now she stood alone under the sweltering sun and prayed to a God she had never believed in. Madam Elvie's place hadn't changed one bit. Rotting stairs and crooked shutters hung limply without a breeze. Vines crawled up the facade, leaves curled and browning in the heat and apparent lack of rain or water.

The stairs groaned and creaked under her weight, and she skipped the middle step entirely, as she feared it would disintegrate if she stepped on it. She knocked on the door and waited with bated breath.

"Well, well, well," Madam Elvie said as she opened the door. "What have we here?"

"I need your help," Lainey blurted, almost interrupting Elvie in her rush to get the words out. "Please."

Madam Elvie scanned Lainey with eyes of the palest blue before she nodded and stepped aside. Lainey followed her down the hall to the room where she had first met the elf. They settled on cushions on the floor, and Madam Elvie wasted no time.

"The curse has been broken. What could you possibly need my help for?"

Lainey pulled Ash's note from her bag and slid it across the stone table to Madam Elvie. "Phoenix is my mate," she explained. "It wasn't just the blood bond you noticed the last time we visited. It was the mate bond."

Madam Elvie took the parchment but didn't open it. "And you want me to break this bond?" Her nostrils flared as she scented Lainey. The beads in her braids clicked as she drew back, her eyes widening in shock. "That bond ..." she muttered. "It's like nothing I have ever sensed."

"I don't want it broken," Lainey quickly answered. "Something is happening to Nix. Ash thinks he's been possessed by a demon?" She phrased it as a question because she'd had no idea demons existed. "He told me to come here and ask you if you knew anything about possession and the demon realm."

Madam Elvie's eyes widened until white showed all around her irises. She placed one hand over the parchment and the other over her throat. "Oh dear," she said quietly before she opened the note and quickly scanned it. "What can you tell me?"

Lainey told Elvie everything, rushing through Phoenix's gradual withdrawal to him forcing himself on her the other day. Describing the lack of fire that usually sparked in the depths of his eyes drew tears to her own, but she blinked them away. It was harder to talk about the bond and how she could barely feel it anymore. The bond was such a personal thing, and it made her shift uncomfortably on the cushion to admit the lack of its presence. By the time she finished, her shirt was sticking to her back and her heart was pounding behind her ribs.

Elvie studied her with an intensity that made her eyes appear to glow. No. Not appear to glow. They *were* glowing. The blue was shimmering and fracturing like cracking ice. "May I place my hands on your chest?" Elvie asked after an uncomfortable silence.

Lainey swallowed but nodded. She leaned back on her hands to give Elvie better access. Elvie knelt on the floor next to Lainey and placed her hands on Lainey's chest. She was positive Madam Elvie could feel her heartbeat racing under her palms.

"Relax," Madam Elvie said quietly.

It was the most normal and serious tone Lainey had heard from the elf, and it made it difficult to calm her racing heart.

"I cannot hear the bond over the beating of your heart. Take a deep breath and imagine yourself relaxing on a nude beach with hunky naked men surrounding you."

Lainey choked but complied, pulling air into her lungs. She held it for a few seconds before exhaling. With her eyes closed, Lainey pictured not a nude beach but the field behind the orphanage and the tall grasses that swayed in the breeze. She could almost hear the tweeting of the birds that sang during the day and the crickets that chirped at night. It brought about a feeling of longing she hadn't felt for a place before. It was almost like she was homesick.

"Good," Madad Elvie murmured softly.

There was a slight vibration in her chest, like the bass that rumbles from speakers that are turned up too high. It spread deeper into her and flowed out through her limbs. It hit again and again. The pattern and feeling almost lulled her to sleep. When Madam Elvie pulled her hands away, the echo of the vibrations lingered.

Madam Elvie returned to her cushion and peered at Lainey with her brows drawn low over her eyes. "That bond ..." She shook her head. "There is something going on that is not like anything I have ever felt."

"What does that mean?" Lainey was unable to keep the fear from making her voice tremble.

"I'm not sure," Elvie admitted. "Give me a couple of days to research this."

"Is there anything I can do to help?" Lainey couldn't sit around and do nothing while her mate and their bond were at risk.

"Come back tomorrow morning. We can work together."

Lainey hesitated to stand from her cushion. "So the demon realm is real? A demon could really be possessing Nix?"

"There are five realms. The human and faerie realms you are familiar with," Elvie explained, folding her hands on the table. "There is also the demon realm, or Hel, the angel realm, Celestia, and the realm of the dead. The angels have kept a close eye on the demons, and everyone leaves it up to them to take care of the problems the demons cause."

"Do all of these ... creatures ... cross into the human realm?" Lainey asked.

"They can. Where do you think your worst criminals come from? Murderers, rapists, and the occasional politician, these are typically demons wreaking havoc. The angels will only get involved if there is a risk of the demons exposing the other realms."

"So it's likely a demon has crossed into the faerie realm and possessed Phoenix?" Hope. Hope that she could get her mate back was so strong, it was hard to breathe.

"It is more than likely after what I have read in you."

Goosebumps prickled Lainey's arms and made the small hairs stand on end. "What does that mean?" she whispered as she wrapped her arms around her middle.

Madam Elvie cocked her head, reminding Lainey of a bird of prey, and her goosebumps intensified under that glacial stare. "I'm not sure," she admitted again. "I'll do my best to get to the bottom of it, though."

Resigning herself to having to wait for answers, Lainey stood. "Thank you," she said to the elf. "Truly. I appreciate the help."

Madam Elvie nodded, and Lainey let herself out. Even outside in the sun and heat, Lainey couldn't shake the chill that had seeped into her bones. She had a feeling she would not like what Madam Elvie discovered. And to think anyone she passed on the street could be an angel or demon ... Lainey shook herself. She didn't have the energy to process that right now. She needed to focus on finding a place to stay that wouldn't cost an arm and leg.

As she headed back toward the penthouse to work on this, she paused. An uneasy feeling had settled over her as she walked and increased the closer she got. Her time in the Faerie realm, practicing her magic, had increased her fae instincts. And currently, something inside her was telling her to stop.

Lainey crossed the street and walked around another apartment building so she could approach the penthouse from a different angle and remain hidden. In the shadows, Lainey stopped and peered around the corner of the building. At first, she didn't notice anything, but the longer she watched, the more aware she became. There were two people standing at each front corner of the penthouse.

They lounged against the brick, looking for all the world like they were doing nothing nefarious. But every so often, they would glance at each other, then peer behind them to the back corners of the penthouse Lainey couldn't see. They wore all black, long pants and shirts even in the heat of the summer sun. Lainey couldn't make out the details, but she saw a gold-colored insignia on the breast of each shirt.

Phoenix knew. And he'd sent his men for her.

They had found her.

LAINEY

Two days since she'd left Faerie.

Slinking back into the shadows, Lainey thought through her options. She couldn't go back to the penthouse. Luckily, she'd grabbed everything she thought she might need just in case before leaving this morning. She even had a few extra changes of clothes in her backpack. What she needed now was a place to stay. She could go to a hotel, but she only had enough money for a couple of weeks, and she didn't know how long this whole thing would take.

With a silent prayer, Lainey pulled Nix's phone from her back pocket. She hoped he had his dad's information saved somewhere on the device. There was nothing under "dad" in his phone besides a phone number. Knowing she at least had that as a last resort, she pulled up the tracking app. There were three people saved in the app. Ash, whose phone was dead, said the location couldn't be found. And Nix's dad, whose dot showed he was on the other side of Central Park from where she was currently.

The third made her pause. Beck. He was currently in downtown New York. She silently thanked Phoenix for tracking Beck. Now she could stay far away from him.

Turning around, Lainey made her way down the block before heading for Central Park. She walked quickly and kept her eyes on her surroundings, but she saw no more black-clad fae. Using the app, she narrowed down Nix's dad's location, while also making sure Beck's dot stayed far from her. As she crossed through Central Park, she was thoroughly regretting her clothing choices. Ash's black T-shirt drew the heat from the sun, her jeans were sticking to her legs, and her hair hung thick and heavy on her neck. By the time she reached the place where the tracking app said she would find Nix's dad, she was a sweaty mess.

The townhome was a typical brownstone found in New York City. It was graceful, despite its age. Lainey was sure the architectural touches around the doorframe, windows, and roof had some fancy name that belonged to an art movement like renaissance or colonial, or something like that. Similarly styled brownstones lined the street in either direction. It was a quaint, quiet little area of the city.

Climbing the stairs, Lainey paused before knocking on the door. She had never met Nix's dad. She didn't think Nix had ever mentioned her to his dad. For all she knew, he could be as awful as Beck. She ran through her options again and decided this was the best one. Besides, maybe she could get some advice about ruling a kingdom from him.

Her fingers shook as she reached forward and knocked. She held her breath, and her nerves fluttered through her when she heard footsteps on the other side of the thick door. It swung open, and Lainey stared at the man ... fae ... on the other side. Nix clearly got his looks from his dad. They had the same dark brown hair that burned red when it caught the light. While his dad's light brown eyes were not as fiery as Phoenix's, they still shimmered with his power. Both were of a similar build, with wide shoulders and a narrow waist. It was almost painful to look at him.

His dad squinted at Lainey and braced a forearm on the doorframe. "Can I help you?"

Lainey let a small burst of her magic free, just enough for him to pick up on. His eyes widened, and he straightened, crossing his arms over his chest.

"My name is Lainey. I ... I'm Nix's mate, and I need help." Her voice wobbled, and she wiped her palms on her jeans.

He exhaled sharply and scanned her from head to toe. "Isn't that one of Ash's shirts?"

Lainey couldn't help but grin, even though it faded quickly. "It is. I had nothing else to wear."

She held her breath until Nix's dad stepped aside and opened the door wider.

Amusement glittered in his eyes as he ushered her inside. "Come in. It would seem there is much to talk about."

✦ ✦ ✦ ✦ ✦ ✦ ✦

LAINEY SAT on the couch with a glass of ice water sweating in her lap. She was perched on the edge of the cushion, back straight and shoulders tight. Every muscle tense and already aching from sitting up so straight. Nix's dad, Brand, sat across from her. She looked around the room to avoid the image of Nix years down the road. The townhome was simply furnished in grays and blues, the cool color tones the opposite of what she would have pictured for a fire elemental. A few plants sat in the windows and on the hardwood floor.

Lainey glanced at her feet resting on a blue and cream rug. She took a deep breath before finally focusing on Brand.

"You're nervous?" he asked, one ankle crossed over his knee as he relaxed in his chair.

"A little. It's like meeting your boyfriend's parents, essentially."

Brand snorted. "I'm sure his mother gave you a fine first impression."

"She's dead," Lainey blurted, then cringed. She couldn't

imagine he had any feelings for the woman who'd sired his youngest child, but she still could have shown some tact.

He laughed softly. "It's okay. I figured when the gate opened, that meant she was dead. And no, I didn't mourn her loss. The things she did, the things she had planned to do?" He shook his head. "It's a good thing she is gone."

Lainey returned her focus to the rug. She followed the swirling pattern with her eyes until it disappeared under the couch. She didn't know what to say, so she shrugged her shoulders. Her fingers were getting cold from the icy glass, but she was too scared to set it down. She had never had a boyfriend she cared about so much that meeting the parents was important. Seeing as Nix was so much more than her boyfriend, she was particularly paranoid about screwing things up.

"Lainey, you can relax," Brand said quietly. "I may be Phoenix's dad, but he got his reserved nature from his mom. Things don't have to be formal here."

She looked from the rug to Brand and really took in his features, looking past the resemblance to Nix. Her shoulders lost their tension, and she exhaled. Something about him made her relax. He was kind. The faint lines around his eyes and mouth hinted at his smiling nature. And his eyes, as much as she tried to avoid looking at them, were soft and inviting. It helped to calm her nerves further.

"How is my son?" he asked.

How to answer that question? "Well, not good, actually," was the only thing she could think to say.

Brand leaned forward in his chair, some of the light leaving his eyes. "What do you mean? You broke the curse. Why haven't you returned to the human realm? According to everything I heard from Phoenix before you guys left, I thought that was the plan?"

"Yeah, it was the plan originally. But Phoenix took Esmeray's place after we removed her. He's the Unseelie King."

Brand released a soft laugh. "That sounds like something he

would do. Ambition is also something he got from his mom. Unseelie King, huh?" His eyes narrowed as he studied her. "As his mate, that would make you queen."

"Something like that," she muttered.

"Something like that?" he repeated, one brow raised. "I'm pretty sure that's exactly what that means."

Lainey shifted under his stare. She knew he wasn't seeing a queen when he looked at her. "Because I'm not a queen," she admitted, shoulders sagging under the weight of that truth. "A year ago, I didn't even know fae existed. I have no clue how to be a queen, or even a fae." Once she got rolling, she had a hard time stopping. Everything she'd been feeling just came pouring out of her mouth. Brand's kind nature seemed to pull it from her, and she could do nothing to stop it. "In fact, I'm not even a full-blooded fae. I know nothing about the faerie realm. How the hell am I supposed to rule it when the people know I'm a fraud?"

"How's Phoenix handling it? He knows nothing about ruling either. He may have an advantage, knowing about Faerie, but this is his first time being in the realm—that he remembers, at least."

"Well, that's why I'm here," she said slowly. "Ash sent me back to get help. He thinks Nix has been possessed by a demon."

Brand reared back, his light brown eyes flaring a softer flame than Phoenix's fire. His grip on the armrests of the couch turned his knuckles white. "Phoenix has been possessed by a demon?" he rasped.

"Ash thinks so. So does Madam Elvie. I went to see her today to see if she could help."

"Madam Elvie," Brand murmured. "She is the elf who helped place the curse?"

Lainey shook her head. "That was her sister, Essie. Elvie helped us figure out how to get into Faerie and break the curse without my death."

"And she thinks she can help?"

Lainey shrugged and finally set her water glass on the end table. "She told me to come back tomorrow to help her."

Brand sat quietly for a moment. His eyes zoned out as he stared at the rug and ran through whatever thoughts were in his head. When he lifted his gaze, his jaw was set. "What help do you need from me?"

"I need a place to stay," Lainey replied, her shoulder curving inward as she wrapped her arms around her middle. "I think Nix knows I'm back here. When I returned to the penthouse, I found Unseelie guards outside. I didn't know where else to go."

Brand leaned forward again, his eyes intense. "Did he hurt you?"

She swallowed. "Not really," she whispered. "It's been more emotional hurt than physical." She wouldn't mention how he almost assaulted her. That pain was still too fresh to deal with. "But if he is possessed, it's not really him." At least, that's what she kept telling herself.

He rubbed his hands over his face before standing and reaching out a hand to Lainey. Her fingers shook as she took it, and he pulled her to her feet.

"You're more than welcome to stay here. You are, after all, basically my daughter-in-law." He gave her a smile that crinkled the corners of his eyes.

She couldn't help the tears that built along her lashes. He genuinely meant that. She couldn't explain it, but she felt more connected to him than she did to her own dad. Maybe it was because there was still so much between her and Zephyr that she needed to unpack. Or maybe it was just because Brand had raised Phoenix, and she loved Nix with every cell in her body. Whatever it was, she was glad she'd made the decision to come here.

As one tear slipped free and fell down her cheek, Brand pulled her in for a hug. It wasn't as good as Ash's hugs, but it was a close second. His fire magic burned hot, and the warmth surrounded her. She felt herself relax for the first time in a very long time. Nothing could beat dad hugs, she decided.

Brand pulled back but kept his hands on her shoulders. He lowered his head so he could meet her eyes on level. "Stay here,

Lainey. And tomorrow, I'll go with you to Madam Elvie's. We'll get Phoenix back."

Her heart soared, and that damn bubble of hope grew a little bigger.

ASH

One day since Lainey had left Faerie.

Ash flinched as the sound of breaking glass echoed from Lainey's room. Nix had been on a path of destruction since Lainey left a day ago. Quick thinking had been the only thing to save him from Nix's anger. When he'd been questioned, Ash lied. He'd acted distraught that his charge had escaped without his notice. He'd laid into the guards around the palace and even had a few of them flogged. It didn't sit well with him, and he hated himself for doing that, but he needed Nix to trust him.

Within seconds of finding out, Phoenix immediately sent his personal guards—ones who had been hired recently and in Ash's eyes, were most likely not trustworthy—to the human realm. Ash prayed Lainey was being smart and staying under the radar. He honestly didn't know what this Phoenix would do if Lainey was captured and brought back to the Unseelie Court. It made his stomach churn to think Nix would hurt her, but he knew the demon inside him wouldn't hesitate.

Ash was walking a fine line. He needed to keep Nix's trust, but he also needed to dig deeper. He hoped Madam Elvie could find a solution, but he didn't want to rely solely on her. He needed to find people he could trust. There was no way he could keep an eye on Phoenix at all times. He needed help.

Zephyr was his first choice, and the most logical. The chances Lainey's dad was behind any of this were slim, but Ash had to make sure. His second choice was Warren. He'd been thorough when he screened the guards who would protect Lainey, and even after he'd chosen, he had kept a close eye on them. Warren genuinely seemed to care for Lainey and her happiness.

A whooshing sound came from Lainey's room, and smoke curled under the door. A demon in possession of a fire elemental? This could get nasty. Demon Phoenix threw the door open and stomped into the hallway, wisps of smoke following in his wake. He didn't spare a glance for anyone, just stormed down the hall, his anger a tangible thing. Inside Lainey's room, flames wreathed her bed. They licked at the wooden headboard and smoke curled to the ceiling.

Warren brushed past Ash and extended a hand. Water droplets formed in the air, getting larger and larger until a giant wall of water undulated in the space before him. He sent it crashing into the flames, and they snuffed out with a hiss. Smoke quickly filled the room, searching for an escape. Ash retreated into the hallway and found Zephyr standing against the wall with his arms crossed.

"Your room?" Zephyr asked and nodded his head toward Ash's room next door.

Ash led the way and held the door open for Zephyr. They both collapsed into chairs, and Ash ran his hands down his face. He was exhausted.

Zephyr cut right to the chase. "You know where she is."

Ash said nothing. While he assumed Lainey's dad was innocent in all of this, he had to make sure before he showed his hand.

"Is she back in New York?" When Ash still didn't reply Zephyr pushed up from the chair. "Damn it, Ash. She's my daughter, I deserve to know." Zephyr paced back and forth in front of the fireplace a few times before returning to the chair. He leaned his elbows on his knees and fixed Ash with a penetrating stare. "I lost one daughter already, and I almost lost Elena. Please, tell me what you know."

He almost cracked. It had to be horrible losing a child and not knowing where the other was. Ash felt for the man. "Who says I know where she is?"

Zephyr snorted. "You're protective of her. If you didn't know where she was, you would be tearing the realms apart trying to find her."

He wasn't wrong. "Look, I want to tell you, but I can't. I need to know I can trust you. Right now, the only person I trust is myself."

Zephyr sat back and leveled another stare at Ash. "It's Phoenix isn't it? There is something going on with him. There has been for a while now, if I were to guess."

"Fuck," Ash muttered and rubbed his hands over his face again. He really couldn't do this alone, and Zephyr seemed like the safest option. He hoped he wasn't making a colossal mistake. "I think Nix is possessed by a demon."

Ash watched Zephyr's reaction closely. First, the man's eyes widened in surprise, and he sat back in his chair. His mouth dropped open before he snapped it shut again. Then his eyes took on a distant look while his brow furrowed, as if he were thinking back to all the time he had spent with Nix, trying to line up what he saw with what he now knew.

"Holy shit," he breathed. "Everything makes sense now." He shook his head, his expression a mix of wonder and horror. "You sent Elena away for her safety, didn't you? Has Phoenix hurt her?"

Ash shook his head. "I don't think he's hurt her physically. He tried once, right before I sent her away. But he's hurt her emotionally. And she kept mentioning the bond, saying it felt like it was being torn apart, which seemed strange to me. I didn't think something like that could happen to a bond?" He phrased that last bit as a question, hoping Zephyr would have some knowledge that Ash was lacking.

"I haven't heard of that happening. Bonds can be broken by a healer with both parties present and willing, but I have never heard of one breaking on its own. Then again, I'm not sure what happens if one partner is possessed by a demon." He exhaled heavily and leaned back in his chair again. "What do you plan on doing about it?"

"Well, I sent Lainey to New York, not just for her safety but to ask Madam Elvie if she knew anything about possession. I'm hoping she can help us. In the meantime, all I can think to do is keep my eye on Nix and try to figure out what the demon is planning."

Zephyr nodded. "I'll do what I can to help."

"Don't get anyone else involved. I have no clue how deep this infiltration goes. I don't want to risk it getting back to Nix that we're aware of what's happening."

"I agree. Do you think it was Phoenix who ordered the poisoning at the Seelie Court?"

Ash shrugged. "I honestly don't know, but it seems likely. I just wish I knew what his goal was with Lainey. Does he want her dead or broken? And why?"

"It's good you sent her away." Zephyr stood and headed for the door, but paused as he reached for the knob. "And, Ash? Thank you for looking out for Elena. It really means a lot to me."

Ash nodded. He would always look out for her. That's what friends did.

• • • • • • • •

TWO DAYS since Lainey had left Faerie.

"I thought you should know, I overheard Lord and Lady Davers talking at breakfast," Zephyr said as he and Ash crossed the training yards the next day, heading back to the palace. "Lady Davers is upset because a guest arrived late in the night. She is apparently a beautiful woman who poses a threat to her daughter's chances of winning over Phoenix."

Ash snorted and shook his head. Vultures, all of them. "Who is this beautiful fae who is going to steal Nix from Lainey *and* Lady Davers's daughter?"

"Well, that's the thing. I don't know." Zephyr shrugged. "I've never heard of her. She arrived well past midnight last night with her brother. No one appears to know who they are or where they came from, but Phoenix seemed to have been expecting them. Rooms had already been prepared before their arrival."

"What are their names?" Ash asked.

"Selene and Andras Mordreth."

Ash pushed open the door nearest the practice yards. Darkness enveloped them as they stepped inside the palace, and it took a few moments for Ash's eyes to adjust after the bright morning sunlight. Zephyr followed in silence as they both thought through the possibilities of who these two new visitors could be.

He'd been making it a priority to check on the men he'd had punished for Lainey's so-called escape. It still didn't sit well with him, what he'd done to them. He'd spent much of the last night awake, thinking over different paths he could have taken to avoid having innocent men whipped for his choice to help Lainey. But in the moment, he hadn't been able to think of any better alternative.

"You did the right thing," Zephyr muttered as they made their way through the quiet halls.

"What do you mean?" Ash asked.

"Having those men punished," Zephyr replied. "You did the right thing. I know it's bothering you and that's why you are checking on them. But if you hadn't done that, your head would be on a spike right now. And what good would that do Elena?"

He was right, but that didn't make it any easier.

"What's Phoenix up to now?" Ash asked as a change of subject.

"He should be meeting his advisors. However, as unpredictable as he is, he could be doing anything."

Ash grunted. "I need to find him and report on our *progress* on finding Lainey." He used finger quotes to show that progress was merely fictional. They weren't actively doing anything to search for her. They already knew where she was, and based on Nix's reaction of sending men to New York, he clearly suspected as well.

"With any luck, he'll be with our two newest visitors," Zephyr said.

As it turned out, luck was with them for once. Ash and Zephyr found Nix in his council room, surrounded by his newly appointed advisors, whom Ash had no doubt were just as evil as the demon possessing him. There were also two fresh faces seated at the table.

Selene was beautiful, he had to admit. Her pale skin contrasted with her raven-black hair that fell well past her shoulders in a shiny curtain. Her lips were painted ruby red and her dramatically kohl-lined eyes were the darkest brown imaginable. She wore a simple but elegant dark red dress that hugged every curve and left nothing to the imagination.

Seated next to her, Andras shared the same pale skin and raven-black hair as his sister, but where hers was straight, his was styled in messy waves to his shoulders. He wore a black jacket over a white shirt, unbuttoned to show black tattoos on his chest. His gaze was cast down on the table, so Ash couldn't see his eyes, but he noted the cut of his jaw and the chiseled features of his facial structure.

He tried to get a read on them, testing the air for the vibrations and scent of their magic, but there were too many other people in the room. All of their combined magics jumbled everything too much to make out individual signatures.

"Ash." Phoenix nodded at an empty chair at the table.

Ash closed the council room door behind him, shutting

Zephyr out. Having Lainey's dad around wouldn't win him any points in trying to gain Nix's trust.

"Do you have an update on my wayward mate's whereabouts?" Nix's voice was cold and uncaring, lacking the fire that made him who he was.

It took every ounce of self-control to not react to those words and that tone. As a fire elemental, Phoenix always ran hot, and not just temperature-wise. He was hotheaded, full of fire, and quick to react with anger or violence. This Phoenix was the exact opposite, cold and detached, with no hint of emotion. It was painful to see his best friend changed so dramatically.

Ash shook his head. "No update. I questioned the guards responsible for the perimeter lookout the night she went missing, and they all claimed to have seen nothing unusual. I'll keep searching, though."

Phoenix grimaced but nodded. "Do that."

He turned his attention to someone farther down the table, and Ash let out a quiet breath. It was disconcerting having Nix watch him when Ash knew it was really a demon looking out of those pale brown eyes.

He glanced at Selene again. She sat quietly next to Nix, and Ash didn't miss the way Nix ran his finger down her arm. A satisfied smile pulled up the corners of her red lips. Ash swallowed down his distaste and transferred his attention to Andras, only to find the man already staring at him.

One corner of Andras's mouth was curled in a small grin. His irises were pale blue, almost white, encircled in a dark blue ring. When their eyes met, a jolt worked through Ash's body, stopping in his chest. His heart pounded an erratic rhythm behind his ribs, and it took a tremendous amount of effort to pull his gaze away from that icy stare.

Even as Ash fixed his attention on the fae down the table talking about something he couldn't have cared less about, his breathing was still uneven, and he could swear he still felt Andras staring at him. He wiped his palms on his thighs and forced his attention to the conversation going on around the table, ignoring the shivers racing over his skin.

Ash's attention was drawn to more important matters as conversation shifted to plans to bring back all the members of court who'd defected after Esmeray was killed. The ones who refused to swear to Phoenix, before the demon. If they were planning on bringing them back, things were going to go downhill fast for Unseelie. Ash had to find out what their goal was. Why had a demon taken over Phoenix? And was this a rogue demon or had it been sent to Unseelie by a higher power of Hel?

While Ash's thoughts wandered, the conversation shifted once again. He tuned back in when he heard Lainey's name.

"I think my brother should help with the search for your mate," Selene said in a low, sultry voice.

Ash barely contained his reaction. Why the hell would she want her brother to help search for Lainey? The first reason he could think of was so he could kill her as soon as she was found. Like hell that was going to happen. Ash narrowed his eyes as he saw Andras flinch when Selene placed her hand on his arm. It was barely noticeable, but he caught it.

Andras's gaze flew to Ash's, and something dark slithered in the depths of those icy blue orbs before he quickly broke eye contact.

"I think that is a wonderful idea," Phoenix said. "The more people looking, the quicker she can be returned to me."

Like she was some possession. Ash gripped the arms of his chair to keep himself from launching across the table and wrapping his hands around Nix's throat.

"Ash, why don't you take Andras to the barracks? Maybe he can get some different answers out of the guards."

Nausea turned in his gut, but he nodded and stood from his chair. Andras shared a quiet conversation with his sister before he, too, stood and followed Ash out of the room.

ASH

THIS WAS A HORRIBLE IDEA. ASH KEPT REPEATING THAT to himself over and over as he led a silent Andras through the palace. Even though he didn't say a word, Ash could feel his presence behind him, like a dark cloud hovering near the sun, threatening to block the light. He reached out with his magic to gauge what kind of fae Andras was, but there was nothing. No wind or water, no fire or earth. No magical signature at all. There was no sign of fae magic in Andras. A sliver of fear wormed its way through Ash, and he missed a step.

He slowed to let Andras walk next to him. They were about the same height, Andras had maybe one inch on Ash's six-foot-five frame. He could feel the heat from Andras's body, and that surprised him. With the lack of magic, Ash imagined he would be cold. Like a vampire. He snorted to himself, and Andras eyed him curiously.

"So," Ash said, "where are you from?"

Andras tensed slightly before responding. "My family is from a small town in Unseelie. Most have never heard of it."

Um, right. There were a few towns in Unseelie, all of them small, and all of them were on the maps. Ash didn't push it. Two could play this game. "What brings you to court?"

"Our parents always had dreams of us coming here. Unfortunately, they didn't survive the curse. My sister and I came to honor them," Andras said, his words slightly accented but devoid of emotion. So flat, nothing suggested he'd recently lost his family.

Ash's family had been split up by the curse, and even now, he had no idea where his dad was. When he talked about it, he couldn't keep the emotion from his voice no matter how hard he tried. Ash didn't believe Andras's story one bit.

"I'm sorry to hear about your parents," he offered.

Andras shrugged his shoulders but didn't respond.

"So, how did you and your sister gain favor with King Phoenix so quickly?" So much for not prodding.

"Our ... our uncle used to be part of Esmeray's court. Before she went mad, that is. He left when things started getting bad."

Another lie. Ash could tell, even if he couldn't pinpoint how he knew. He felt it in his chest, like he had some inner lie detector that buzzed every time Andras spoke.

"Who is your uncle?" Ash asked.

"I don't think you would know him. He hasn't returned to court."

Ash bit the inside of his cheek to keep from smiling. Andras was not a good liar.

They reached the doors that led to the training yards, and for the second time that day, Ash stepped outside to the sounds of weapons and the grunts of guards. He eyed the barracks in the distance, and his stomach sank. What would Andras do to question the guards? He hadn't gathered enough about the man during this brief conversation to determine what kind of person he was.

With a spur-of-the-moment idea, Ash spun around and walked backward toward the nearest empty training ring. With his arms spread wide, he gave Andras his best winning smile.

"How about a friendly duel? It's been a long time since I practiced with someone."

Something sparked in Andras's eyes at the mention of a duel, and that half smile curled the corner of his lips again. "Are you sure you want to do that?"

A surprisingly pleasant shiver traveled down Ash's spine at the deep baritone of Andras's voice. "Oh, I'm positive."

He spun and grabbed a sword from the rack of weapons on the side of the field. The sharp edge glittered as it caught the sunlight, and Ash ran his thumb over the edge pressing just before the point of breaking his skin. No wooden practice weapons for this.

He moved to the center of the ring and watched Andras prowl to the rack himself. He ran his hand over the various options before selecting a slim, curved sword. Nerves fluttered in Ash's belly as Andras approached, and only partly because of the duel about to take place.

He hadn't been lying when he'd said it had been a while since he'd trained. Working with Lainey had taken up a lot of his time, and he hadn't been able to practice as much as he would have liked. In New York, he'd trained with Nix and his dad, but that seemed like ages ago.

The afternoon sun beat down on his head, and he leaned the sword on the edge of the barrier surrounding the practice ring to tie his hair back with one of Lainey's hair ties. It was too short for all of it to go back, so the bottom layer fell out almost immediately. He then grabbed the hem of his shirt and pulled it over his head before tossing it to the side. While he stretched his arms and torso, he watched Andras discard his own jacket and shirt, and the weird feeling in Ash's stomach increased, a mix of swooping excitement and nausea.

Black tattoos covered Andras's chest and arms. They almost looked like a language, but it was nothing Ash had ever seen before. He couldn't stop his gaze from roaming lower to Andras's chiseled abs and the waistband of his black pants sitting low on his hips, displaying a deep V that made Ash's mouth water. Ash swallowed and quickly averted his gaze before Andras could notice. Picking up his sword, he swung it a few times to warm up and get used to the weight.

He smirked at Andras before asking, "Ready?"

Andras nodded, and they faced off. Both made a few test moves toward the other, gaining an understanding of how the other fought. Once they fell into the movements, Ash had to admit, Andras was very well trained. Better than him, in fact. He moved like smoke, flowing from one move to the next with an ease that turned the fight into a beautiful dance.

Ash did his best to not get distracted by the muscles bunching and tensing under Andras's pale skin, but he couldn't seem to keep his attention on his target.

"Fuck," Ash muttered as he conceded a step to his opponent's onslaught.

Andras went on the offensive, and Ash blocked each hit with a grunt before he got the upper hand and turned the tides back on Andras. They went back and forth across the training field, swords clashing as they sparred. The sun beat down, and sweat quickly coated both of them.

The longer they sparred, the more he learned about the man Andras was. It was amazing what you could determine about a person by watching them fight. Andras was cautious but not afraid to take an occasional unexpected chance. He remained focused on the fight, and when he advanced, he did so with determination and an air of absolute certainty. Ash found it fascinating to watch the man let go of his armor as he fell into the moves of swordplay.

In a maneuver Ash hadn't expected, Andras disarmed him and pressed him against a post of the fence ringing the field. His sword edged into Ash's neck while his body pressed tight to Ash's. Ash raised his hand to grasp the wrist holding the sword, and Andras's pulse beat wildly under his thumb. Their chests rose and fell together, brushing against each other with each inhale. Sweat plastered strands of Andra's hair to his forehead, and Ash's fingers itched to brush them away.

There was something captivating about him that Ash couldn't put a name to. Neither of them said anything, but Ash couldn't resist the pull to lower his eyes to Andra's lips. When he returned his gaze to Andras, the man's icy eyes were hooded, making Ash's blood simmer in his veins. Neither of them could hide the effect this had on them. Ash felt Andras's cock hardening against his own, and his breathing hitched.

"Ash!"

The spell broke, and Andras pulled away, lowering his sword to his side. Ash turned and found Warren jogging toward them. He quickly retrieved his shirt, adjusting himself as subtly as he could.

"Ash, you're going to want to see this. The village is on fire." Warren stopped in front of Ash, but he kept his focus on Andras.

Andras paused while pulling his shirt over his head. Most people would have missed it, it was so subtle, but Ash was even more tuned in to the man's movements after what had just happened between them. Was that worry he detected in the lines of Andras's body? But worry about what? Getting caught?

Ash returned his attention to Warren and asked, "The entire village?" He deposited his sword on the rack, then raised the hem of his shirt to wipe the sweat from his eyes.

"The southwest corner," Warren replied. "The queen's observatory will give you a good vantage point."

Ash made his way toward the palace with Warren at his side. He could sense Andras following behind, a weird mixture of heat and a void of nothingness where his magic should have been. It wasn't until he was halfway up the winding steps to the observatory that he realized he had just given Andras the location of Lainey's safe space.

He stepped out of the stairwell and past the shattered door, kicking up dust in his wake. The telescope gleamed dully in the sunlight filtering through the windows. He wanted to fix that old thing as a surprise for Lainey, but he had no idea where to start. Nor the time.

Ash turned at Andras's soft gasp and found the man wide-eyed with wonder as he took in the telescope. The carefully blank expression Andras wore around Ash had fallen away, replaced by something that made Ash's chest ache. Andras stepped forward and reached out a hand to the telescope. He ran his fingers over the aged metal and crumbling pieces of wood. Ash tried to ignore the image that formed in his head of those fingers running over his skin.

"Does it work?" Andras asked quietly, but there was no mistaking the hope in his voice.

"No," Ash replied, "it's broken."

The longing on Andras's face made Ash wish the damn thing worked. Why did he care so much about what Andras thought? Why did he want to tell him the telescope worked so he could see the first genuine smile grace those lips?

"I wonder what started it?" Warren asked, his question breaking through Ash's uncomfortable thoughts.

He spun around and joined Warren at the windows overlooking the front of the palace grounds. The wall surrounding the Unseelie palace was massive, with sporadic, tall, pointed spires that housed the lookouts. The black stone usually seemed to suck in all the light despite the bright sun overhead, but today, there was no sun. A dark gray cloud of smoke hung over the village, blocking out the light. Orange flames burned through the southwest corner of Unseelie. Villagers ran from the fire, while water fae ran toward it.

"How many water fae do we have?" Ash asked Warren.

"Enough to handle this fire."

Andras approached the windows, and Ash watched him closely from the corner of his eye to gauge his reaction. He took a deep breath and swallowed before turning for the door. "I need to speak with my sister," he said, then vanished down the stairs.

"What do you think of him and his sister?" Warren asked as soon as Andras was out of earshot.

Ash frowned. "I don't know. But something isn't adding up." Turning his attention back to the window, Ash sighed. "I want guards to go through the damaged buildings as soon as the fire is extinguished. Search for any wounded and bring them to the barracks. Set up a check-in and gather the names of any missing fae. Check with villagers not impacted by this and see if they can help provide shelter, food, and clothing." Before Warren could turn away to carry out his orders, Ash grabbed his arm. "And Warren, find out what caused this."

THREE DAYS since Lainey had left Faerie.

Ash made his way through the palace, ignoring the frenzied court members who ran around gossiping about the fire and spreading rumors as to the cause. Warren hadn't been able to find the cause yet, but he was working on it. The energy in the palace was palpable. He still didn't know who he could trust or who was involved with the demon plot, and the extra excitement made him weary.

But he was on edge for a very different reason this morning. There had been a raven sitting outside his window when he woke. The thing had been staring at him, and as soon as Ash acknowledged its presence, it took off with a flap of its wings.

His mom had always believed in omens and portents. She'd sworn the day the curse locked the gates, there were ravens perched on the roofs and steps of every fae home in the city. He didn't know whether that was true, but he couldn't shake the uneasy feeling that had settled within him at the sight of the bird outside his window.

As Ash came to an intersection in the hallway, he slowed. Harsh, angry whispers echoed from the other hall. He strained his ears to hear the words, but the people arguing were speaking too quietly, like they wanted to keep their conversation secret.

He turned the corner and stopped in his tracks. Andras was hunched down to his sister's level, and Selene had her red-painted nails dug into the fabric of Andras's jacket. As soon as they noticed him, they straightened, and their conversation fell silent. Selene plastered a fake smile on her face while Andras stared wearily at Ash.

"Good morning," Selene said in her deep and sultry voice that made Ash's skin crawl.

He gave them a polite smile and nodded before replying, "Not sure how good it is, but morning."

Selene laughed, a surprisingly high tinkling sound. "You're so right. It is quite sad about that fire."

She looked anything but sad. Ash narrowed his eyes at her, and Andras must have noticed his reaction. He placed his hand on his sister's back.

"Selene," he warned.

"Right," she said and shook herself free of his touch. "We must be going. Have a good day."

"You too," Ash murmured.

He watched them walk away for a second longer before continuing on his way to the council chamber with thoughts swirling through his head. Those two showing up unexpectedly and no one knowing who they were, then the unexplained fire. It all seemed tied together. And he had a feeling Nix was at the center of it all.

Ash found Zephyr leaning against the wall opposite the council room, his arms crossed over his chest and his blue eyes—so similar to Lainey's—narrowed at the door.

"Any news?" Ash asked as he stopped next to him.

Zephyr shook his head. "Nothing. Phoenix has been holed up in there all morning. The mysterious siblings just left not too long ago, but neither spared me a glance."

"I ran into them," Ash muttered, rubbing at the stubble along his jaw. "I feel like all the pieces of a puzzle are laid out in front of me, but I can't put them together to see the entire picture. It's driving me insane."

Zephyr opened his mouth to reply, but the council room door opened, and Phoenix strode out.

Ash straightened and gave his friend a once-over. He looked rough. His clothes were too big on him, hanging on his once bulky shoulders and arms. His hair was longer and unkempt—something that would have driven Nix mad. Dark, bruise-like shadows had appeared under his eyes, and his cheeks were sunken in. His usually tan skin was pale—almost sickly.

This drastic change had happened so fast. The last time Ash had seen Nix, it hadn't been this bad. It looked like he was being eaten alive, all of his health and vitality slowly disappearing as the demon inside him devoured his very essence. A sense of urgency he hadn't felt before rushed through Ash at the sight. Was this normal? There was so much Ash didn't know about demon possession, but he felt the blade poised over his neck now, the seconds counting down. They were running out of time.

Ash gritted his teeth and contained the shiver that tried to run down his spine. He nodded his head respectfully at Nix, grimacing internally as he realized he was bowing to a demon.

"Ash. Good. Follow me," Phoenix said coldly before striding down the hall without another glance behind him.

Ash clapped Zephyr on the shoulder before falling in with the rest of the trailing entourage. Lady Davers was sulking and whispering fiercely in her husband's ear. Ash couldn't pick out all the words she said, but he heard *marriage, daughter,* and *hussy,* and could only assume she was fuming over Selene's appearance at court and how much it disrupted her plans for her daughter marrying Nix.

Ash wondered briefly if he could trust the Daverses, but quickly dismissed that idea. Even if they had nothing to do with this demon shit, they clearly wanted Lainey out of the picture, and Ash would never tolerate that.

The entourage followed Phoenix through the palace, and it

didn't take long for Ash to realize where they were going. When Phoenix opened a heavy metal door and began the climb up hundreds of steps, it confirmed his suspicions.

The tallest spire of the palace housed the war room. At the top of the winding stairs, a round, open room with floor-to-ceiling windows overlooked Unseelie. It had been added to the palace at a later date, the height obstructing part of the view of the observatory, which was the reason the observatory had fallen into disuse. The view from this room was breathtaking—when part of the village wasn't smoldering. A large wooden table took up most of the space with a rack full of maps along the only bit of wall not made of windows, near the door.

One of Phoenix's newer council members—a fae Ash had only seen in passing and didn't trust—strode to the maps and pulled one from the rack. He spread it over the table, using various weapons to weigh down the edges. The image depicted was the section of the village that had been burned by the fire.

Nix stood in front of a window with his hands clasped behind his back as he stared out over the view. Every instinct in Ash was telling him to go stand by his friend. In normal circumstances, he would have been there, shoulder to shoulder with his best friend as they observed the chaos outside the walls. He didn't know what to do with himself in this situation. Would everyone expect him to do that, knowing they were best friends? He really didn't want to be any nearer the demon than he had to be.

He was spared from deciding when Phoenix turned from the window and approached the table.

"What was the cause of the fire?" he asked with no emotion in his voice.

"We haven't figured that out yet, Your Majesty," Lord Davers replied.

"And the amount of damage?"

"The entire southwest section of the village is gone," another council member replied.

"Casualties?" Phoenix's gaze was fixed on the map, body eerily still as he stared, unblinking.

Lord Davers replied again, "Twenty-three so far, and I expect the count to continue to grow." He, at least, sounded grim as he studied the map portraying the section of burned village.

Phoenix snagged a dagger and twirled it between his fingers. "Who gave the orders to the guards to put out the fire and start rescuing villagers?" He lifted his gaze to Ash, like he already knew the answer to his question.

Fingers of dread gripped Ash's spine. "I did," he said.

Demon Nix studied Ash, his gaze cold and piercing. It took all of Ash's training to not squirm under that unyielding stare. After what felt like hours, Nix dropped his gaze back to the map. "Pull the guards back."

"What?" Ash spluttered. "The villagers need their assistance. Are you going to send others out there instead?"

Nix turned toward the door, his entourage falling in line behind him. "With the court divided, we don't have the resources to spare. We need to be proactive and not throw resources away when they could be better used elsewhere."

Phoenix and the entourage exited the war room, but Ash couldn't make his feet move from their spot. Leave the villagers to deal with this catastrophe on their own? They would never survive. The village was already hurting for supplies after Esmeray's reign; this would completely decimate them.

Why was everyone else so okay with this? Ash stared out of the window, charred remains and smoke curling to the sky, not registering in his vision as the wheels turned in his head. Did they know what was happening? That Nix was possessed? He ran his hand through his hair and sighed heavily, suddenly extremely tired. Had the members of the court willingly allied themselves with a demon? Did they have their own plans that he knew nothing about? This was too much for him. He hadn't been trained for any of this, and he didn't know what to do. All he knew was that he needed to save Nix.

If he hadn't already been completely sure something was possessing Nix, this encounter would have sealed the deal. Never would Nix have allowed something like that to happen to innocent people. As if the stakes hadn't already been high, this raised them even more. The press of time seemed to speed up, and Ash felt every second like a blade to his throat.

LAINEY

THREE DAYS SINCE SHE'D LEFT FAERIE.

It took her a moment to remember where she was when she woke up. Lainey glanced around the room decorated in neutral colors with bland artwork hanging on the walls. It was completely different from her rooms in the palace. The realization of how much she missed Unseelie gave her a sharp ache in her chest.

It wasn't just Nix and Ash that she missed. It was her bedroom with the gold painted stars on the ceiling. She missed the orphanage and the town on the outskirts of the palace. The fae who inhabited the town were so unlike the court. She missed their welcoming smiles and friendly waves. Her feet itched to walk down the broken cobblestone street to the small bakery that made the best chocolate pastries, or the flower shop with enticing scents that always permeated the air around the store.

Sighing, Lainey climbed out of bed and quickly brushed her hair and teeth in the adjoining bathroom. Once she was halfway presentable, she followed the scent of freshly brewed coffee to the kitchen. At the bottom of the stairs, she heard voices coming from the direction of the kitchen, and she slowed her steps. She couldn't make out the second voice or what they were saying, but she knew the first belonged to Phoenix's dad, Brand.

Lainey rounded the corner and came to a screeching halt. Her hand wrapped around her throat on instinct, and she took a step back, even as her body wanted to lock up and freeze her in place. Her pulse beat madly under her fingers, and she fell so hard into her memories, she stumbled against the wall, reaching blindly for something to hold on to.

The blood seeped between her fingers, warm and sticky, as she lay on the hard ground. Roots dug into her back, and leaves brushed her cheek as they fell. Her lungs screamed for air, but when she gasped, it was a wet and choked thing. Like smoke, every thought slipped through her fingers, floating away into the universe. But there were still emotions. Still fear. Still regret. Burning bright like a star about to go out, and then ... dimming. Fading. Dulling into the darkness that lingered around the edges of her vision. Waiting to claim her.

"Lainey," a voice said at the same time a hand gripped her shoulder. "Lainey," the voice repeated.

The gentle shaking drew her out of her memories, and she blinked to clear her vision. Brand stood in front of her with worry creasing his brow. He was blocking her view of the reason she'd had that flashback.

"Beck," she said in a strangled whisper.

Brand frowned and turned his head to peer behind him. "Do you two know each other?"

Lainey's grip tightened on her throat. "He almost killed me," she whispered. "He killed my sister."

Brand's face drained of color, and he gasped. "What?" he yelled. Turning to face his son, Lainey noticed red creeping up the back of his neck. "Beck! What is she talking about?"

Beck shrugged. "I was trying to break the curse."

"You murdered someone? And you tried to murder your brother's mate?" Incredulity painted Brand's words, and anger made them tremble.

Over Brand's shoulder, Lainey saw Beck's eyes widen.

"Mate?" he repeated, surprise lighting his eyes. "In my

defense, I didn't know they were mates." He shrugged nonchalantly.

Brand growled low in his throat and turned back to Lainey. His jaw was tense, but he gently pried her hand away from her throat and led her to the kitchen table. "Sit, Lainey. We will work this out. Do you like coffee?"

She nodded numbly, never taking her eyes off Beck. He watched her with boredom lining his features. Dark blue eyes stared at her with no remorse or caring. He ran his hand through his light brown hair and slumped further in his seat, posture pure arrogance and "who gives a fuck". Her fingers were cramping from how hard she was clasping them together in her lap, the urge to launch herself across the table and wrap them around his throat was so strong.

Brand poured a cup of coffee and set it in front of Lainey with cream and sugar. "Explain," he said in a no-nonsense tone of voice Lainey gathered was reserved for fathers to their children.

Beck sighed dramatically. "I was trying to break the curse," he said again. "Failed at doing so, obviously."

Lainey saw red. His words and the way he said them, like it was no big deal, made her shake. She wished she had a knife, or even a fork. Anything pointy to stab him with would have worked. With a jolt, she remembered her magic. She gathered it to her and threw it at Beck, wrapping it around him and squeezing tightly.

He didn't have time to react before her wind surrounded him like a boa and started constricting. His eyes bulged, and he struggled, writhing in the binds of her magic, trying to escape. She'd wrapped it around his mouth so she didn't have to hear him talk anymore, and all that he could get out were grunts and growls.

Lainey squeezed even tighter. She imagined him popping like a grape and couldn't keep the smile from her face. The anger in Beck's eyes disappeared, replaced by fear as he realized just how much she wanted to kill him.

"Lainey!" Brand jumped forward and grabbed her shoulders, giving her a little shake. "Lainey, let him go!"

Her chest heaved with the gasping breaths she was taking. "He killed my sister. He slit my throat. It's the least he deserves." She didn't recognize her own voice. It was cold and detached. That darkness she'd been keeping at bay slithered through her. It reveled in the violence. Begged for more.

"I get it," Brand said calmly. "I understand you want him to hurt, but you don't want to kill him. You would be no better than him if you did."

She laughed without humor. "Oh, but I really, really do." The darkness rejoiced at her words.

Flame sparked to life in Brand's palm. Lainey barely noticed it. Her eyes were glued on Beck, who was turning an interesting shade of purple. Would he literally pop and explode if she squeezed hard enough? Or would his insides just collapse in on themselves?

"He is still my son Lainey," Brand said evenly. "Let him go. We will deal with this. He won't get away with what he did. I promise."

The flame in Brand's hand grew, climbing up his forearm, and the heat seared Lainey. She tore her glare from Beck and looked toward Brand. His eyes shone with regret, and she knew he wouldn't hesitate to hurt her to save his son. She needed Brand's help too much to make an enemy of him. Not to mention, he was her father-in-law.

"Fuck," she growled and reluctantly released her magic, shoving aside the growing darkness, which flailed in despair at her giving in.

Beck gasped and fell forward, clutching his chest. He heaved in huge lungfuls of air, and Lainey glared at him. Each breath he took was one her sister was no longer taking. How was that fair? Why did he get to live and Emma didn't? Tears burned her eyes at the unfairness of it all, but she blinked them away.

Brand didn't spare his son a glance as he pulled a chair around and sat between them. "I'm truly sorry for what my son has done to both you and your sister. I know apologies don't change what happened, but know that I do not stand for that kind of behavior." His voice was firm yet kind. "Had I known what was happening, I would have put a stop to it. He won't hurt you again. You have my word."

Beck grunted as he finally straightened. Lainey looked at him, *really* looked at him, for the first time. She could see the resemblance between him and Phoenix. They had a similar facial structure and build. His hair was lighter than Nix's with none of the reddish tint. He must have gotten his eyes from his mom. They were a beautiful shade of dark blue.

"Now," Brand began, drawing her attention away from the murderer. "Before we head to Madam Elvie's, tell me everything you can about Phoenix and why you think he's been possessed by a demon."

Beck jerked back in surprise, and the little color he had regained after Lainey's attack drained from his face again. "Demon?" He swallowed, and his gaze bounced between Lainey and his dad.

Lainey narrowed her eyes at him. "Yes, a demon. What do you know about it?" she asked accusingly.

His wide-eyed stare shot to Lainey. "Why would I know anything about that?"

"Oh, I don't know, maybe because you seem to have it out for your brother and his mate?" Lainey clenched her hands on the edge of the table and glared at Beck. Her magic swirled angrily in her veins, begging to be let loose again. The darkness egged her on.

Beck threw up his hands in surrender. "Whoa, back up, princess. I may have done some shitty things, but I had good reasons for doing them. I would never let my brother get possessed by a demon."

"Both of you, calm down," Brand interrupted in a soothing

voice. "Arguing and playing the blame game won't do anything to help Phoenix."

Lainey exhaled and stared at the table, shame heating the back of her neck. Of course, Brand was right. She needed to focus on the bigger problem. She could deal with Beck after she saved Nix.

Brand glanced between Lainey and Beck until he was sure they would behave. "Now," he said once satisfied, "we need to head to Madam Elvie's. Beck, are you coming with us?"

Lainey jerked in her seat. No way was she working with Beck. She opened her mouth to argue but snapped it shut at one glance from Brand. She huffed and crossed her arms over her chest. "I don't trust him," she mumbled.

"I didn't ask you to trust him," Brand replied. The look he leveled at his son could have withered even the heartiest of flowers.

In Beck's defense, he only slightly flinched under that stare.

"I will tolerate no bickering," Brand continued. "I understand there is a painful history between you guys, but my other son needs help, and I intend to help him. You will not get in my way."

Properly chastised, Lainey nodded and mumbled her agreement. She wouldn't let her anger for Beck distract her from saving her mate.

⁂

"OH, WELL, ISN'T THIS INTERESTING?" Madam Elvie grinned at the three guests standing on her dilapidated porch. "I do so love drama." She stepped aside and ushered everyone in.

Lainey chose a dark blue cushion to sit on and eyed the massive stacks of books and scrolls piled on the table and scattered across the floor. Beck took a cushion as far from Lainey as he could get, while Brand sat on one between them, ready to be the mediator. Elvie lowered herself into a seat across from them and said nothing. She smiled and folded her hands on the table.

"So ... uh ..." Lainey began. "What do we do?"

"Tell me again everything that has happened." The elf looked entirely too excited by the prospect of drama.

Lainey took a deep breath and retold her story. When she finished, she could feel Beck's gaze on her, and it made her skin crawl. She dared a glance in his direction and found a troubled expression on his face.

"When I tested your bond," Madam Elvie said, "I felt something disturbing. A mate bond cannot be broken or worn away. A healer can remove a bond with the permission of both parties, and both must be present for the breaking."

Lainey nodded. She knew that much already. But her bond didn't feel broken or worn away. It felt like a tattered ribbon blowing in the breeze, unraveling more and more each day.

"Your bond felt ... shredded, for lack of a better word," Madam Elvie said. Her brows were drawn down over her pale blue eyes, and a thoughtful expression pulled her mouth into a frown. "There was something dark in the pieces of the bond, more noticeable in the frayed edges, but it was as if it were alive, or sentient."

Fear bubbled in Lainey's chest. "Alive? Like I have a parasite or something?" She swallowed thickly, fighting back the sudden urge to vomit.

Madam Elvie bobbed her head from side to side. "In a way. I'm not sure how to explain the feeling I got from it. I don't think it is a presence so much as an echo. Something that has traveled from Phoenix and attached itself in order to destroy the bond."

Lainey pressed a hand to her chest, as if she could hold the pieces of the mate bond together. "How do I stop it?" she whispered.

Madam Elvie sighed. "I am not sure. If we remove the demon from Phoenix, will that stop the bond from breaking? Will it continue, even after you free Phoenix? These are things we will need to research." She waved her hand to indicate the stacks of books and scrolls. "These all came from Faerie and are older than Faerie itself. No one knows where they came from. They were just

... there. If there is a way to save Phoenix and your bond, it will be in these books."

"So we just start reading?" Brand asked as he eyed the numerous ancient texts. "That will take us forever."

"Then we better get started!" Madam Elvie crowed.

ASH

Six days since Lainey had left Faerie.

"Fuck!" Ash inspected his arm and the thin slice that was already leaking blood.

Andras chuckled darkly and lowered his sword. "That's the third time I've drawn blood. Do you surrender?"

Ash growled, "Never!" He lunged forward, fully expecting Andras to jump back. Instead, faster than Ash could track even with his fae sight, Andras lifted his sword and blocked Ash's attack with an easy smile.

Ash growled again and backed away before turning and stomping to the weapons rack. The man was infuriating. Ash had never fought against someone so well trained, and almost every sparring session left Ash conceding defeat with his tail between his legs. If it weren't for the complete joy he got out of spending time with Andras—shirtless—Ash would have quit sparring with him days ago.

Ash slammed his sword back onto the rack and grabbed a towel he'd hung over the fence. He grimaced as he wiped the blood off his arm, shoulder, and chest. They were shallow cuts, a sure sign of Andras's amazing control over his sword, but they hurt nonetheless. Mostly because Ash hadn't landed a single hit on the dark-haired man.

"Nice work today," Andras said, as he replaced his own weapon much more calmly.

Ash grunted but couldn't stop from glancing at Andras. Sweat glistened on the panes of his tattooed chest and slid down the grooves of his abs. His pale skin had darkened a bit from the time they had spent sparring outdoors, but he was still much paler than Ash.

Ash had suggested the daily sparring to keep tabs on Andras, and to figure out what his and his sister's plans were. So far, he'd gleaned nothing useful except a few tidbits about Andras's personality. He was punctual—always on time, if not early. He was quiet but not shy, and he always thought through what he was going to say before he said it. He also hadn't questioned the guards yet, even though Phoenix had commanded him to. And the most intriguing thing Ash had noticed: he gave none of the women at court a second glance, even though they fawned over him.

Shaking off his grumpiness at losing—again—Ash forced his attention to Andras's face. "What are your plans for the day?"

Andras shrugged his shoulders before tugging his shirt over his head. "My sister has things she wants to discuss, but other than that, I was going to spend some time in the library."

"Mm," Ash hummed. "How is your sister doing? I haven't seen her around much."

The thought ignited fire in his veins. The reason Selene had been missing around the palace was because she'd holed herself up in Phoenix's quarters. After Nix had burned his and Lainey's rooms, he'd commandeered the wing of the palace Esmeray had inhabited. He'd moved Selene into the wing with him, and neither of them were seen very often after that, except during council meetings. Ash swallowed back the nausea in his gut.

Andras didn't reply right away. He nodded, and his eyes took on that distant look they usually did when he thought through his next words. Ash gave him the time he needed, but one day, he would pressure Andras for answers in hopes of getting something useful.

"She's doing well," he said slowly. "She has been working closely with King Phoenix, trying to find a happy medium in regards to bringing old court members back."

It took all of Ash's self-control to not snort. *Working closely, indeed.*

"What do you plan on doing today?" Andras asked.

Ash almost missed a step. Usually, it was Ash engaging in conversation, and Andras following his lead. He couldn't think of a single time Andras had asked him a question.

"I'm meeting with Zephyr," Ash replied carefully. "I want to see if he has heard anything on Lai—Queen Elena's whereabouts."

Ash noticed Andras watching him from the corner of his eye with a crooked smile. Andras hummed in his throat, but he clearly didn't believe what Ash had said. Why did lying to Andras make him feel dirty?

Ash shook off the feeling as they parted ways inside the palace, Andras heading toward his rooms and Ash heading toward Zephyr's. He did need to talk with Lainey's dad, but not about her. There was nothing to discuss there, unfortunately. Ash couldn't let his thoughts linger on her without worry taking over, making him nauseous.

"You're bleeding," Zephyr said, nodding his head at Ash's shirt as Ash pushed into his room.

He'd pulled his shirt on, but not before his wounds had healed. The red stains bloomed like gory flowers on the white fabric.

Ash grunted. "Andras is a damn good fighter."

"Among other things?" Zephyr asked with a twinkle in his eye.

"Watch it, old man."

Zephyr chuckled and tossed an ice cube at Ash from the glass in his hand. Ash settled onto the couch and kicked his feet up onto the coffee table. He sighed as the pressure was relieved from his aching muscles.

"Did you learn anything today?" Ash asked as his head flopped back onto the cushion behind his head.

"Actually, I think I did. I heard the name *Halphas* uttered multiple times today. I may be wrong, but I'm almost positive he's a demon."

Ash chewed on the inside of his cheek as he thought. While Ash had been sparring with Andras, Zephyr was using his sylph magic to listen in on conversations between members of Phoenix's council. So far, it had led to nothing useful. But this ... this might have been the lead they needed.

"Okay," Ash said as he stood from the couch with a slight groan. "I'm going to bathe, then I'll head to the library and see if I can find anything on that name."

✦

ASH STEPPED out of the bathing room and stretched his arms over his head, leaning from one side to the other, groaning at the pull of sore muscles. His focus snagged on movement by his window, and he froze. A raven sat on the ledge. This was the third time he'd seen a raven in his window. The other two times, it had flown off as soon as Ash noticed it. This time, it stared back with unblinking black eyes.

Ash grabbed a towel and wrapped it around his waist before slowly approaching the bird. A crease formed between his brows the closer he got to it. The raven tilted its head before it squawked and took off in a flap of wings. A single black feather drifted through the open window and landed on the floor. Ash picked it up and twirled it between his fingers. The black shone in the sunlight, a faint blue shimmer threaded through the vane. Ash brought the feather to his nose and inhaled. He couldn't identify the scent, but it made his heart stutter in his chest.

With a frown, Ash set it on his nightstand and got dressed. He gave the feather one last glance before leaving his room and making his way to the library.

When he stepped inside, he couldn't help but smile as he thought about the last time he'd been here. The memory of Lainey with her skirts hiked up around her knees, lying in a pile of dusty books, broken wood around her, was etched into his brain forever. And all that for a smut book. Damn. He missed that girl. He sent up a quick prayer that she was safe and getting the information they needed to save Phoenix and Unseelie.

Ash hunted down the crotchety librarian and found him reading a scroll in his office. "Excuse me," he said politely. "I was wondering if you could hel—"

Master Corbin didn't tear his attention from the scroll he was studying, but he held up his hand and cut off Ash mid-question. His shrewd eyes moved back and forth as he continued to read, paying Ash no mind. Ash crossed his arms over his chest and leaned against the doorframe, trying to remain patient. There was no point in pissing off the old fae; it would only slow him down even more.

After what felt like an age, Master Corbin lifted his head with pursed lips and a glare. "What is so important that you would interrupt me?"

Ash bit back his retort about doing his job and instead bowed his head. "I would appreciate it if you could point me in the direction of the books on demons."

He wasn't concerned about Master Corbin talking and spreading rumors. The old librarian was too unpleasant for people to actually want to talk to him. It made him a safe bet for getting information without the risk of discovery.

"You think that is more important than me doing my job?" Master Corbin raised one hairy eyebrow and harrumphed. "What could you possibly need information on demons for?"

Isn't helping readers part of his job? Ash managed not to sigh as he pushed off the doorframe. "Morbid curiosity."

Master Corbin huffed and shoved past Ash, heading to the large map of the library that was inlaid in the floor. He tapped a section with his toe. "Here you will find everything we have on demons. Mind, it is not much. They are a secretive people."

"Thank you for your help." Ash bowed his head again. "You are certainly the kindest and most helpful librarian in the realms."

Master Corbin stared at Ash without expression before turning on his heel and heading back to his office. The door didn't quite slam behind him, but it was close.

Ash studied the map, plotting the quickest route to the section Master Corbin had indicated. Once he committed it to memory, he made his way through the shelves. His mind was trying to focus on so many things. Phoenix. Lainey. Andras. The feather and the raven. Demons. There was too much. *I'm going to wind up with gray hair at this rate.*

In the human realm, his life had been fairly simple. He and Phoenix had basically just been living the dream life. Drinking, watching football, going to concerts, hooking up with girls and guys. They'd had no worries. His short time in Faerie had been a sharp contrast to that cushy life. The queen's well-being was his responsibility. Now he was trying to save his best friend and the Unseelie people from a demon. A demon that would most likely not be content with just Unseelie. Once he had what he wanted here, where would he go next? Seelie? Earth? There was too much at stake. So many innocent people at risk who didn't even know about the realms and the magic in the world they lived in.

Ash came to the section of the library with the books on demons, and he trailed his fingers along the spines, pulling down those he thought might be useful. With his arms full, he found a seating area not too far from the demon section and dropped everything on the low table. The black couches in the library were comfortable, and Ash sighed as he sat and pulled a book toward him, flipping it open and scanning its contents.

After an hour of scouring pages with no luck, he heard footsteps nearby. Ash looked up to find Andras emerging from an aisle with his own armful of books. The man stopped as his icy gaze landed on Ash. He rolled his shoulders and set his stack next to Ash's. "Mind if I join you?" he asked quietly.

Ash hesitated. He needed to say no. The material he was researching was too sensitive, and he couldn't let Andras catch wind of it. Even as he was opening his mouth to say no, different words popped out instead. "Of course." Ash snapped his mouth shut. *What the hell was that?* In an effort to keep his reading material secret, Ash slid his books farther across the table.

Andras gave him a small smile before sitting on the couch across from Ash. "What are you looking for?" Andras indicated Ash's pile of books.

"Oh, this and that," he hedged. "What about you?"

"Same."

They stared at each other for a moment, the air charged with so many things. Attraction, curiosity, uncertainty. Ash was the first to break eye contact, and he subtly tried to read the titles on Andras's books, but it was no use. They were too old and worn, the letters faded to intelligibility.

Silence fell around them as they dug into their reading. Ash was almost relaxed with the sounds of soft breathing and pages turning. At least until he felt a prickle on his skin, and he knew Andras was watching him. It took all of his self-control to keep his eyes firmly glued to the book. When he noticed Andras was no longer turning pages of his own book, he couldn't fight it anymore. He glanced up and caught Andras's gaze.

They got sucked into the moment, looking at each other. Ash let his eyes rove over Andras's face, cataloging his features and trying to decipher what his feelings meant. Were those butterflies in his stomach? That was something he'd never experienced before with any of his partners, male or female. And his heart, it was fluttering madly like a bird trapped in a cage. As often as he'd messed around with people in the human realm—Nix calling him a "man whore" was pretty accurate—he'd never had this kind of visceral reaction before. It was all very unsettling considering he had no idea who Andras was, and he was certain the man was hiding something important.

Andras's gaze dropped to the book on Ash's lap. He'd closed it, marking his place with his finger, and the cover was now clearly visible. Andras's eyes widened, and he stiffened.

"Demon hierarchy?" he asked quietly but intensely. His gaze lifted to Ash's ,and it burned straight through him.

Oh, fuck. Ash scrambled to find a reason for reading about demons, but he came up empty. "Morbid curiosity?" he said with a guilty grin. He knew Andras wouldn't fall for it the same way Master Corbin supposedly had.

Andras lowered his brows over his eyes, creating shadows in their icy depths. "Why are you studying demons, Ash?"

It was the first time Andras had said his name, and shivers worked over his skin at the sound of it on Andras's tongue. He shook his head, clearing it of the lust that had suddenly fogged over his mind, and moved the book more firmly onto his lap, hiding his very obvious reaction.

Ash didn't answer the question. There was nothing he could say, and the damage was already done. He would have to keep a closer eye on Andras and maybe force some information out of him.

Andras looked at Ash with a kind of openness he had never seen from the man. "Be careful, Ash." He stood and gathered his books. "Don't let anyone else see you reading that," he cautioned, then walked away.

Ash swallowed and rubbed his hand down his face. Well, that had not gone very well. But if Ash hadn't already guessed, that interaction just solidified his theory. Andras definitely knew something, and Ash was determined to get it out of him.

ASH

SEVEN DAYS SINCE LAINEY HAD LEFT FAERIE.

Ash grabbed his books and headed for Lainey's observatory, deciding that would be the safest place to continue his research. As he climbed the spiral staircase, he knew he wouldn't be alone when he reached the crumbled door. Andras's scent floated in the air, a citrus and spice aroma that was definitely still fresh and definitely delicious.

Ash stepped through the doorframe and stopped. Andras was kneeling on the floor in front of the telescope. He was shirtless, wearing loose cotton pants and no shoes. The sight of his bare feet was strangely intimate, and heat crept up the back of his neck. Andras peered over his shoulder at Ash in the doorway. His black hair caught the light streaming in from the windows, causing some strands to shimmer blue.

"What are you doing?" Ash asked, then cringed when it came out sounding accusatory.

Andras sat back on his heels, tapped a tool on the palm of his hand, and said "I'm trying to fix this." Ash could only stare as Andras's cheeks infused with red in an adorable blush. "If you want me to quit, I will," Andras added hurriedly. "I meant nothing by it. I've just always wanted to look through one."

Ash shifted the books to one arm and waved dismissively. "By all means, if you can fix it, go for it."

Andras's attention fell to the book, and his expression shuttered. "So, you are continuing with your research?"

Ash cleared his throat. "Um, yeah."

He could see the questions building in Andras's eyes, so he quickly turned and set the books on the floor. After spreading out a blanket Lainey had left behind, Ash sat and threw himself into his research, ignoring Andras's questioning gaze. Andras went back to work on the telescope, and the sound of clinking tools was oddly soothing as Ash continued his reading.

He was flipping through the third book, quickly losing hope, when the name *Halphas* caught his eye. Sitting up straighter, he read through the two paragraphs detailing the demon. Halphas was a demon of fairly high rank in Hel, and was known for supplying weapons and ammunition, as well as armies for wars.

Ash's blood froze in his veins. If Zephyr had heard that name multiple times during his spying, it couldn't have been a good sign. Was demon Nix attempting to bring an army into Faerie? And with Andras and Selene's sudden appearance at court, paired with the fire, there were too many coincidences to not be connected.

Ash watched Andras. The man was lying on his back under the telescope. He thought through everything he knew of Andras, and admittedly, it wasn't much. As a fae, Ash had pretty good instincts. He'd grown used to trusting them, and so far, they'd rarely led him astray. Unfortunately, his instincts were a mess where Andras was concerned.

His timely appearance at court, and his less-than-believable reasons for being there, made Ash's instincts scream *red flag*. Not to mention, he was incredibly skilled with the sword. His sister was on the top of Ash's list as a suspect in all of this. And there were those warnings he gave Ash after he saw the book on demons.

On the other hand, he was quiet and thoughtful. He never

said anything that expressly made Ash worry. And he was currently lying on the ground trying to fix a telescope. He didn't seem evil, and Ash's instincts said he wasn't. But was that just because Ash thought he was attractive?

There was no denying it to himself. There was a chemistry between them that drew Ash to Andras, always searching for more. More conversation, more sparring, more secretive glances. More shirtless interactions. He thought back to their first sparring match, when Andras pinned Ash to the fence with his sword against his neck. Ash hadn't been the only one turned on.

A loud clink and a curse drew Ash's attention to Andras. The other man grunted and attempted to reach something he'd dropped on the floor that had rolled away, while holding another piece of the telescope against the giant frame.

"Do you need help?" Ash asked and stood. He snagged the bolt from the floor and knelt next to Andras.

"Thank you," he replied and held his arm out.

Ash pressed it into his hand, letting his fingers trail along Andras's palm as he pulled away. Andras's fingers contracted, and Ash heard his sharp inhale before he went back to work on the telescope.

"Could you hold this here for me?" Andras asked tentatively.

Ash scooted in until his knee brushed against Andras's thigh. He reached out to hold the metal piece to the frame as Andras tightened the bolt. Ash had seen Andras shirtless many times now, and each time, he found himself distracted beyond reason. The lines of his tattoos seemed to come alive as the muscles of his arms shifted and he tightened the bolt. It made Ash swallow, his mouth suddenly dry, and he had the hardest time dragging his gaze away.

Ash helped Andras with the telescope far longer than he should have. He had so many things he needed to do, but he couldn't make himself walk away. They passed the time in comfortable conversation, avoiding any topics that were too personal, such as where they lived, their magic, their current goals and jobs. Andras was still quiet and thoughtful with his responses, but he'd opened up more.

Even discussing nothing personal, Ash learned a few things about Andras. He gathered from the sorrowful expression that occasionally crossed Andras's face when talking about different adventures he had been on that he was missing someone. Ash didn't enjoy thinking Andras had someone he missed so fiercely.

It was obvious during these stories that Andras wasn't talking about someplace in Faerie, but Ash didn't press. He just enjoyed listening to him talk, and he enjoyed sharing his own stories from his time in the human realm. The give and take in the conversation, and the interest Andras showed in everything Ash spoke of, was something he'd only experienced with Phoenix and Lainey.

"So, how much longer do you think you'll need to fix this?" Ash asked during a comfortable silence between conversations.

Sitting next to Ash, Andras inspected the telescope with pursed lips. "Maybe another week? The eyepiece will be the most difficult to figure out."

Ash barely heard Andras's response. His attention had drifted to those pursed lips and stuck there. So enticing and plush, with the perfect cupid's bow. Ash had never wanted to kiss someone more than he did in that moment. He noticed Andras had fallen silent and quickly snapped his focus to Andras's soft blue eyes. His breath stuck in his chest as Andras's gaze darkened and dipped toward Ash's mouth.

Anticipation shot through him, a lightning bolt that awakened every nerve ending, leaving them begging for Andras's touch. He held his breath as he leaned in and slowly closed the distance between them, giving Andras time to back away.

He didn't. Instead, Andras leaned forward as well, and Ash felt a surreal sense of rightness as their lips met in a soft brush. His eyes closed and he leaned in to the kiss, increasing the pressure. Andras's fingers trailed lightly over Ash's cheek, the touch cool yet burning at the same time.

Before Ash could deepen the kiss, Andras abruptly pulled away. His eyes were wide and wild, his lips pressed into a thin line, his chest rising and falling as if he'd just run miles. Ash felt the distance between them immediately, and he hated it. It was wrong. The distance between them was all wrong.

Andras shook his head, his black curls hiding his eyes. "That ... We ..." he stopped and swallowed thickly before standing. "That can't happen again."

Andras left through the crumbled door without a backward glance. Stunned and confused, Ash sat on the floor by the telescope, staring at nothing. Those four softly spoken words echoed through his head as if Andras had shouted them.

That can't happen again.

TEN DAYS since Lainey had left Faerie.

Even days after their kiss, Andras's words echoed through Ash's head, creating an empty pit in his stomach that churned. They hurt with an ache he wasn't used to, more than he thought words ever could, especially because he barely knew the other man. It was something in his gut, something his instincts wouldn't let drop. While Andras was definitely hiding things, Ash had a feeling not all of those things were bad.

They'd attended many council meetings together since that kiss, and the tension in the air between them was suffocating. It was surprising no one else had noticed it. There was a current that practically vibrated with need whenever they glanced at each other. Despite the obvious connection and desire, Andras's face remained cold and impassive. It was impressive, actually, how well he controlled himself around Ash. Ash, on the other hand, could barely keep his eyes from Andras. He used every opportunity to sit near him, despite Andras's chilled demeanor.

When he wasn't ruminating on that kiss, Ash spent every waking moment within Phoenix's orbit. He was doing everything in his power to make everyone believe he had no idea what was going on with Nix. Joking and laughing with the demon was the hardest thing he'd ever done. It took all of his focus to appear relaxed and friendly. Despite his efforts, he was no closer to worming his way into Phoenix's inner circle of mis-trusted advisors.

Warren had reported the other day that a guard who was also a fire elemental believed the fire in the village had been lit intentionally. So now Ash was trying to determine how to handle that. He'd never pulled the guards back from helping, even though Demon Nix requested it. Ash wouldn't have been able to sleep at night—the couple of hours he managed, anyway —if he had left the villagers to deal with it themselves. Telling Demon Nix these findings would only draw attention to that fact, and he doubted anything good would come of it. Not to mention, Nix was fire elemental. They were rare, and even though there were other ways to start a fire, Ash was still suspicious.

Exhausted, Ash walked through the halls of the palace, severely missing his best friends. He rubbed his chest, at the spot that was now empty and cold, the spot where his friends should have been. Despite the horrors they had faced in their adventures in the human realm and when they'd first arrived in Faerie, they were some of his favorite memories. Lainey and Nix were his chosen family, and he missed them both tremendously.

The sparring sessions with Andras, and the time they had spent in the observatory or library, didn't replace Lainey and Phoenix but had been a nice addition. Unfortunately, the day after that kiss, Andras hadn't shown up at the fields or the observatory, and he hadn't shown up any day since then. If Ash were being honest with himself, he was lonely.

While he wasn't as out of his element as Lainey had been, this was still his first time in Faerie. This was his first time with this much responsibility. Not only Lainey's life, but Nix's as well. And the rest of Unseelie, apparently. He missed the simple times in the human realm. He missed electricity, showers, music. He missed not having to watch over his shoulder constantly.

Voices echoing down the hall drew Ash from his woe-is-me thoughts. He slowed his steps and strained his ears, his instincts telling him he needed to hear this conversation.

"You will do it, Andras, because I commanded you to." It was Selene's voice, low and sultry but seething with anger. "You know what will happen if you don't."

"I said I will, so back off," Andras hissed.

"It sure doesn't look like it," Selene drawled. "In fact, it looks to me like you need a reminder. Shall I have a message sent? Would you risk it for a pair of pretty eyes?"

"Don't you fucking dare!" Andras's voice rose in volume, the urgency ringing through the words. "I said I'll do it. I'm making sure I get all the information I can from him. Give me time."

"Dear brother," Selene chuckled darkly, "you don't get to tell me what to do."

The whisper of blade sliding free from its sheath had Ash moving before he realized it. He rounded the corner and came to a stop. Selene had Andras pinned against the wall, a slim dagger in her hand glinting in the light as she pressed it to Andras's side.

Andras stared down at his sister with barely contained hatred and a hint of fear. The anger radiating off of him was palpable. His chest heaved with heavy breaths, and his clenched fists shook at his sides.

Andras's attention slid to Ash, and his eyes widened. Selene whirled around and attempted to hide the dagger in her skirts while planting a fake smile on her face. It fell flat. Her expression tightened, fine lines marred the smooth skin near her eyes and mouth, and her eyes almost glowed with rage.

She turned back to Andras and said quietly but fiercely, "See that it's done." Then she stormed down the hall in a flurry of red silk.

Ash kept his gaze pinned to Andras. He was going to get to the bottom of this. Now. He motioned with his head for Andras to follow him, and luckily, he did. If he had refused, Ash wouldn't have hesitated to make a scene in the hallway. He led Andras through the palace to the hidden door of Lainey's observatory.

Clouds blocked the light of the moon from illuminating the space, and the telescope sat in the shadows like a slumbering beast. Ash used his magic, harnessing a bit of energy from lightning to create balls of light to float around the space. The tense lines of Andras's body were clear in the light of Ash's glowing orbs as he walked the length of the curved walls.

"I'm giving you one chance to tell me what's going on," Ash threatened quietly. "One chance before I do something you and your sister won't like." He was bluffing. He had no clue what he would do.

Andras paused but kept his back to Ash. His shoulders rose on an inhale, then dropped. "I can't do it," he whispered. "I can't do it, but Selene will kill her if I don't."

Ash approached slowly, his magic ready. "What are you talking about, Andras?"

"Selene," he said in a broken whisper. "She has my twin sister locked away somewhere. She'll kill her if I don't do what she asks."

Oh, shit. "And what does she want you to do?"

Andras huffed a humorless laugh. "For starters? Kill you."

Well, fuck. "And after I'm out of the way?" He tightened his hold on his magic.

"I can't tell you." He turned around, and unshed tears glistened in his eyes. "My twin is my best friend. She is the other half of me. Selene will destroy her if I tell you."

"Okay, how about this question. What are you?" Ash knew he wasn't fae. There was no way, unless he knew how to hide his magical imprint.

"I have a feeling you already know the answer to that question." Andras's voice was low and quiet, barely audible in the silence of the room.

Ash opened his mouth, but his words were forgotten as

Andras appeared to shimmer. It was like looking down the street on a hot summer day and seeing the pavement undulate back and forth. When the shimmering faded, he stood before Ash in his true form.

Two black horns parted his dark hair and curved up and back along the length of his skull. Faint iridescent blue stripes glistened along their length in the glowing orbs of Ash's magic. Andras's usually icy blue eyes were even paler, and they glowed like a predator's in the low light. Everything else was the same, yet not. There was an otherworldly air about him that sucked the breath from Ash's lungs.

"Demon," Ash whispered.

LAINEY

ELEVEN DAYS SINCE SHE'D LEFT FAERIE.

Lainey was crawling out of her skin. Her frustration had reached a boiling point, and she was desperate for *anything* that would help her save her mate. It had been a week and a half of nothing but boring history on demons and Hel. They hadn't found anything remotely useful about possession or severing a connection with a demon. Just political history, random textbooks and novels, and the occasional poetry book. Most of it was in languages they couldn't read, so Madam Elvie was doing the majority of the work.

"This looks interesting," Brand muttered one day as he pored over a crumbling ancient scroll, the gloves everyone was wearing to help protect the old documents not doing much to keep it safe. He grimaced and gently lifted the parchment toward Madam Elvie.

The elf's eyes widened in shock. "That is certainly interesting, and definitely a lead."

"What is it?" Lainey leaned forward eagerly, heart thumping in her chest at the prospect of answers.

"An official document from Hel. A proclamation by a ..." Madam Elvie smiled. "A demon seer."

"A demon seer?" Lainey asked.

"How do we know it's official?" Skepticism threaded heavily through Beck's voice.

"You can smell the brimstone on the parchment still. Only an official document of the demon realm would still smell of brimstone." Madam Elvie set the scroll down carefully. "As for a demon seer, it would make sense that each race would have their own seers," she said, more to herself than anyone else.

"What does it say? It's written in a language I've never seen," Brand said.

Madam Elvie waved her hand dismissively. "What it says is not important. It proves there are seers in the demon realm. They could help you."

"You mean ... You can't possibly be saying ..." Lainey trailed off, unable to fully wrap her mind around what Madam Elvie was proposing.

"A vacation, of course!" Madam Elvie cackled.

Beck barked a humorless laugh. "You *are* insane. There is no way she would survive a trip to Hel."

"Not alone, no. But with help ..." The elf trailed off, glancing at Beck with a raised brow.

"Uh-uh, nope. Not happening. I am not going to the demon realm." Beck crossed his arms over his chest and sat back on his cushion.

"Go to the demon realm?" Lainey asked quietly. She would do it. If that was the best hope of saving Phoenix and their bond, she would go to hell for him. "How would I even get there?"

"There is a portal somewhere in the Catskills," Madam Elvie said, rubbing her chin. "I just have to remember where exactly."

"You're not seriusly considering doing it, are you?" Beck asked incredulously. "You're all insane."

"I would do anything for Phoenix," Lainey said vehemently. Turning her stare to Beck, eyes narrowing in a glare, she spat, "I'm sure it's nothing you would understand. You are heartless, after all."

Beck flinched at her words—barely, but it was there.

"Lainey, let's think about this for a moment," Brand said.

"No," she said shortly, cutting her hand through the air for extra emphasis. "I can't wait any longer. Every day, my bond with him grows weaker. What happens when it disappears? What happens to me when I lose the connection to my mate?"

No one said anything, but Lainey didn't need them to. She wouldn't survive that loss. Physically, she wouldn't be able to continue if the bond was destroyed. She could already feel the ramifications of the bond weakening. Pain, weakness, darkness, insanity. It was all slowly creeping into her consciousness. She knew it would overcome her if the bond was broken.

"How about a compromise then?" Brand leveled a stare at Lainey. "Let's return to Faerie first and talk to Ash. I would feel better, and I'm sure you would too, if Ash went with you. Then we can use the portal in Faerie."

Lainey contemplated this. It *would* make her feel better to have Ash by her side. There was no one she trusted more. But was he needed more in Faerie? She supposed there was no harm in returning there and talking to him at least. "Okay. We can talk to Ash first."

Brand's shoulders slumped as he exhaled. "Good. Thank you."

"If you return to Faerie first, you need to make sure you mask your bond. The moment you step through the portal, Phoenix will be able to sense you," Madam Elvie cautioned.

"How do I do that?" Lainey asked.

"Imagine draping your bond in a heavy blanket. But make sure you cover every inch."

"That's all?" Lainey practiced now, imagining a thick wool blanket covering the bond, tattered ends and all. It seemed simple enough.

"That is all. Easy peasy." The elf clapped her hands once and pushed up from her cushion. "Well," Madam Elvie said, "it sounds like you have a plan." A grin split her face, and she eagerly rubbed her hands together. "Make sure you take a lot of salt, and enjoy your trip."

Twelve days since she'd left Faerie.

"I'm coming with you," Brand announced the next morning. "To Faerie, at least. Not the demon realm."

Lainey set her coffee down and smiled. "That would be great, actually. Nix and I could both use some advice on ruling Faerie." She swallowed and tried to not let her fear show.

She hadn't let herself think of the fact that she was going to be traveling to the demon realm. All last night, she had forced her thoughts in other directions whenever they had wandered to the task at hand. She refused to let the negative thoughts and self-doubt take over. She'd had enough of being the damsel in distress. No longer would she rely on someone else to save her. She was going to save herself. And Nix in the process.

Beck sauntered into the kitchen, his brown hair mussed and sticking up in all directions. Lainey quickly averted her eyes when she realized he was shirtless. His muscles were no less defined than his half-brother's, but where Nix was more bulky, Beck was more lean.

"I'm going as well," he announced as he poured himself a cup of coffee. "To Faerie and Hel."

Lainey whipped her head around so fast, she winced as pain shot up her neck. "What?" she screeched as she rubbed the aching spot.

"You'll need help." His voice was blasé and uncaring, but his shoulders were tense.

"Absolutely not." She crossed her arms over her chest. "I wouldn't travel to the demon realm with you if my life depended on it, which it does."

"What if your mate's life depended on it? Because, in case you've forgotten, it also does." The little smirk Beck gave her, combined with raised brow, made Lainey see red.

Brand sighed heavily and rubbed the bridge of his nose. "Guys, please."

Beck sat at the table across from Lainey and leveled a stare in her direction. "Believe it or not, I'm not trying to be an ass. You just learned about the Faerie realm. You don't even have full control of your powers. How do you expect to traverse Hel? A place with magic you know nothing of and have never encountered?"

"I had pretty good control of my powers when I almost killed you yesterday," she muttered under her breath.

"Lainey, I think Beck should go with you." Brand ignored Lainey's muttered words, but his eyes were kind when he looked at her. "After you went to bed last night, we talked, and we both decided it was the best course of action. I know there's a lot of things you two need to work through. Maybe this will be a good time to do that."

Hurt flared in Lainey's chest. They'd talked about this without her, like she was a little girl who couldn't make her own decisions. "I see," she said quietly. Quickly, she finished her coffee and stood from the table.

Before she could leave the kitchen, Brand said, "I know he's your mate, but he's my son. I want him back as much as you do. And ..." He exhaled and looked down at the table. "You're my daughter now. I want you to make it through this alive." His eyes swirled fiery copper when he lifted his head. "Beck is going with you."

She just nodded and left the kitchen. He was right. They both were. She knew nothing of the demon realm, even less than she knew of Faerie. It was smart to have the extra help. But how was she supposed to deal with that help being the person who'd murdered her sister? The same person who slit her throat? Lainey's hand wrapped around her neck as she climbed the stairs.

The skin was smooth under her fingers. Phoenix's healing blood had made sure of that. But she remembered what it felt like. The knife slicing through her skin, her blood spilling from the wound.

"Emma," she whispered brokenly. "I am so sorry he got away with it. I'm sorry he gets to live when you don't. I'm ..." She trailed off as a single tear rolled down her cheek.

She let the tear fall. Had she ever cried for Emma? At first, she'd been too numb. Then everything had happened—Phoenix, finding out about Faerie, the portal, breaking the curse. Then it had all been about learning to be queen and trying to adapt to a new life. She really hadn't ever cried for Emma's loss. So, she let the tear fall and didn't wipe it away, but no more followed.

Lainey turned to the door at the sound of a throat clearing. The man in question stood at the threshold. His jaw was clenched so tight, a muscle feathered under the skin.

"We leave in an hour. Get ready."

"Why do you insist on coming with me?" she asked, eyes narrowing in distrust. She didn't want to be alone with him, much less in a world where literal *demons* roamed.

"Phoenix is my family," Beck said quietly but resolutely. "It's not his fault he was born into the situation he was. I may not agree with everything my dad did, but at the end of the day, Phoenix is blood."

She nodded. "Just like it wasn't Emma's fault she was born into the situation she was. That didn't matter to you, though. You still killed her."

His eyes were cold and hard as he said, "That's not the same thing. You know nothing about ..." He shook his head and trailed off. "You wouldn't understand."

"Maybe not, but I understand that *you* are a murderer. Emma's blood is on *your* hands. It is *your* fault my sister is dead. *Your* actions took my only family from me. One day, you will have to face those facts, and I don't think you'll be so blasé about it then."

Beck's jaw tightened further, and he left her staring at the open doorway, seething with rage at the whole situation.

That rage continued to simmer on low heat as Lainey packed the few things she had—toothbrush and toothpaste, brush, some of Ash's band tees, leggings, and the most important things: an old-school iPod loaded with music, a docking speaker, and a solar charger.

She'd picked one up at a pawnshop after selling the damn crown and downloaded all of her and Ash's favorite music onto it so they could listen in Faerie. She hoped it would work. It didn't require wi-fi or data, no electricity to charge it with the solar charger, and the headphones were the old-school plug-in kind.

They walked in silence through Central Park, with Brand a buffer between Lainey and Beck. Any time she caught sight of Beck in his cargo pants, Henley, and combat boots, she wanted to punch him in the face. Repeatedly. With a knife. She wasn't sure she'd make it through this without actually hurting him. Not that he didn't deserve it.

"It's been a long time since I passed through the gate tree," Brand murmured as they stopped before the giant oak. Awe slackened his face, and his eyes shone with wonder and unshed tears. "I'm going home," he whispered, so quietly that Lainey almost didn't hear him.

The tree didn't have quite the same impact on her. "Well. This tree certainly holds fond memories. Doesn't it, Beck?" Lainey asked, tone so sweet it was almost acidic. She forced herself to look at him, to watch his steps falter, if only just so she didn't have to see the place where he'd once slid a knife across her throat.

He continued his march forward, ignoring Lainey's words.

"Yeah," she continued, nodding her head and releasing a wistful but sarcastic sigh. "So many wonderful memories. You know, it's a miracle the tree doesn't weep blood. I mean, those roots must have absorbed quite a bit between Emma and me, wouldn't you think?"

"Lainey," Brand chastised.

He leveled a look at her, a similar one he'd given Beck the other day, one that made her want to cower. But she wasn't a child, and he wasn't her dad. She huffed and stepped past him to follow Beck.

By the time Lainey and Brand caught up to Beck, he had already pressed his hand to the tree and pushed open the door. Golden flames lit the torches and flickered in the breeze blowing through the park. Beck didn't wait. He began the climb down the steps carved into the tree, and Lainey followed. Brand was slower to join them, and Lainey assumed it was because of his reverence at passing through the gate and returning home.

Going down the steps was much easier than going up when she'd returned to the human realm, but it took just as long. Down and down, until she once again wondered if the steps would spit them out in hell. That would have been helpful, considering that was their ultimate destination.

When they reached the bottom, Beck held out an arm, stopping Lainey from pushing through the door. "Wait. Let my dad and me go through first. If the demon was smart, he'd have guards posted at the gate in case you returned."

Lainey frowned but agreed. She waited impatiently as Brand and Beck entered Faerie. How long should she wait? It seemed like she'd stood there forever by the time Beck opened the door and held it for her to step through.

"It's a good thing you waited," he said, breathing heavily. "There were three guards waiting, and they didn't bother to ask questions before they attacked us."

Lainey stepped through, and her gaze landed on the three dead guards on the island surrounding the gate tree. She didn't recognize them and assumed they were demons. Ignoring the crawling of her skin, she walked to the stone bridge spanning the river and crossed to the mainland of Faerie. She inhaled the fresh air and could have sworn she could smell the shimmer that permeated all of Faerie, a citrusy, floral scent. Her magic swooped in her veins, rejoicing at returning. She couldn't help but tip back her head and close her eyes. A content smile pulled up the corners of her lips, and she let the sun beat down on her from high above.

Home. This was home.

ASH

Ash had already suspected that, but seeing it in front of him made him pause. A million questions assaulted him. *Is he part of this whole thing with Phoenix? What's his overall goal? Can I trust him?*

What do I do now?

Ash looked at Andras, really looked at him. Fuck. He was beautiful. Without his glamor, Andras was absolutely stunning. And Ash could finally get a read on his magic. It was wild and untamed. It reminded Ash of cold mountains and blustery winter days. While Ash's magic always felt *green* to him, Andras's was icy white. It was still nature, just the beautifully deadly side of nature. It called to some primal part of him.

Ash narrowed his eyes at Andras. The demon hadn't moved. He held himself perfectly still, waiting for Ash to do or say something. A sudden suspicion wormed its way into Ash's gut. Without thinking, he raised his hand and wrapped one of Andras's black curls around his finger, studying the way the black turned blue in certain light.

"Raven-black hair," he muttered to himself.

Andras's muscles tensed, and his eyes widened. Ash could tell he wanted to step back, to put distance between them, but he held himself immobile.

"You can shift," Ash said. It wasn't a question, and Ash already knew the answer. The man ... demon ... before him, could shift into a raven. "You've been watching me."

Worry flashed in Andras's gaze, as if he were waiting for Ash to attack. He did no such thing, though. He twirled the hair around his finger and met Andras's blue eyes, waiting for his explanation.

"Yes," Andras sighed, his whole body seeming to deflate with the exhale. He slid down the wall behind him so he was sitting with his forearms resting on his knees.

Ash debated for a moment before moving to sit next to him. He was careful to keep enough distance between them that they didn't touch, but that didn't stop the weird pull he felt on his magic.

"I don't even know where to start," Andras said in that quiet way of his.

"From the beginning?"

Ash turned to Andras and was rewarded with a smile. It was small, but it almost took his breath away. What would a genuine smile look like?

"My mother died when I was ten," Andras began. "She was murdered by a fae in Hel."

Ash jerked back and stared at Andras. "A fae in the demon realm? Is that common?"

"It wasn't uncommon before the curse, but when the gates were locked, the fae who were in Hel were stuck there. They thought we locked the gates, trapping them in our realm. We had no idea what was happening in Faerie or the reason the gates had been locked, but we knew we had nothing to do with it."

Ash listened intently. He hadn't realized it had been *all* gates to Faerie that were locked with the curse. It made sense, though.

"The fae became angry," Andras continued. "When we could

do nothing to unlock the gates, they grew violent. My father is a duke. He's well known in society and became a target for attacks. My mom ..." He trailed off and swallowed thickly. His eyes closed, thick dark lashes fanning against his pale cheeks. "My mom got caught in the crossfire."

Ash wasn't breathing. He watched Andras closely, and it took all of his restraint to not reach out and comfort him.

"My mom was a beautiful person. She was the glue that kept my family together. Without her ..." Andras shook his head, pain pinching his features. "I had my twin. We turned to each other, and we kept each other from going down a dark path." He opened his eyes, and they were cold and hard as he stared straight ahead. "My dad and Selene got lost in their grief. They let it change them. They became bitter and angry with the fae and all of Faerie. A group of demons formed who began spreading all kinds of vitriol, amping people up and making them even more angry. My dad and Selene joined them. My dad rose higher in the ranks of that group, and when the gates re-opened, he sent Selene over to enact their plans."

"And Faerie was weak after the curse," Ash picked up. "So it was easier to infiltrate."

"It was too easy," Andras agreed. "With the court split and a new untrained king ..." He shrugged.

"What is the end goal?"

"To destroy Faerie. And then, I wouldn't be surprised if they set their sights on the other realms."

Ash's stomach dropped, and a cold sweat broke out over his skin. That's what he had been afraid of. "And what about you? What role do you play in all of this?" He watched Andras closely for any signs of deceit. He saw none.

"Selene needs me. I ... I am one of the most powerful demons of our time, and I have certain training under my belt." He shook his head, then let it thump back against the stone wall behind him.

"What kind of training?" Ash asked, gaze narrowed on the demon.

"Assassin."

Ash studied his profile. With his mouth downturned, eyes closed, and shoulder slumped, Andras didn't look like someone who was enjoying his job. "You don't seem thrilled to be doing any of this," Ash said quietly with a furrowed brow.

"Because I don't agree with it," Andras said with a harsh laugh. "It wasn't Faerie's fault that all of this happened. The gates are open now. I just want everything to go back to normal."

"Then why help her?"

"My twin."

Oh. Ash had forgotten that part. "Selene has her?"

He nodded. "She knew I would never agree to any of this, so she took Zurie. I don't know where she is or how she is being treated. But I know Selene, and I know it can't be good."

"Why the fires outside the walls?"

"Distraction and destruction. It's a way to keep everyone's attention on the village and hopefully off of the king so they don't realize what's happening. It also helps move the demons' goals forward. Destroy everything."

"And then your focus will shift to the Seelie Court," Ash assumed.

"Correct."

Ash rubbed a hand down his face. "What about the demon possessing Nix? How can I save him?" He didn't really think Andras would tell him, but he had to try.

Andras shrugged. "I honestly don't know. Selene was in charge of that. It would all depend on the type of demon possessing him. Not all demons have the ability. It's the less civilized and more monstrous ones that do the possessing."

"So you're supposed to take me out to ... what? What's the reason for killing me?"

"You're too much of a threat. You care about the king, and we can't have you getting it in your head to save him."

"You realize those thoughts are already in my head?"

Andras huffs a humorless laugh. "Yes. And I should have killed you already."

"Why haven't you?" Something swirled in Ash's gut he couldn't identify. Andras was supposed to kill him, but instead, they'd spent time fixing a telescope, sparring, and kissing?

Andras turned to look at him. "I don't know." His brow furrowed, pulling low over his icy blue eyes. "I just ... can't."

"What are your plans for Phoenix and Lainey?" He had to know, even though he already suspected.

Andras said nothing. He looked at Ash with an expression that said, *I can't tell you, but you wouldn't like it.*

"You realize I can't let you do anything to them, right? I will do whatever needs to be done to protect my friends."

"I understand."

Where did that leave them? Andras's words after the kiss came back to him. *This can't happen again.* Ash ran his hands through his hair before standing and heading for the door. But something stopped him in his tracks. He knew if he walked out that door, he would lose the connection he had found with Andras. It would be like shutting a door on this part of his life. His heart raced in his chest, his magic—his soul—rebelling at the thought. The remaining wood of the doorframe cracked and crumbled under his punishing grip, the dust falling to the floor.

His muscles shook, strained so tight, he thought he might pull something. But no matter how hard he tried to tell himself to take that step, to leave the room—and Andras—behind, he couldn't do it. He couldn't make his body obey the command. And deep down inside, he didn't want to. Andras had become an addiction, a drug he couldn't go without. His quiet voice, careful glances, and small smiles were teases that hinted at so much more. And Ash wanted *more.*

"Ash." Andras's voice was low and carried a hint of desire.

His name on Andras's lips snapped something inside him. He whirled around and stalked toward Andras, his steps echoing in the quiet room. Andras stood, and his eyes, lit from within with a predatory glow, watched each step Ash took. Ash could've sworn he saw excitement and lust flash in those glowing, pale eyes.

Ash reached Andras and wrapped his hand around the demon's throat, pushing him against the wall. Andras's eyes flared with heat, and his lips parted on an inhale. Anticipation curled in Ash's gut, need coursing through his veins, and he couldn't hold back any longer. He kissed Andras. It wasn't a gentle kiss. It wasn't the soft brush of lips the first one had been. This kiss was rough and demanding. A battle for dominance neither man wanted to lose.

He tasted like winter, and it was so good. Ash knew he would never get enough of that taste. He moved his hand from Andras's throat and slid both hands through his black wavy hair, fisting it tightly. Andras sucked in a breath, and something sparked deep within Ash's chest.

Andras's hands gripped his hips and tugged him closer, and they both groaned. His body was hard against Ash's, muscles bunching and contracting under Ash's hands. *What am I doing?* He was kissing a fucking demon and loving every second of it. Every touch, every brush of Andras's tongue against his, was driving him higher and higher, and he wanted more.

With a sudden urge, he reached up, grabbed Andras's horns, and tugged his head closer, kissing him harder. Andras growled deep in his chest and pushed off the wall, spinning them so Ash was pinned against the black stone. Ash didn't even feel his head thump back against the unforgiving surface. His focus narrowed on Andras's lips and tongue as he trailed kisses down Ash's neck. Hands slid under Ash's shirt, fingertips trailing along his taut muscles and sending shivers racing over his skin.

Ash was pretty sure his heart was about to beat right out of his chest. It pounded erratically behind his ribcage, stuttering at each touch of Andras's skin against his. Andras dipped his hand under the waistband of Ash's pants and palmed the hard length of Ash's cock.

"Oh, fuck," Ash groaned. His hips bucked off the wall, searching for more contact.

Andras smirked as he knelt on the floor in front of Ash and tugged down his pants. His palms slid up Ash's thighs, and his eyes glowed as he eyed Ash's already dripping arousal. This wasn't happening. Ash was sure he was dreaming as Andras wrapped his hand around his hard length and stroked from base to tip. And when Andras opened his mouth and swirled his tongue around the tip of his cock, tasting his precum, Ash barely kept himself from thrusting his hips forward.

There was not a single thought in Ash's head as Andras took him into his mouth. He sucked and licked and stroked until Ash's legs quivered as they tried to hold him up. The heat and gentle pressure, with the occasional rough squeeze and hint of teeth, was driving Ash closer and closer to that edge. It became harder to keep himself still, and he grabbed Andras's horns and thrust his hips, watching Andras swallow him completely.

The sight almost made him come. Andras's pale blue eyes, hooded with arousal, peering up at Ash through dark lashes. Ash's hands wrapped around those black horns. Andras's perfectly bowed lips wrapped around his cock. Ash shuddered and groaned. And when Andras slid his hands behind Ash's thighs and prodded his back entrance with a finger, Ash lost it. He held Andras's horns tightly and came so hard he saw stars.

"Andras," he groaned as the last tremors worked through his body.

Andras watched Ash through it all with unblinking eyes that burned with desire. He swallowed and pulled back when Ash stilled, wiping his bottom lip with his thumb and grinning wickedly.

"I like hearing you say my name like that," Andras said quietly, his voice low and rough. "Like … a prayer."

Ash's chest heaved as he gulped in breath and tried to calm his racing heart. He decided there, in that moment, he would worship this demon if he asked for it. He could see Andras's erection pushing against his pants as he knelt on the floor. Even after that orgasm, desire curled low in his stomach at the thought of tasting Andras.

He pushed Andras's shoulders and smirked when the demon's eyes widened in surprise as he fell backward. He straddled Andras's waist, and his stomach fluttered as Andras groaned at the contact. Ash leaned down and kissed him. It wasn't as rough and demanding as before, but it was just as deep and life-altering. Never in his life had he felt like this while kissing someone else. The way his magic stirred in his veins and the way his heart skipped as it pounded in his chest. It was all-consuming.

Andras rocked his hips, searching for more contact, and Ash smiled against his mouth.

"Is there something you want?" Ash asked. He trailed kisses down Andras's neck, nipping and biting as he went.

Andras pushed Ash's shoulders, trying to shove him lower, but Ash resisted. "Your mouth on my cock," Andras growled with another push.

Ash chuckled but complied. He yanked down Andras's pants and swallowed when his erection sprang free. Ash swirled the tip of his finger around the head, gathering up the moisture beading there before bringing it to his mouth and sucking the flavor off. Fuck, he needed to taste more of that.

Without any more teasing, Ash sucked Andras into his mouth, and they both groaned. It wasn't long before the demon was writhing under Ash, and Ash watched him come undone. It was hard for Ash to wrap his head around. This man ... this demon ... who could best him in the sparring ring was completely brought to his knees by Ash's mouth and tongue.

Andras slid his hands into Ash's hair and pulled. He forced Ash's head down, and his hips bucked wildly as he came. Ash swallowed all of him, milking him to the last drop. When Ash sat up on his knees between Andras's legs, he let his gaze wander over the other man's face.

Andras's chest heaved, and a small smile played about the corners of his lips. His eyes were closed as he lay in a boneless heap on the floor. Ash swallowed at the sight. He was so beautiful. Andras's pale blue eyes opened and landed on Ash without err. Ash smiled and laid next to him on the floor, shoulders and legs touching.

Neither said anything. Ash didn't think he could ignore this. He wouldn't be able to walk through the door and pretend this didn't happen. Andras's taste still lingered on his tongue, and it hadn't been nearly enough. He was already craving more. Andras was a beautiful, dangerous drug.

The silence was comfortable, and Ash was content lying next to Andras, listening to their breaths mingling in the quiet. Still, Ash had a question. He propped himself on his elbow so he could see Andras. He lifted his free hand and gently ran a finger down one of the black horns. Andras shivered.

"Are they sensitive?" he asked.

"Not sensitive, exactly." Andras's voice was rough—with emotion or desire, Ash couldn't tell. "I can feel them, but it's just like an extension of me. Light touch tickles. A knife would hurt. Just like any other part of my body."

Ash traced the deep blue circular rings and watched Andras's face relax at the touch.

"Do the blue rings mean anything? Do all demons have horns? Do they all look alike? I have so many questions." A sheepish grin spread across Ash's face with the rapid-fire questions.

Andras chuckled. "We all have horns, just different kinds. The rings indicate our affinity and the strength of our power. The more rings, the more powerful the demon."

Ash studied Andras's horns. The rings started at the base, hidden under the black waves, and traveled to the very top. "So ... I take it you are a very powerful demon, then."

Andras smirked cockily. "Few have as many rings as I do."

"And the blue? What is your affinity?"

He hesitated, not meeting Ash's stare. "Nature."

For some reason, Ash wasn't surprised. "Snow in particular?"

Andras's focus snapped to Ash. "How ..."

Ash shrugged. "Your magic feels like a snowy mountain, or a tundra. Your scent and taste are like winter. It reminds me of nature, like mine, but cold and wild rather than green."

Andras stared at him, and Ash couldn't decipher that look, the slightly widened eyes and parted mouth. Was it fear? Uncertainty? Ash shifted and glanced away before sitting up. Before he could stand, Andras sat up and cupped his cheek, his eyes burning straight through Ash.

"Don't," Andras said softly. "Don't pull away now."

How could he not, though? Andras's goal was to destroy Faerie. Not by choice, but still. How could Ash let things go any further? Unless ...

"Let's work together," Ash said, sitting on his knees and begging Andras with his eyes.

"What do you mean?" Andras tilted his head to the side, reminding Ash of the raven he could shift into.

"You don't want to hurt Faerie. I don't want you to hurt Faerie. Let's work together to stop your sister and the rest of the demons." Excitement made his words rush out of him in a jumble.

Andras's eyes shuttered. "My twin," he whispered. "I can't risk her."

"We won't. We'll figure something out. With both of us working together, I'm positive we can stop Selene and make sure your twin is safe in the process." He held his breath, not daring to let himself hope.

If Andras didn't agree, Ash wasn't sure what he would do. He couldn't let anything happen to Nix or Lainey. He would do anything to prevent them from getting hurt. Even if it meant hurting Andras—and that thought almost destroyed him. His magic roiled, and he had to swallow back the bile that climbed up his throat.

The demon nodded his head slowly. "Okay, but if at any point there is a risk to Zurie, I will do whatever is needed to keep her safe."

Ash exhaled, and his shoulders relaxed. "I understand."

LAINEY

"WE SHOULD STOP HERE FOR THE NIGHT," BECK SAID AS he let his backpack drop to the ground.

Lainey shook her head. Only partly because she refused to agree with anything that came out of his mouth. "We can go a little farther."

"Lainey," Brand said quietly. "It's getting dark, and we don't know how far we would have to go to find another safe spot for the night. You don't know the dangers that can be found in Faerie."

Oh, but she did. Two of them had almost killed her when she'd first arrived. It was for that reason that she reluctantly set down her bag. As soon as she'd set foot in Faerie, an incessant tug had began pulling her toward her mate. It had been so long since she'd felt anything from the bond. She tried not to let worry overtake her. Why was she feeling something now? What was going on with Phoenix that she suddenly felt pulled to him? She hoped desperately that the blanket she'd draped over the bond was doing its job concealing her from Nix.

Brand started a fire, and Beck pulled out the food they had packed. Lainey sat as far from Beck as possible while remaining near the fire. She wasn't hungry, but she ate anyway. Brand had been forcing her to since she'd arrived at his house.

She just wanted to get to Unseelie. What had happened since she'd been gone? She desperately wanted to know what state Unseelie was in and how her mate was faring.

Lainey laid in the grass, letting her fingers trail over the soft blades as she stared into the vast starry sky. She'd had a hard time keeping her thoughts off of Nix since she returned, and her magic felt closer to the surface. Maybe that was the reason she could feel the bond so clearly.

"We should reach Unseelie tomorrow," Brand said. "We need to have a plan when we get there. And we need to figure out how to get word to Ash."

"I have an idea," Lainey said to the night sky. She didn't mention she wasn't sure if her plan was even feasible. She was just going to hope and pray it worked. There weren't many options when she couldn't show her face in the palace, and the circle of people they could trust was basically nonexistent.

"Are you going to share it with us?" Beck asked.

"Not with you, no." Lainey scowled at Beck's voice. Whenever he spoke, she wanted to scream and rage, throw things, kick, maul his face. These past few days had been a trial in patience, and she wasn't sure she could keep going like this.

Brand sighed heavily. Lainey wasn't looking at him, but she could picture him rubbing the bridge of his nose and beseeching the heavens above for peace. She smiled at the image. Annoying Brand as often as she could had become her secret goal.

"Look," Brand said with his infinite patience. "Let's just get to Unseelie and assess the situation. We can plan once we have more information." Brand had been spending as much time as he could with Lainey, getting to know her and telling her stories of Phoenix growing up. She felt closer to him than she did her own dad.

Lainey settled further into the grass, enjoying the way it tickled her neck. It smelled like Ash, though, and her heart squeezed painfully at the thought of him. She hoped he was okay, and she couldn't wait for one of his hugs. Wrapping her arms around herself, Lainey counted the stars to draw herself into sleep. She lost count around three hundred and was still wide awake. Sighing, she sat up and faced the flames. She imagined they were Phoenix's and let herself bathe in the heat of them. She really fucking missed him.

"You should be asleep," Brand said quietly.

Lainey glanced over and found him leaning up on one elbow, eyes creased with worry.

"When you agreed to marry Esmeray," Lainey began cautiously, "did your mate agree to it?" She couldn't imagine ever agreeing to something like that.

Pain flashed in Brand's eyes before he got himself under control. He sat up and faced Lainey. "No, she didn't agree. But it was something I had to do."

"What happened?" Lainey whispered.

"She had the bond broken. I agreed because, how could I deny her the chance to find love somewhere else, even if it wasn't me?" He rubbed his chest as if he could still feel the pain from that broken bond.

"Did it hurt?"

He huffed a humorless laugh. "More than anything I've ever felt. I wouldn't wish that pain on my worst enemy."

Brand studied Lainey as she rubbed at her own chest. For her, the pain was still fresh. It was actively tearing her apart every second of the day. She could feel each thread slowly unraveling, and there was nothing she could do about it.

"We'll get him back, Lainey." Brand laid a gentle hand on her knee.

The kindness in his eyes and the surety in his voice made tears build on her lashes.

"What if it's too late for the bond?" It was one of her biggest fears. What if they saved Phoenix only for their bond to be gone? What would happen then?

"Would you love him even if you didn't have the bond?"

She nodded.

"Exactly. The bond doesn't make you love him. It doesn't make him love you. You don't need the bond to be with him, Lainey."

Ash had said the same thing essentially. She knew that, but it didn't ease any of her fear. "Can a bond be rebuilt after it's broken?"

"Under normal circumstances, no. Having a healer break a bond is permanent. However, your situation is different. I don't know if rebuilding will be possible or not."

Her words were too heavy to get out, so she said nothing. An oppressive weight settled over her entire body.

"Try to get some sleep," Brand said gently. "We have a long day of traveling ahead of us."

Lainey nodded and silently laid back down in the grass. She didn't sleep, though. Instead, she tossed and turned, the pressure sitting upon her as she realized the bond seemed even thinner than it had the other day. Urgency settled in her, and her need to save Phoenix consumed her thoughts.

"Oh, fuck," Lainey whispered as she lay on her belly on top of the hill.

"That's not good," Beck agreed on the other side of his dad.

Lainey scanned the village spread out before her. In the distance, smoke curled over the roofs, and she could just make out charred frames peeking between some buildings. "Are they burning the village?" she whispered.

"Yeah, it appears so." Brand slid halfway down the back of the hill before standing and walking the rest of the way down.

Lainey took one last glance at Unseelie, fear and dread coiling in her gut, and followed Brand.

"This complicates things," Brand said once they were all safely hidden from view. "We can't go strolling into the village when we don't know what we're going to find. How many more demons have arrived? Are they patrolling the village? We need to get some information before we go in."

Lainey had initially planned on sneaking into the orphanage

...

"The orphanage!"

Fear exploded inside Lainey as she thought about the smoke clouding the sky. Was the orphanage okay? Had the children been hurt? Before Brand or Beck could do anything, Lainey flew to her feet and took off running. She ran faster than she ever had in her life. As her feet pounded on the ground, she distantly heard Beck calling her name, but she ignored it. The orphanage had to be okay. The kids had to be okay. Lainey ran to the edge of the village and didn't slow down until she was in an alleyway between two buildings, crouched behind a stack of disintegrating crates.

"What the fuck are you thinking?" Beck growled as he slid down behind her.

Chest heaving, she gulped down air and glanced behind Beck but didn't see Brand. "Where is your dad?" she gasped.

"Not coming. He can't risk being seen, and neither can you!" Beck whisper-yelled. His face was red, and Lainey didn't think it was from the exertion of running. Beck was furious.

"I have to make sure the kids are okay," she said more to herself than Beck. "I have to make sure the villagers are okay. I will not sit around and do nothing while my people suffer." She was their queen, after all. It was time she started acting like it.

"You won't be helping them if you get yourself captured by a fucking demon," Beck muttered, but his shoulders were set like he'd already accepted she wouldn't change her mind.

Lainey tuned him out and carefully picked her way down the alley. When she reached the end, she cautiously poked her head around the corner and checked both ways. The streets were unusually quiet. Typically, fae would have been about their business, shopping or selling their wares. But the village was a ghost town. She almost expected to see a tumbleweed blowing down the street.

She kept slinking through the alleys, Beck always on her heels, until they reached the part of town where the smoke was thickest. Peering around a corner, she had to slap a hand over her mouth to keep from gasping out loud.

Unseelie had never been prosperous. The streets had never been beautifully paved and lined with colorful flowers. Buildings had always been rundown and dilapidated. But the scene before Lainey's eyes was heartbreaking. The air was thick with the scent of fire, and the sky was a sickly shade of gray. Ashes rained down like snow and coated the ground in a sick parody of a winter landscape.

And the buildings. Every one of them was a burned-out husk. Charred wood and ash were all that was left of this corner of the village. Her heart beat frantically as she thought of all the loss. All of the homes, shops, and establishments that had been lost in this fire. All the fae who didn't make it out alive. What had caused this?

Her eyes welled with tears, but they didn't last long. Soon, fire erupted in her veins. She may not have been the best queen to have ever graced Faerie, but she *was* their queen. She'd taken vows to protect these people, and she had failed. At the first sign of trouble, she'd run. Shame coated her insides, and she let her anger burn brighter. She would make this right. She swore to herself in that moment, staring out at the desolate vision of Unseelie, that she would bring Unseelie back from this.

Beck placed his hand on her shoulder, and it wasn't until then that she realized she was shaking. Balling her hands into fists and shrugging off his touch, Lainey dashed into the street and left a cursing Beck behind. She ran, keeping to the shadows cast by the remaining buildings, until she came to another alley. Ducking inside, she marched the length of it, continuing to ignore Beck.

"Lainey, stop!" he hissed.

She did no such thing. Instead, as she peeked her head around the corner, she raised her arm and gave Beck her middle finger.

Lainey continued this way through the village, avoiding any of the usually busy areas, with Beck following behind her, spewing curses at her back at every opportunity. When the orphanage came into view, she let out a relieved breath. It was still standing. But she needed to make sure the people inside were safe too.

They made their way to the back of the building, and Lainey peered into the kitchen window. Relief almost dropped her to her knees when she saw Mira standing at the stove. Lainey tapped on the glass, and Mira spun around. Her eyes went impossibly wide before she rushed forward.

"What are you doing?" Mira hissed after she'd opened the window. She grabbed Lainey's arm and pulled her through. Halfway, though, she seemed to remember who Lainey was, and she gasped. "Oh, I'm sorry!" She raised her arms and backed away.

Lainey huffed and climbed the rest of the way through on her own. Once inside, she stepped to the side so Beck could follow. It gave her immense joy to see Beck's disgruntled expression at having to squeeze through the narrow space.

"Your Majesty, what are you doing? It's not safe for you here." Mira turned to the window and closed it, pulling the curtains shut to keep anyone from seeing inside.

Lainey couldn't resist. She rushed forward and wrapped Mira in a hug. The green-scaled fae was stiff at first, then relaxed and hugged Lainey back.

"Are you okay, my queen?"

"Please, Mira, call me Lainey. And yes, I'm okay. There are people I need to talk to, though. Is there someplace safe where I can do that?"

Mira nodded and led them through the orphanage, closing curtains along the way. She settled them into a room on the second floor. It was a small library of sorts, with a couple of shelves sporting various children's books. Lainey sat on a chair well away from the windows.

"I need ... I need to talk to Ash." This was the part of her plan she wasn't sure would actually work, but she had to try. She pointed to a window that overlooked the field behind the orphanage. "Beck, can you make sure there is no one outside?"

Beck peered around the curtain, then nodded. "All clear."

"Keep looking. Let me know if you see anyone." She walked to his side and pushed open the glass, eyes scanning the sky instead of the ground.

There was a tree not too far from the orphanage, and it was there she focused her magic. She sent a small current of wind to swirl through the tree. The leaves fluttered, and she narrowed her eyes, searching for movement. As soon as she saw it, she wrapped her wind around it and brought it to herself.

A small brown bird landed softly in her palm. It cocked its head from side to side, small black eyes blinking curiously at her.

"Can you understand me?" she asked the bird.

It blinked and chirped. Did that mean *yes*?

"Okay," she drawled softly. "Um, if you can understand me, I need you to go to the palace. Find Ash. He's an Earth Elemental, about this tall." She raised her arm to show how tall Ash was. "He has blond hair to his shoulders, and really pretty green eyes."

Beck snorted, but she ignored it.

"Find him, and tell him to come here to the orphanage. I need to talk to him."

The little bird chirped twice, then flapped its wings and took to the sky. Lainey watched, and sure enough, it was heading toward the palace. *Holy shit, is this actually going to work?*

"You know, you could have asked me to do that," Beck said.

Lainey stepped away from the window and glared at him. "Like I'd ever ask you for help."

She settled in the chair facing the doorway and waited.

ASH

FOURTEEN DAYS SINCE LAINEY HAD LEFT FAERIE.

It had been a long fucking day.

Ash let the door to his room slam shut, and he went straight to his little stash of alcohol. Faerie wine wasn't his favorite, but it would do in a pinch. He poured himself a glass and downed it in two gulps. After the day he'd had—listening to reports of buildings razed to the ground, fae beaten and murdered, and watching Phoenix ignore all of it—he was going to need more than one glass. Ash was pouring his second when he caught sight of a raven in his window.

"You might as well come in," he said, and poured an additional glass for the demon shifter.

The raven ruffled its feathers as if annoyed, then flew to the ground. Before it landed, a small flash of light erupted through the room, then Andras was standing there in all of his naked demon glory.

Ash pulled his lower lip between his teeth and sauntered over to Andras, thoroughly appreciating the sight. He handed Andras the wine and snagged a pair of sweats from the back of a chair.

"You can wear these ... if you want." He winked at Andras and tossed him the pants.

Andras's pale blue eyes gleamed, and he smirked as he tugged them on.

"Shame," Ash said and shook his head. He collapsed onto the couch with a groan. "What an absolutely shitty day."

"Would it improve your day if I took off the pants?" Andras asked as he sat next to Ash.

Ash's gaze slid to Andras, then lower to his lap. "Absolutely."

Andras snorted. "I agree. It was an absolutely shitty day, and this shit is awful," Andras said as he swirled the last dregs of wine in his glass.

"What do you drink in the demon realm?" Ash snagged the glass from Andras and refilled both.

"I guess the closest thing to it in the human realm would be whiskey. It's called hell fire."

"Mm, then this definitely isn't up to your standards," Ash laughed. "It is pretty awful, but at least it's strong."

"Cheers to that."

He held his glass out, and Ash clinked his against it. Silence settled between them, and Ash's shoulders relaxed, his mind quieting. Each refill of their glasses brought Ash closer to Andras on the couch as more and more of his inhibition disappeared in a sea of alcohol. When Andras trailed his hand up Ash's thigh, Ash tensed.

He'd never been shy around other people. Nix jokingly called Ash a man-whore, but he wasn't wrong. Fae were naturally more beautiful than humans, and being fae in the human realm, Ash'd had no difficulty finding willing partners.

For some reason, though, he felt unsure around Andras. Not unsure of Andras but unsure of himself. It was the first time in his life he was questioning each move he made, each word out of his mouth. It was unsettling, and he wished he could just let go of that uncertainty and self-doubt.

"S-sorry," Andras stammered and quickly pulled his hand away.

"Fuck ... Sorry ... That's not ..." Ash groaned at his own

stupidity. He felt like he was in high school again, like an awkward, gangly teenager with their first crush.

Fuck that. He'd never been awkward or gangly before, and he wasn't going to start now. He set his glass on the table and grabbed Andras's horns, pulling him in for a kiss. Andras's glass thumped on the rug a second before the demon moved to straddle his waist. Andras threaded his hands into Ash's hair and deepened the kiss. They both groaned when Andras rocked his hips against Ash's.

Ash ran his hands up Andras's sides to his back, then back down to grab his ass. He ground Andras against him at the same time he lifted his own hips.

"Fuck, Ash," Andras breathed. He dropped his hands to Ash's waist and slid them under his shirt.

Ash let his head fall back against the couch and focused on Andras's fingers as they drew his shirt up and over his head. He couldn't get enough of Andras's skin against his own, or the taste of him in his mouth. There was no way Ash could stop this.

Ash fisted Andras's hair and tugged his head backward, exposing his neck. "Bedroom?" he asked breathlessly against the soft skin of his throat.

Andras didn't answer, but he stood and tugged Ash to his feet. Ash's heart beat madly in his chest as he led Andras to his room. He fought the urge to wipe his palms against his pant leg. Was this really happening? And why did he feel like an inexperienced teenager? Butterflies seemed to swoop in his stomach with nervous excitement.

In the bedroom, Andras clasped Ash's face in his hands and kissed him deeply. Ash's head swam as he walked Andras backward until he bumped into the edge of the bed. With a gentle shove, Andras fell onto the mattress. They both took a moment to catch their breath before Ash slowly unbuttoned his pants and let them slide to the ground. Andras's eyes tracked his movements hungrily, and the desire darkening his irises made Ash burn from the inside out.

Ash placed one knee on the bed and trailed his fingers over Andras's torso. He traced the black tattoos that stood out starkly against his pale skin. Seeing the goosebumps that popped up at his touch and the way Andras was looking at him through hooded eyes made Ash's heart stutter. It was hard to breathe through the tightness that settled in his chest. He curled his fingers in the waistband of the sweats and tugged them down Andras's legs, and he had to stand to stare at the demon sprawled naked in his bed.

He looked like a classically carved statue. A very sexy statue with his lean-cut muscles and pale complexion. A lock of his dark hair had fallen forward, and Ash leaned down to brush it from his face. Andras grabbed his shoulders and tugged Ash down. He toppled forward, breath hitching in his chest as he landed on top of the demon. Ash groaned at the sensation of their skin touching in so many places. He settled himself on his elbows and looked at Andras with a question clear in his eyes.

Andras answered by rocking his hips, and Ash saw stars. Lightning shot through his veins, every nerve ending tingling with anticipation. He reached between them and grasped both of their lengths in his hand, squeezing gently as he jerked them both off. Andras's head fell back onto the pillows. His lips parted as he breathed deeply, and Ash nipped at his lower lip. A low moan slid up Andras's throat, and he spread his legs wider, a clear invitation that sent shivers racing over Ash's skin.

"Are you sure?" Ash asked roughly, grabbing a bottle of lube from the nightstand and popping the cap.

"Fuck, Ash." Andras huffed a laugh. "Yes, I'm sure. Stop with the chivalrous bullshit and fuck me."

Andras's low growly words shot straight to Ash's cock, and it twitched in his hand against Andras's. He poured a generous amount of lube into his palm before running a finger down to Andras's hole. Andras groaned as he slowly pushed his finger inside, then followed it with a second. Ash leaned forward and scraped his teeth against Andras's nipple as he prepared Andras to take his cock.

"Damn it, Ash. Stop playing." Andras spread his legs wider and lifted them to his chest, demanding Ash make his move.

Ash chuckled but removed his fingers and added more lube. He stroked his length, precum beading at the tip, before leaning over and guiding himself to Andras's entrance.

This wasn't his first time doing this, and he could tell it wasn't Andras's either. Still, to say it had never felt so amazing was an understatement. The way Andras clenched around Ash like a vice was almost too much for him. He had to stop and take a deep breath, or he knew this would all be over before it even began.

He watched Andras's face as the other man took him deep and stroked his own cock at the same time. With his eyes hooded and dark with desire, lower lip caught between his teeth, and a slight flush turning his cheeks pink, he was absolutely beautiful, and Ash wanted to see this euphoria lining his features every fucking day. The thought made him falter, his chest tightening inexplicably. His subconscious had already decided this was not a one-and-done. *When did that happen?*

"You're holding back, Ash," Andras breathed heavily. "Fuck me like you mean it."

Ash chuckled darkly and complied with the demon's commands. He pounded into Andras, skin slapping as he thrust harder and harder. It didn't take long for either of them to reach their orgasm. Ash's barreled through him so hard, he blacked out. When he came to, his forehead was resting on Andras's shoulder, and Andras was gripping his ass tightly, breathing heavily.

"Holy shit," Ash mumbled as he slowly pulled out and rolled over onto his back. His heart pounded in his chest, and fine tremors worked through his limbs.

"That's ... that's one way to put it," Andras rasped, head falling against the pillows.

Andras lay limply next to Ash, and they were quiet as the sweat cooled on their bodies and their breathing returned to normal. When Ash was sure he could walk without falling flat on his face, he grabbed a wet cloth from the bathroom and tossed it to Andras. Back in bed, Andras hesitantly rolled over into Ash's side. Ash smirked and tugged Andras close, wrapping his arms around the demon and tangling their legs together. Andras liked to cuddle.

He tried to ignore the way Andras sighed as his head settled on his chest. He tried and failed. That sigh made his stomach do a strange flip. Ash buried his nose in Andras's hair and inhaled his scent. Snow and mint filled his lungs and set his soul on fire. His grip on Andras tightened without him realizing he'd even done it.

Andras's finger trailed over the tattoo on his chest, the touch light and sending shivers through him.

"What does it mean?" the demon asked quietly.

"I can shift into a fox," he answered. "I knew what I was in the human realm, I could feel the animal inside me, but I could never access it. It wasn't until I came to Faerie the first time that I could actually shift."

Andras stilled, and his head lifted off Ash's chest. There was something in his eyes that gave Ash pause.

"What is it?" Ash asked.

"N-Nothing," Andras stammered and shook his head. He laid back down and continued tracing the tattoo, more reverently this time.

"What's Hel like?" Ash asked. He slid his hand up Andras's back and wrapped a curl around his finger.

Andras hummed in the back of his throat. "Not like Faerie. From everything I've heard, it's more like the human realm. While Faerie was locked down by the curse, Hel was able to continue to grow by learning from the humans. Faerie also has that ..." He waved his hand in the air absentmindedly. "That ... whatever in the atmosphere that causes electronics to not work. The demon realm doesn't have that."

"You have cell phones?" Ash asked incredulously.

Andras chuckled, the sound rich and deep. "Yeah, we do. And I fucking miss mine. I feel naked without it."

Ash trailed his hand down Andras's back and squeezed his ass. "I won't complain about you being naked."

That chuckle again. "I'm sure you wouldn't."

"I'd like to see it one day," Ash said quietly.

"My ass? I think it's too late for that. You've done more than see it."

Ash smacked the ass in question. "The demon realm, crow."

"Call me crow," Andras growled and pinched one of Ash's nipples. "I'd like to take you one day, though." After another moment of silence, Andras said, "Tell me about them."

Ash knew who he meant without asking. "Nix has been my friend since we were kids. We did everything together. We learned about Faerie, magic, and who we were. We had each other's backs and went through some shit together. At this point, Nix is more my brother than my friend." He stopped to swallow the lump in his throat talking about Nix created. He really fucking missed him. "He's a good guy. There is no one more loyal than him. He's hot-headed and stubborn, but he would take on the world for you if you asked him."

Andras kept tracing the fox on his chest, listening to every word Ash said. "And Queen Elena?"

"Lainey." He huffed a small, amused laugh. "Lainey came along about a year ago. We caught wind that Nix's half-brother had somehow gotten through the gate. He was looking for a way to break the curse. Unfortunately, we couldn't stop him in time to save her sister, but we were able to save Lainey." He shuddered at the memory of Lainey in front of the gate tree, blood spilling from her neck and Nix going absolutely feral when he saw her. "Lainey is tough. She's been through hell, but she never let it keep her down. It's not easy for her to let people in, but when she does, the light she shines on them is almost blinding. I consider myself blessed to be able to stand in her light."

"They sound like great people," Andras said quietly.

"They are. That's why I can't let anyone hurt them." He took a deep breath, the absence of his friends in his life leaving him empty. "They're my family. If anything happened to them, it would destroy me."

Andras didn't reply, but he placed a kiss on Ash's chest, right over his heart.

"What about your twin? Zurie?" Ash asked, pushing aside the heaviness that settled over him whenever he thought of Lainey and Nix.

"She's ... well, she's a little crazy." Andras chuckled. "She's tiny, but if you ever say that to her face, she will rip you a new one. People underestimate her, and that is their first and last mistake. She is fierce in everything she does. I always worry about her. She's constantly getting into some kind of trouble. When we were kids, I spent all my time keeping track of her and making sure she didn't get caught when she did something she shouldn't have." The smile was evident in his voice as he talked. "She's my other half. I'm not complete without her."

"We'll get her back," Ash promised, running his fingers through Andras's hair.

Silence fell around them, and Ash yawned, the Faerie wine, sex, and long day catching up to him. He wiggled down onto the mattress, tugging Andras closer. With his eyes closed, his other senses heightened. And it was with Andras's scent, the sound of his breathing, and the beating of his heart against Ash's chest that Ash fell asleep.

⁂

ASH WOKE to the feeling of Andras trailing kisses down his ribs and abs. He groaned and stretched, lifting his hips eagerly. Andras chuckled and looked at Ash through lowered lashes.

"Good morning," Andras said, the gravel in his voice only adding to his sexy, disheveled morning appearance.

Before Ash could respond, someone pounded on the door to his room.

"Ash! Ash, open up!" Zephyr's muffled voice came through the wooden door.

"Fuck," Ash said as both he and Andras jumped from the bed in a flurry of sheets.

He grabbed their pants from the floor and shoved one pair at Andras as the demon hurried to the bathroom. Ash tugged his pants on while hopping one-legged to the door.

"I'm coming, chill." He checked to make sure the bathroom door was closed before he let Zephyr in. "What's going on?" He rubbed his hand through his hair, attempting to tame the wild mess.

Zephyr peered at Ash, and his nostrils flared as he scented the air. Whatever he smelled made the corners of his eyes crease. "It's awfully late for you to just be waking up." The accusation in his voice was crystal clear.

"Fuck off, Zephyr. Yesterday was hard." Ash crossed his arms over his chest, daring the older man to say something.

"Yeah, well. Today won't be any easier. Look outside."

Ash swallowed, dread curling in his gut as he made his way to the window. Bile burned up his throat, and he gripped the edge of the sill so hard, it cracked.

"Are those ..." He trailed off, unable to voice his fears.

"Villagers, yes."

Ash had no words as he took in the scene. At least fifteen villagers—both men and women—had been strung up by the large tree in front of the palace. With his fae vision, he could clearly see the burns and lashes covering their naked bodies. A commotion to the left of the tree pulled his attention that way, and he wished it hadn't.

Another broken and beaten fae swas being dragged toward the tree. He fought with every bit of strength he had left, but it was no use. The rebel fae—or demon, Ash had no idea—tightened the rope around his neck, and Ash sank to the floor of his room, unable to watch. He covered his face with his hands, rubbing his eyes roughly, wishing he could wipe that sight away.

"This is going to destroy him," Ash whispered brokenly. "When we save Nix, knowing he condoned all of this. It's going to destroy him."

Zephyr placed his hand on Ash's shoulder. "We'll cross that bridge when we come to it. For now, we can only focus on what we can do. Get dressed. Meet me in the library."

Ash nodded numbly, and Zephyr left without another word. The bathroom door opened, and the scent of snow and mint surrounded him as Andras sat next to him. It was like a balm for his hurting soul.

"We're going to figure this out," Andras said quietly and rubbed his palm up and down Ash's thigh. "We'll save them both."

He didn't need to tell Ash who he meant. Phoenix and Zurie. The two most important people in their lives.

As they sat on the floor, with Ash trying to pull himself together, a small brown bird flew through the window and landed on Ash's knee. He looked up and cocked his head to the side. The bird chittered at him, and Ash used his magic to decipher the message.

"Who wants to meet me?" he asked quickly, lungs constricting with fear.

The bird chirped, and Ash's heart stopped in his chest.

"Lainey," he breathed.

ASH

Ash stripped out of his pants and folded them with the second pair he'd carried with him to the back of the palace grounds. He continuously scanned his surroundings to ensure no one saw him. When he was positive it was safe, he tossed the small bag containing the two pairs of pants and two shirts over the wall surrounding the palace, using a bit of magic to get it high enough. A raven landed on a low branch, head cocked to the side as it watched Ash. He winked at it, then shifted.

On four paws, he turned to a tree closer to the wall and began scaling it with his claws. It was harder than he thought it would be. He'd researched foxes almost religiously when he'd realized he could shift into one. It turned out only gray foxes could climb trees, but Ash was a golden fox with fae intent. He made it work.

By the time he reached the limb he needed to jump to the top of the wall, he was panting, sides heaving and mouth open. He had to stretch his paws, retracting and extending his claws to work out the ache in them. The raven flew to him and landed on his back, nipping at his ears until Ash batted it away with a paw.

When he was ready, Ash took a running leap from the tree limb to the top of the wall and propelled himself forward, landing softly on the other side. The raven swooped down and took one more nip at his ears, this time emitting a soft warbling sound before flying back to the sky. Ash yipped and grabbed the small bag he'd tossed over in his jaws. It was awkward, but he managed a fairly quick trot around the palace wall.

He was aiming for the backside of the orphanage, and when the building came into view, he slowed. His heart pounded but not from exertion. *Is Lainey really here?* Anxious energy made his fur stand on end as he stopped behind a tree near the orphanage. He changed back to his human form, and the raven flew down, shifting before it landed, revealing Andras.

"Really, with the ears?" he asked with a raised brow as he tossed Andras some clothes.

The demon shrugged with a sly grin. "They're cute, with the furry black tips. I couldn't help myself."

Ash snorted and waved to the horns sprouting from Andras's head. "As cute as those are, don't forget to hide them. I imagine they won't go over well until people get to know you." Ash smiled as Andras ducked his head. "Aww, you're blushing." His smile grew to a full-blown grin as the red deepened.

Andras cleared his throat and shrugged his shoulders. "No one's ever called them cute before." He reached a hand up to finger one of the curving black horns.

"Really?" Ash had a hard time believing that, but Andras's reaction was so pure and innocent, it made his heart thump in his chest. He reached up with both hands and grasped the horns tightly. Tugging Andras's head to his, Ash said, "I love your horns." His voice was rough and laced with desire. He kissed Andras deeply until they were both gasping for air.

Ash forced himself to step away from the demon, and he watched in awe as Andras's form shimmered. It was like a blanket covered him, concealing the horns and making him appear more ... human. His eyes darkened to a more natural pale blue, and the sharpness of his features smoothed out. He was still beautiful, just a different sort of beautiful.

Ash swallowed and shook himself. He needed to get his head

back in the game. Andras was one of the few things that could distract him from Phoenix and Lainey. And if Lainey was here in Faerie, it meant she either had information they needed or something had gone very wrong.

Ash stepped from behind the tree and approached the orphanage. The back door opened before he could knock, and a green-scaled fae with purple hair ushered them inside. She led them upstairs and waved to a door.

"She's in there," she said, brushing her purple hair over her shoulder.

Ash took a deep breath and pushed open the door. He'd only just stepped past the threshold when a force barreled into him and knocked him backward. He wrapped his arms around Lainey and squeezed her tightly. Sobs shook her entire body, each one a knife to his chest.

"Lainey," he breathed into her hair.

She only held onto him tighter, and Ash held on just as tight. When her tears stopped, she pulled back enough to look up at him. Her blue eyes swirled with so much emotion—relief, sadness, fear, happiness. Ash used his thumbs to wipe her tears away and kissed her forehead.

"Are you okay?" he asked, voice rough with emotion.

She nodded. "Yes. I have so much I need to tell you. And so many questions." A shudder wracked her body, and she hugged him again. "I missed you so much, Ash."

"Gods, I missed you too, little half-breed."

She huffed a laugh at the use of his nickname for her and stepped away. Ash had been so wrapped up in Lainey, he hadn't taken the time to scan their surroundings. He'd just assumed Andras would have his back if something went tits-up. His attention landed on Lainey's companion, and he stiffened, tugging Lainey behind him.

"What the fuck are you doing here?" he growled, reaching for a dagger he didn't have and cursing himself for not bringing any weapons.

Andras must have sensed his unease, because the demon stepped to Ash's side, and he glimpsed black claws tipping his fingers. He quickly grabbed Andras's arm and squeezed, letting him know he was showing his other side. The claws disappeared, but Andras remained tense with his pale eyes narrowed on Beck.

Lainey moved around Ash and placed her hand on his chest. "Relax, it's okay ... ish."

Ash dropped his gaze to Lainey. "What do you mean? Why is Beck here?"

She sighed heavily, and her shoulders slumped. "Let's just all calmly introduce ourselves?" She raised an eyebrow at Andras, and the demon gave her a small smile and bowed his head toward her.

"This is Andras, you can trust him," he said to Lainey. "Andras, this is Lainey."

"Queen Elena," he said with a hand over his heart. "It's a pleasure to meet you."

Ash snorted, and Lainey elbowed him.

"No need for all that," she said with pink cheeks. She glanced at Ash. "Are you positive we can trust him? Who is he?"

"I'm positive," he replied. "He knows everything."

Lainey swallowed and nodded. She waved a hand at Beck with an eyeroll. "This is Beck," she said to Andras. "You can't trust him."

"Oh, for shit's sake," Beck grumbled, throwing his hands in the air.

"Well, she isn't wrong," Ash growled. "Last time I saw you, you'd slit Lainey's throat and left her for dead. Why the hell are you here?"

Beck crossed his arms over his chest and lifted his chin, looking down his nose. "In case you've forgotten, Phoenix is my brother. I can't just ignore the fact he's been possessed by a demon."

"You didn't seem to care too much when you tried to murder

his mate!" With his fists clenched at his sides, Ash took one step forward.

Beck matched his step, eyes narrowing on Ash. "I didn't know Lainey was his mate. Dammit, *they* didn't even know they were mates when that happened."

"But you just want us to forget that, if it hadn't been for Nix, Lainey would be dead right now? Like her sister?" Ash's face was tight with anger, his blood boiling hotter in his veins with each word out of Beck's mouth. "Why the fuck do you think I would let all that slide?"

"I don't really think it's up to you, is it?" Beck sneered, taking another threatening step forward.

"Like hell it isn't!" Ash's body vibrated with the need to put Beck in his place. This fucker thought he could just pretend he hadn't completely ruined Lainey's life. It incensed Ash, made him grind his teeth together in rage.

"Guys!" Lainey screamed. "Please, just stop!"

Ash snapped his mouth shut but continued to glare at Beck, muscles straining to throw a punch.

"Look, Beck is here, and unfortunately, he's not going anywhere," Lainey said resolutely, plopping onto the couch in a very un-queenly manner. "Believe me, I've tried. So just stop with the arguing because it won't get us anywhere." She looked up at Ash with a pleading expression.

He sighed and relented. Fighting with Beck wasn't going to help them get Nix back, and he didn't want to hurt Lainey any more than she already had been. Besides, just because he stopped arguing now didn't mean he couldn't accidentally trip with a knife in his hand and stab the bastard later.

Ash turned to the couch to sit next to Lainey but paused when his gaze landed on Andras. The demon was tense, staring at Beck with unveiled anger. His icy-blue eyes slid to Ash, and he raised a brow. His question was clear. *Do you need help taking care of him?* Ash's lips twitched, trying to pull into a smile. He gave

Andras a subtle shake of his head, warmth spreading through him at Andras's willingness to help.

"What can you tell me about what's happening here? It seems like everything's gone to hell." Lainey's hands fidgeted with a stray string on her T-shirt.

"Hey! That's my shirt!" Ash pointed an accusatory finger at Lainey.

She glanced down at the vintage Blink-182 tee she was wearing and smiled. "Thanks for letting me borrow it."

He rolled his eyes and flopped onto the couch next to her, nudging her with his shoulder. However, as soon as he thought about trying to tell Lainey about Phoenix and Selene, all levity drained from him. *How the hell do I tell Lainey her mate is probably fucking a demon?*

"Well, you're right," he began. "Everything has gone to shit. Some demons from Hel have invaded and are planning on wiping out all of Faerie. Besides the demon possessing Nix, there is another demon leading the charge in the palace with Nix."

He kept the details to a minimum. He couldn't tell Lainey how he knew Selene was leading this. That would give way to too many questions about Andras. And he couldn't bring himself to tell Lainey her mate was spending a lot of time with her. Seeing the heartbreak in her eyes would destroy him. It was selfish of him to keep it secret, and she'd probably be pissed at him when she found out, but fuck it.

"And Nix?" she asked quietly, barely breathing.

Ash sighed and ran his hand through his hair. "I see less and less of Nix peeking through. He's still in there, I know he is, but the demon is taking over more and more." He closed his eyes, suddenly so very tired. It was hard to keep his head from thumping back on the cushions. "Nix is letting the raids on the village happen. He isn't trying to help the villagers at all. And no matter how hard I try to get inside his trusted circle, I can't." Bracing himself, he opened his eyes to see Lainey's reaction.

Her face was pinched with worry, skin paler than usual. She was probably thinking the same thing he had thought that morning: This was going to destroy Nix when they saved him.

"What about you? Did you find anything to help us?" Ash's tone was hopeful, despite how he tried to temper it. If Lainey had come back empty-handed, he wasn't sure where that left them.

"I think so, but it won't be easy." She glanced at Beck before leaning against the back of the couch with a sigh. "Madam Elvie believes we can find a ... a demon version of her in the demon realm. They should be able to help us find a way to free Nix from the demon controlling him. The only problem is, we'd have to go to the demon realm. I promised Brand I wouldn't go without talking to you first ..." Lainey trailed off when she noticed the strange expression on Ash's face.

His mouth had dropped open, eyes wide. His focus shifted to Andras, who was gripping the arms of his chair tightly, but his eyes were gleaming with both excitement and fear.

"What is it, Ash?" Lainey sat up straighter, turning to lean forward into his space.

Ash raised a brow at Andras, silently asking permission to reveal this massive truth. He could see Lainey out of the corner of his eye, her head bouncing between Ash and Andras. Andras gave a small nod, forcing his hands to relax. Ash knew this was a hard decision for him. His twin's safety was always the first thing he thought of. Ash made a mental note to make sure Andras knew he would never risk someone so important to him.

Ash took a deep breath, and said, "I can get us to Hel, and I can get us a guide."

Lainey's mouth dropped open. "H-How?"

Ash peered back at Andras and offered him a small smile. Andras released a breath, and his form shimmered. This time, it was like a blanket being removed. His features sharpened, his eyes paled, and those black curving horns parted his hair and curled along his skull. Ash couldn't help but stare, and his heart thudded in his chest when the demon looked back at him. Beautiful, sexy, dangerous.

While Ash was staring at Andras with awe—and desire—Lainey and Beck were not so impressed.

Lainey jumped from the couch with a screech and backed away from Ash with wide eyes. She stepped toward Beck, who stepped in front of Lainey protectively, and something ugly writhed in Ash's gut at the sight. He was the one who was supposed to protect Lainey. Not Beck. Not the guy who had almost killed her.

Instead, Lainey was staring in at Ash like she didn't know who he was. Mistrust and fear shone through her swirling blue eyes, and her hair lifted from her shoulders as her magic rose to the surface.

"Fuck, Lainey, it's not what it looks like." He raised his hands in surrender. "Let me explai—"

Beck cut him off with a growl. "There is nothing to explain." With his teeth bared, Beck looked positively livid, setting his feet like he was prepping for a fight. "You brought a demon here. Clearly, you're on their side."

Ash and Andras stood, and Ash took a step in front of the demon as Beck's wild gaze traveled to him. Frustrated and sick of hearing Beck talk, Ash used his magic to draw a vine from a potted plant in the corner. It erupted through the soil and slapped Beck across the face. His head snapped to the side, and when his gaze returned to Ash, his eyes burned with the desire to lay into Ash.

"Fuck off, Beck. No one asked you." He stepped further in front of Andras, prepared to take the full force of Beck's magic, which was rapidly gathering around him.

Before Beck could make a move, Lainey placed a hand on his arm. "Let's give him a chance to explain." Her gaze absolutely destroyed Ash. She'd never looked at him with such hurt and mistrust, and it was like a hot brand searing through him.

"I swear, Lainey." He lowered his hands and begged her with his eyes to understand. "I would never do anything to hurt you or Phoenix. You know that. I trust Andras, or I'd never have brought him here to you. Please believe me, Lainey."

"Then why is he here? Why is he in Faerie with the rest of the demons?" Her voice shook, but her eyes were fierce.

"I can't tell you," Ash said. "That's his story, and—"

"She has my twin," Andras interrupted quietly. "The demon running things in Faerie, she has my twin. It's the only reason I'm here. If I hadn't come with her to do her bidding ..." He shuddered, unable to finish his sentence.

Ash refrained from reaching back and grabbing Andras's hand. Barely. But he did step back to stand shoulder-to-shoulder with him. "Look, Andras and I are working together. We're going to make sure his sister is safe and do what we can to save Phoenix. This opportunity to go to the demon realm is perfect. Andras will be able to help us there. He'll make sure we stay safe. He'll know where to find the answers we need to save Phoenix. Lainey, I'd never offer this if I didn't trust him. I'd *never* put you in danger. You *know* that."

Lainey studied Andras. Whatever she saw, her features softened, and she stepped around Beck. "I'm sorry, Ash. I do trust you. It just startled me."

Ash exhaled a relieved sigh. "Thank fuck. Don't scare me like that again." He placed his hand over his heart. It pounded under his palm.

"What?" Beck exclaimed. "You're just going to trust them like that? Lainey, you can't be serious."

Lainey ignored Beck and turned to Andras. "Do you know anything about the demon possessing Nix? Do you know how to save him?"

Andras grimaced and shook his head. "I'm sorry. I don't know anything about it. The only information I was given was what Selene thought necessary. How we save him depends on the type of demon possessing him." He gave her a sad smile. "We need to figure that out first. And a seer will be able to do just that."

Lainey closed her eyes briefly. When she opened them, a determined light burned in their depths. "When can we leave?"

LAINEY

Lainey had no idea what to expect as they all stood in the cellar of the orphanage. Andras had said he was positive being underground would prevent any demons in the streets from noticing a portal opening. Lainey had pulled Ash aside earlier, and he'd sworn again that he trusted Andras. She trusted Ash, so she guessed that meant she trusted Andras too.

She'd watched Andras closely as they prepared to go to the demon realm. He seemed to be telling the truth, but really, how would she have known? She couldn't stop staring at his horns. They curved along the length of his skull, starting right above his forehead and stopping right at the back of the crown of his head. The faint shimmery-blue bands were intriguing. She'd tried to count how many there were, but he didn't sit still long enough for her to keep them straight.

"Lainey, this is a terrible idea," Beck said in her ear. "We need to think this through."

She shrugged him off. Partly because a part of her thought he was right, and partly because she didn't want him that close to her.

"Lainey, seriously," Beck said, stepping closer again. "I'm just trying to keep you safe. Let's give this more thought."

She let his words roll right off of her and looked over to Ash, who was watching Andras intently.

"I asked Brand about your dad," she said quietly.

Ash whipped his head in Lainey's direction. "And?"

She could tell he was trying to not get his hopes up, so she was glad she could give him good news. "He's already returned to the human realm with your mom and sister."

His shoulders relaxed, and the line between his brows smoothed as a weight lifted from his shoulders and one of his worries disappeared. "Thank the gods," he breathed. "Thanks for asking. You didn't have to do that."

She smiled. "Yes, I did. You would have done the same for me." She bit her lip. "How ... how is Zephyr?"

"He's fine, and he's being careful."

"Good," she said, unsure how to react.

"How's Brand?" Ash asked.

Lainey smiled. "He's here. In Faerie. I think he is going to stay hidden for a while, but he's happy to be back. I should find a way to let him know what we're doing, so he doesn't worry."

"I already sent a bird to him with a message before we came down here," Beck said behind them.

"Quit listening to my conversations, Beck." Lainey huffed.

Before Beck could respond, Andras turned to face them. "Are you guys ready? I'm going to open the portal near my apartment. It's probably the best place for us to stay while we figure things out."

Nerves fluttered in Lainey's stomach as she realized she was about to step foot in the demon realm. What would it be like? Full of fire and brimstone? Darkness and shadows?

"Are you sure this is safe for us?" she asked for what seemed like the hundredth time.

"Safe enough," Andras replied. "Like I said, fae weren't uncommon in the demon realm before the curse. If we keep a low profile, you should be fine. Just try not to draw attention to yourself."

"But I'm only half-fae."

He shrugged. "Keep your ears hidden and no one will know. I can sense your magic, and it doesn't feel any different than Ash's."

"What is the demon realm like? Should we bring anything with us? Do we need salt?" All of a sudden, this seemed like an incredibly rash decision. They didn't even have any salt! She briefly considered saying they should wait and plan, but as she thought of Phoenix, and the tattered bond in her chest, she quickly dismissed the idea. They didn't have time to wait.

Andras chuckled. "The salt thing is a myth humans picked up from somewhere. I personally love salt. And we don't need to bring anything. We can get whatever we need there. Hel is not too different from the human realm. We have cities, cars, electricity, running water. It's just a bit ... darker."

Darker? That sounded ominous. But she let her questions go as Andras stepped to the middle of the cellar and held out his hands. A blue shimmery light appeared in the middle of the space. It started spinning, slowly at first, then faster and faster until a wind blew outward from the blue light, blowing her hair away from her face and making her squint. The spinning stopped suddenly, and the light expanded until a vertical blue ... door? ... was in front of them.

"Holy shit," Beck muttered.

"I have to keep the portal open, so I'll have to go through last," Andras said to Ash.

Ash nodded. "I'll go first. Give me a few seconds before you follow, Lainey."

She swallowed but nodded. Her hands fisted against her belly as she tried to fight the nervous nausea that threatened to climb up her throat. Her brain had a hard time comprehending when Ash stepped up to the portal and walked through. Blue light flared as he disappeared, and Lainey gasped. He was gone. Holy shit, he was gone.

This was so different from the gate trees. She'd used and seen those being used, and it was nothing like this. What if he didn't make it? Would he just be floating in some weird in-between space, lost forever? What if Andras couldn't be trusted and he'd just sent Ash to his death?

"Lainey, it's your turn," Andras said. He bowed his head respectfully in her direction.

She narrowed her eyes at him. "If you just sent Ash somewhere to die, I'll kill you."

A smile tugged at his lips. "If I ever hurt him, you have my permission to kill me."

She blinked. What the hell did that mean?

"Last chance, Lainey. It's not too late to stop this." Beck was staring at the portal with open distrust.

Shaking her head, and she took a step forward. She was doing this for Phoenix. She'd do anything to save her mate. Lainey took a deep breath, squared her shoulders, and took one step into the portal.

Blue. That was all she could see as she took another step forward. Blue pulsing light surrounded her, and tingles of electricity swarmed over her skin. It wasn't painful; instead, it was almost comforting. She took one more step, and the light disappeared, the tingles disappeared. She gasped as her surroundings came into focus.

She was in a ... parking lot? It looked a hell of a lot like a small parking lot behind a building. The building was a three-story brick structure, with windows and doors, and balconies. In the distance, she could see taller skyscrapers reaching high into the sky. A sky that was blue, but not. A glowing orange-ish ball she assumed was the sun let off a strangely dim light that made everything appear kind of dark.

The demon realm reminded her of a city, an alternate version —a darker version—of New York.

A chuckle to her left drew her attention, and she hurried to Ash's side, clinging to his arm like a toddler. "Not what you expected?" he asked as he ruffled her hair.

"Where is the fire?" she breathed. "The black craggy mountains spewing lava?"

"I'm sure it's around here somewhere. If you really want to see it, maybe we can take a field trip." He sounded entirely too enthusiastic for her liking.

She elbowed him in the side and took immense pleasure when he grunted and doubled over. Before they could continue their bickering, the portal flared, and Beck stepped through. His hand was on his dagger at his waist, and he scanned his surroundings for danger. He didn't appear surprised by what he saw. Was she the only one who'd expected the dreary, burning visage of hell?

Beck made his way toward them, and the portal flared once more, this time depositing Andras into the parking lot before it winked out of existence. He checked to make sure they were okay, then nodded his head toward the building. "This way."

They followed him through a heavy metal door that looked a lot like the back door to many New York City buildings. Then down hallways that reminded Lainey of nicer versions of her apartment hallways, and up a staircase that looked exactly like staircases she'd used in the human realm. She was completely reeling when Andras used his thumb to open a door on the third floor and ushered them all inside.

"Have a seat. I'll get everyone some water." Andras waved to what appeared to be a living room.

Lainey numbly sat on a black sofa and let her gaze wander the space. Light gray painted walls boasted abstract artwork of lines and colors. A few plants sat in corners and on tables, nothing like the plants she'd seen in either of the realms she'd lived in. They reminded her of carnivorous plants, and she made a mental note to stay away from them. Two black chairs, a glass coffee table, and a white and gray rug that looked ridiculously soft accompanied the sofa.

The space was tasteful and inviting. And nothing like she'd expected.

Andras joined them and handed out bottles of water. Lainey

stared at the label. It looked like a knock-off version of a brand in the human realm. Her wide-eyed stare lifted to Andras, and she gaped. Words were bubbling inside of her, but she couldn't make her brain and tongue work together to speak them aloud.

Andras laughed and sat on the arm of the chair Ash occupied. Lainey narrowed her eyes at them as suspicion grew in her gut.

"Not what you expected?" Andras echoed Ash's earlier question.

She still couldn't form words, so she shook her head instead.

"The curse only locked the gates to Faerie, so we continued growing with the human realm," Andras explained. "We also have a similar atmosphere as the human realm, unlike Faerie. So electronics work here." He held up a device similar to a cell phone.

"Umm ..." She couldn't think of anything to say. She ran her fingers through her hair and winced when they got caught in tangles. When was the last time she'd washed or brushed her hair?

"Maybe a shower would help?" Ash offered with a wry grin.

"Like, a legit shower? Not a bath?" She couldn't hide the hopefulness in her voice.

"A legit shower," Andras replied. "Follow me."

She hesitated, but the thought was too tempting. She'd risk death for a hot shower.

Andras led her down a hallway to a small but nice bathroom. "Everything you'll need is in here." He tapped a cabinet. "The shower works just like one in the human realm. Take as long as you need. We have an endless supply of hot water, being in Hel and all." He grinned at her.

Lainey couldn't help but admire how attractive he was, with those stunning blue eyes, plush lips, and carved cheekbones. The suspicion worming through her grew a little more.

Andras left, and Lainey locked the door, eagerly turning on the water and stripping off her dirty clothes. She was going to be here for a very long time.

BY THE TIME Lainey emerged from the bathroom in a cloud of steam, everyone else had clearly showered using another bathroom somewhere in the apartment. It grated on her nerves that Beck had apparently been provided amenities as well. She wanted him to suffer. If that meant withholding showers, she'd make it happen.

Ash and Andras were sitting next to each other on the couch. And by *next to each other*, Lainey meant she'd noticed there was zero space between them. Suspicion confirmed.

Beck sat on a chair with a plate in his lap, and Lainey glanced at the coffee table and gasped.

"Is that pizza?"

"Yep, and it's delicious. Help yourself." Ash waved to an extra plate on the table.

Lainey grabbed a slice and carefully took a bite. He wasn't wrong. It was quite possibly the best pizza she'd ever eaten.

"Did you raid my closet while you were in New York?" Ash's eyes gleamed as he took in his Silverstein tee on her much smaller frame.

"Yes, and the shirts I brought back are mine now. Thank you very much."

He snorted. "Anything for you, my queen."

Lainey groaned. "No! Don't you dare start that shit." She sat on the floor in front of the couch and set her slice of pizza on the plate. "But I did bring you something, although I don't think it will be as big a deal in the demon realm as it would be in Faerie."

She dug through her bookbag and pulled out the iPod with headphones already plugged in. She handed it to Ash.

He raised one brow. "Is this an old-school iPod? Where the hell did you find one of these?"

"A pawn shop, actually. I also got a speaker it can hook up to, and a solar charger. I loaded all our favorite music on there, so we can listen to it in Faerie."

Ash grinned and scrolled through the bands Lainey had put on it. "Bayside, Blink, Green Day, New Found Glory, Silverstein,

Story of the Year, The Used, Yellowcard. You got all of them, Lainey."

"There were more I wanted to add, I just didn't have the time."

"This is going to make working out so much better." He turned and grinned at Andras. "You are in for a treat."

"Are we going to talk about the real reason we're here?" Beck grumbled from his chair. "Did everyone forget our purpose for coming to this godsforsaken realm?"

Lainey sighed. He was right. As nice as it was to joke with Ash, she had to remember her true mission: Phoenix.

"You need to talk with a seer?" Andras asked.

"Yes." Lainey looked at Andras and narrowed her eyes. His hand was resting on Ash's thigh. She'd have to have a more in-depth conversation with the demon, it seemed. Shaking her head, she continued, "Madam Elvie said they could tell us how to free Nix."

Andras rubbed his chin. "Yeah, you'll want to talk to a seer, but not just any seer. You'll need someone powerful, someone we can trust who isn't part of the movement to destroy Faerie."

"Is that possible? Is there someone who could help us?" Lainey was afraid to get her hopes up.

"There is," he paused and released a breath. "It might be dangerous, though. And ..." He trailed off and glanced at Ash, indecision clear in his expression.

"You don't want to risk your twin," Ash filled in for him.

"Well ... Zurie is a seer. And a powerful one."

Lainey stared at him, her mouth hanging open. "Are you serious?"

"I am, and she'd be able to help," Andras said, nodding his head. "The problem is, I don't know where Selene is holding her."

"So if we find your sister, she can help me find a way to save Nix?" Lainey couldn't keep the hope out of her voice.

Andras nodded again. "Yes."

"But how do we find her?" Ash asked.

"I think I know where to start looking, at least to get an idea of where she is being held, but it's incredibly risky," Andras said. He turned his attention to her. "I'm sure it would make Ash feel better if you stayed here tomorrow. At least until I get an understanding of where things stand here."

She would never admit it, but Lainey was relieved to hear that. Whenever she remembered she was in the demon realm, fear fluttered to life in her stomach. She needed a little more time to come to terms with what she was doing. A day in a seemingly normal apartment would help tremendously.

"As long as you have some books for me to read, I'll happily stay here for a day. But only one day." She pointed a finger at them. "After that, I want to be a part of this. The quicker we can get your sister to safety, the quicker we can find a way to save Nix."

Andras smiled. "Deal."

"How dangerous are we talking?" Ash asked.

"Well, I'm supposed to be in Faerie assassinating you. Instead, I brought you here with two other fae, one of them the queen they are all searching for."

"So what's the plan then?" Ash asked, threading his fingers through Andras's.

Andras pulled his lower lip between his teeth. "I have no idea. I'll think on it tonight."

"Wow, that sounds like a spectacular plan," Beck drawled. He'd been silent through all of this. So much so, Lainey had almost forgotten he was there.

"Fuck off, Beck. If you're not going to contribute, go away." Lainey glared at him, and Beck just rolled his eyes and shook his head.

"We should all probably get some sleep," Andras said, attempting to diffuse the rapidly growing tension in the room.

"Can I permanently put Beck to sleep?" Ash muttered as he pulled Lainey to her feet.

"Yes, please," she said.

"Not in my apartment. I don't want to clean up the mess," Andras said as he led them down the hall and pointed out rooms for them.

Ash hesitated outside Andras's door and Lainey gave him a gentle shove. "Go ahead, sleep with your boy toy."

His gaze bounced down the hall to the room Beck had just entered. "That's okay. I'll stay in your room. I don't trust Beck."

Lainey rolled her eyes. "Great. Now I'm cockblocking you. You better not hold this over my head."

Ash chuckled. "Oh, I most certainly will."

ASH

"WELL, THIS IS DEFINITELY MORE HOW I PICTURED hell."

Ash stood with Andras in front of a black building that looked to have been carved from a massive piece of stone. With its craggy peaks and broken, jagged edges climbing high into the sky, it was the opposite of every other structure Ash had seen so far. Most of the skyscrapers in Hel looked like any that could be found in New York—pale gray, white, even shiny blue glass. This one stuck out like a sore thumb.

"It's our main government office. Essentially the same concept as the human realm's White House." Andras sounded distracted, his eyes not as bright as usual.

Part of that could have been because of the weird sun in Hel. The orange ball in the sky didn't let off a bright light. Instead, it made everything darker. It was early morning, but it felt more like late evening with the dark, shadowed light.

Though Ash had a feeling the shadows in his eyes were because of whatever he was going to face inside that black building. "What's the plan?" he asked again and stepped closer, letting his shoulder brush Andras's in silent support.

Andras sighed. "There isn't a good one. I'm just hoping we

haven't been noticed missing in Faerie yet. I'm going to tell him Selene sent me back for something and hope she hasn't been in contact with him lately. But I'm going to talk to him to see if I can get him to tell me anything that helps us find Zurie. I also want to lay the groundwork for making sure you're safe while we're here."

They'd talked long into the night, making and dismissing plans that would ensure everyone's safety. In the end, they decided Andras would continue to pretend he was getting close to Ash to get information from him. Ash would pretend to be a lovesick puppy following Andras around, spilling said important information. Although, that wasn't too far from the truth.

"All right. Let's do this, then." Ash nudged Andras with his shoulder.

Andras gave him a grateful smile and started up the steps to the looming front doors of carved black stone. Ash took in the intricate designs that reminded him of the tattoos inked onto Andras's skin. Not for the first time, he thought it must have been some kind of language, and he made a mental note to ask Andras what it was.

As they pushed through the doors, Ash ran a finger along the dagger Andras had lent him. His eyes never settled on one thing as he scanned their surroundings for any threats. Most people ignored them entirely. A few blinked in surprise when they saw Andras, but they only bowed their heads respectfully and continued on their way.

Ash watched it all with interest. Andras had said he was one of the more powerful demons in this realm, but he was starting to suspect Andras may have downplayed it a bit. Andras ignored most of the demons, only nodding back to a few of them.

Ash cataloged the various horns that sprouted from everyone's heads. He felt keenly aware of his lack and how that singled him out as something other. Most of the horns he saw were small black points, barely visible through the hair. There were a few with horns shaped similarly to Andras's, curving back over the skull, and some that twisted like a kudu or ram, but none of them had nearly as many colored bands. He saw every color spiraling up the horns, ranging from Andras's dark blue to the palest yellow.

When he wasn't looking at the horns, Ash took in his surroundings. It reminded him of the Unseelie palace. Smooth black stone made up the floor and walls. The modern furniture and artwork were a paradox that Ash had a hard time wrapping his head around. He expected to turn a corner and find a massive throne with the devil seated on top, complete with pitchfork and spiky tail. Instead, all the demons wore business casual clothes in an array of colors.

Andras led them to an elevator and pressed the button. His shoulders were tense, and Ash could practically feel the unease rolling off of him. As soon as they stepped into the elevator, he turned to the demon.

"Are you okay?" he asked quietly.

Andras rolled his shoulders. "Just want to get this over with. I've never had the best relationship with my dad, and my mom's death only made it worse. I just ... I never know what to expect with him. It makes me edgy."

Ash reached out and squeezed his hand. He attempted to let go when the doors slid open, but Andras held tightly, and he pulled Ash down the hall. He stopped in front of a black door with a frosted glass window boasting the name *Badon Mordreth, Chief of Defense.* Well, that certainly made sense.

Andras took a deep breath, his shoulders rising then falling before straightening. He knocked twice, then pushed the door open. Ash kept his free hand away from his dagger, but he was ready. Andras's dad didn't like fae, and he would not be taken by surprise.

A secretary sat at a desk in the middle of the all-black room. Her eyes widened briefly before she stood and bowed to Andras, a blond curl falling over her slim shoulder. "My lord," she said as she stood. "I wasn't expecting you." She glanced at Ash, and her eyes widened even further. Her attention darted back to Andras, and she licked her lips nervously. "Have a seat. I'll let your father know you are here."

Andras led Ash to a white leather sofa while the secretary notified Mr. Mordreth, Chief of Defense. Ash stared at Andras with a flat expression.

"Chief of Defense, eh? Seems like an important job. And all the people bowing to you?" Ash's lips twitched as Andras's face flooded scarlet. "Did you forget to mention something, *my lord*"

Andras's shoulders stiffened further. "Don't," he hissed. "Don't you dare treat me any differently because of my position."

Ash reeled backward. "You really think I'd do that?"

Andras shrugged and looked down at his hands in his lap. Ash opened his mouth to say something, but the secretary had returned.

"He'll see you now, my lord." Her gaze cut to Ash, and wariness flooded her features. "Only you, though."

Andras stood quickly and didn't spare Ash a second glance as he entered his dad's office. Ash sat back on the couch and crossed his arms over his chest. Unreasonable irritation flooded his system. He couldn't have cared less what position Andras held in Hel. But it bothered him that Andras had never told him. It was irrational, and he knew it, but he couldn't talk sense into himself. While he understood Andras's initial reluctance to share information of that caliber, they'd spent more time with each other and seemed to have formed a sort of bond. Hell, Ash had trusted him with Lainey's life. He'd hoped Andras would have trusted him with information about his life like that.

The secretary eyed Ash warily as he scowled at nothing in particular. He wasn't sure why it bothered him so much, but the idea that Andras hadn't trusted him with that knowledge made him itch under his skin. It didn't feel like a betrayal, more like ... more like a shortcoming Ash possessed. Like he wasn't worthy of that knowledge.

He grunted, and the poor secretary almost jumped out of her skin. The longer he sat there, the more he could think, and the more irritated he became. It was a loop he got stuck in—irritated at Andras, then irritated that he was irritated. His fingers tapped on his biceps, and his leg bounced up and down, making the vase of flowers rattle on the coffee table in front of the couch. He needed to get out of his own head. There were more important things to worry about than why Andras hadn't shared that information with him.

When the door to Badon's office opened, Andras stepped out and glanced at Ash, although he looked at a spot over Ash's shoulder rather than meeting his gaze. The tendons in his neck stood out sharply as he nodded his head toward the hallway. "Let's go." His tone was quiet but clipped, and a muscle feathered in his jaw as he waited for Ash to join him before leaving his dad's office.

Ash gritted his teeth as he followed Andras in silence down the hall to the elevator. They didn't speak as they waited, and the tension between them vibrated in the air. Ash struggled to maintain his calm, and that alone almost shocked him out of this funk. He rarely lost his cool, but something about this situation was getting under his skin.

The elevator dinged, and the door slid open. It felt like it took years for the space to widen enough for Andras to step through. Ash followed, and they stood on opposite sides, Ash with his arms crossed over his chest and Andras with his hands shoved into his pockets. At first, Andras said nothing, and Ash ground his teeth together as the tension grew even more.

When Andras finally glanced at Ash, his expression was carefully blank, but he raised one eyebrow as if he was waiting for something.

Ash barked out a harsh laugh. "If you're waiting for me to bow to you and call you *my lord* again, don't hold your breath. You'll be dead before I ever entertain the idea." He leaned against the elevator wall, daring Andras to say something.

Emotion flickered across Andras's face too fast for Ash to read. With a wave of his hand, icy blue light coated the inside of the elevator, and the demon made his way toward Ash to slap the emergency stop button. They jerked to a halt, and Ash caught himself with a hand to the wall. Before he could ask Andras what the hell he was doing, Andras pushed him against the cool surface and kissed him.

Shock froze Ash for a just second, then he slid his hands through Andras's hair and grabbed his horns, tugging the demon closer. Something settled within him, as if all the nervous energy building inside him had just melted away into nothing.

Andras broke the kiss first and rested his forehead against Ash's.

"What was that for?" Ash asked as he ran his fingers through Andras's hair.

"For not treating me any differently."

Ash pulled back as much as he could with his back against the elevator wall. The open, vulnerable expression on Andras's face tightened Ash's chest. "Why the hell would I?"

"Everyone else does." He shrugged. "My mom and my twin are the only ones who have ever treated me like … like a person. To everyone else, I'm either Lord Andras or my father's legacy. Neither of which I want."

"Well, you've seen me with Lainey, and she's a queen. I've never treated her as anything other than my friend, unless we're in public and need to keep up appearances."

"But you're always so protective of her. I don't want, nor need, to be protected just because of a title."

Ash couldn't help but smile. "I protect Lainey because I care about her as a friend. And because she's my best friend's mate, and it would destroy him if something happened to her. I'd protect Lainey even if she were a peasant living on the streets. Title has nothing to do with it."

Andras looked at him with a mixture of hope and disbelief. Ash wrapped his hand around the back of Andras's neck and pulled him in for a kiss.

"I mean it, Andras," he said against his lips. "Nothing has

changed between us because of this. Except maybe me calling you *my lord* in the bedroom." Ash winked at Andras, and relief swept through him when Andras relaxed and smiled back.

"That I think I can handle," he said as he pressed the button for the second floor and the elevator began moving again.

"Did you learn anything from your dad?"

"Nothing," Andras grunted. "I don't think he knows I left Faerie without Selene's consent. And he knows you're here and thinks it's because I'm getting information out of you. We'll have to think of some things to pass along so he doesn't get suspicious. Maybe a mix of truth and lies? Things that won't hurt Faerie but will mess with Selene's agenda." Before the elevator door slid open, he waved his hand again, and the blue light disappeared.

"I'm assuming that handy trick kept people from overhearing our conversation?" Ash asked quietly as they exited the elevator.

"I froze the camera feed and muted the mic. Hopefully, anyone playing back the video will assume I did that so we could have some *quality time* together," Andras said with a wink that made Ash's stomach flip-flop.

This time, Andras led him through the halls to another office door. This one didn't have a nameplate, only a sign next to the handle that said *223.*

Andras peered up and down the hallway before pulling something out of his pocket. "Let me know if anyone's coming," he muttered as he bent to the lock and slid a thin metal pick into the hole.

Ash's brows raised to his hairline, but he scanned the hallway for visitors. "Are you picking the lock to that door?"

"Uhh ... yeah."

Ash spared a glance down to find Andras with his features painted with intense focus, the tip of his tongue adorably sticking out of the corner of his mouth. "And whose office are you breaking into?"

"Selene's."

Ash whipped his head back toward Andras. "Selene's?" he hissed. "Isn't that a surefire way to piss her off?"

"It is. Which is why I'm not using my magic. She has this place warded to detect any hint of magic." He paused and scrunched his brows down just as a soft *click* sounded from the door. "Ha! Got it."

He straightened, and the smile he tossed Ash's way was breathtaking. So far, Ash had seen many small smiles and smirks from Andras but no full-blown smiles. As cliché as it sounded, it was like the sun breaking through the clouds on a stormy day. Ash's heart actually skipped a beat at the sight.

The smile faded, and Andras peered at him warily. "What? Why are you looking at me like that?"

Ash had to swallow before he could speak. "Like what?"

"A mix between awe and like you've just been punched in the stomach."

"I'm just amazed at your lockpicking skills." When Andras turned back to the door, Ash said, "And I want you to smile more."

ANDRAS FLOPPED onto the couch as soon as he stepped foot inside his apartment. It was the most human reaction Ash had seen from him, and if it weren't for the utter despair in his eyes, Ash would have enjoyed watching him.

"I don't know what else to do," Andras groaned.

Ash sat on the couch by Andras's sprawled legs and gripped his thigh. "Let's keep thinking. Don't give up, Andras."

Drawn by the noise of their entry, Lainey and Beck sauntered into the living room.

"No luck?" Lainey asked quietly as she sank into a chair. She held a book in her hands, but Ash couldn't read the title through her fingers.

"Nothing from my dad or Selene's office." Andras let his arm fall across his eyes.

Lainey bit her lower lip as she thought. "I'm assuming Selene would pay someone to do her dirty work where your twin is concerned, correct?"

Andras grunted.

"Did you check her files for payroll?" Lainey asked, setting her book on the coffee table. "She'd have to keep track of something like that."

"We looked through her bank statements and payroll information. There was nothing there." Ash rested his head on the back of the couch as he rubbed his eyes. An ache was steadily building behind them. "I guarantee she's doing it under the table. She wouldn't want that information going public."

Beck shifted in his chair. "Yes, but she'd still have to have some kind of record of it. Some way to show money is going out and into someone else's account." He sounded like he was speaking to an insolent child, and it made Ash sit up straighter.

During their conversation, Andras had removed his arm from his face. When Beck finished his thought, he sat up so fast, his head cracked against Ash's.

"Holy fuck!" Ash yelled at the same time Andras groaned, "Shit, fuck, ow."

Pain made lights flash behind Ash's tightly closed eyes. A sharp ache radiated outward from his forehead, growing in intensity. He held his forehead with one hand, while his other fisted against his mouth. He couldn't open his eyes to check on Andras, but based on the groans coming from the demon, he was hurting too.

"What the fuck, Andras? Are you trying to kill me?"

"Argh! Why is your head so fucking hard?" Andras moaned. "I think you fractured my skull."

"*I* fractured *your* skull?" Ash cracked one eye open and glared pathetically at Andras. "That was your fault. Why did you launch yourself off the couch like that? A little warning would have been nice."

"Why was your head so close to mine?" Andras countered.

"It wasn't! Not until you ejected yourself from the couch cushions."

"Are you two quite done?" Lainey asked from her safe spot in the chair.

Ash turned a baleful eye on her. Amusement lit her eyes, and dammit if it didn't make his heart skip a beat. When was the last time he'd actually seen something other than heartache in her eyes? If giving himself a concussion made her happy, he'd knock his head against a wall every damn day until they got Nix back.

He returned his attention to Andras, who was rubbing a red spot on his forehead. "You're lucky you didn't hit me with a horn. You could have taken my eye out! You need to be more careful with those things."

Andras sighed. "Could you be more dramatic?"

"Don't ask him that. He'll take it as a challenge," Lainey chimed in dryly.

Andras huffed a laugh. "Damn, I think I already have a knot forming."

He was right. Ash could see the reddened bump growing above his left eye. He felt his own forehead and found a similar bump.

"Are you guys done being babies? We'd like to know what idea popped into Andras's head." Beck sat in the other chair with his arms crossed over his chest, clearly unamused.

Andras ignored Beck's hostility and turned to face Ash. "You and Lainey are absolutely correct. She wouldn't be paying someone to do her dirty work where anyone could find the evidence. It wouldn't be in her office in the government building. She'd keep all of that in her office at home. At our dad's."

ASH

ASH EYED LAINEY AS SHE STRAPPED A DAGGER TO HER thigh. If she wasn't his best friend's mate, he'd have admired the picture she painted. Sexy, badass Queen of the Underworld. Instead, nervous energy curled in his gut.

"There is no way I can convince you to stay behind?" he asked for what seemed like the hundredth time.

She didn't even bother to glare at him. "I'm not answering that ... again."

Ash sighed and walked over to her to help ensure her straps were all tight and intact. She slapped his hand away.

"I'm perfectly capable of doing this myself. You taught me how to do it, after all."

He gave her a flat stare, and she rolled eyes but relented. While his fingers worked the leather straps, he glanced at Andras. The demon also painted quite the impressive picture. His horns gleamed in the light as he bent his head to strap on his own daggers. Andras in leather was everything Ash never knew he needed. A glance in the other direction showed Beck getting ready for their mission as well, putting on his borrowed leathers and weapons.

Ash tried not to think about how everything could go

horribly wrong today. Andras's dad's place was well guarded—with people and magic—and they didn't have much of a plan besides sneaking in, getting what they needed, and sneaking out. Because Andras had grown up in the house, he knew the floor plan, the basic rotation of guards, and locations of cameras, but that didn't ease the worry gnawing at Ash.

"Should we wait a day or two? Make better plans? Scout ahead of time?" he asked, again, for the hundredth time.

Both Lainey and Andras shook their heads. They were too eager to get back the people they loved. Waiting another day wasn't an option for them, despite how much Ash disagreed with rushing in without a more solid plan. He'd tried—multiple times—and failed—multiple times—to convince them otherwise. Beck had remained quiet on the matter, and Ash had a feeling he was conflicted. He didn't want to wait any longer, but he also didn't want to be reckless.

Ash sighed in resignation. "Let's just get this over with, then." His nerves were fired up, and he couldn't remain still. If he did, he was positive the growing itch under his skin was going to make him explode. Moving helped to ease the anxiety building in his system. He couldn't remember a time he'd felt so anxious about something. Even when they first came to Faerie, even when they took on Esmeray. He'd been nervous, but not to this point of nausea. It wasn't sitting right with him.

As they made their way through the demon city, Ash wished he could take in the sights, but he couldn't bring himself to care. Cars drove past, similar to cars in the human realm but with no familiar makes or models. Buildings looked like structures in New York, and the demons on the streets looked just like humans, albeit with horns sprouting from their heads. Any other time, he would have loved to observe the ebb and flow of the city.

When they turned onto the street Andras grew up on, Ash let out an appreciative whistle. Clearly, Andras came from money. All the houses were mansion-like, with sprawling manicured lawns and gated driveways. They skirted the perimeter of Badon's house, avoiding the range of the cameras on the fence.

"Here," Andras said as he stopped in front of a section of fence that was no different from the rest. "This is the one blind spot we can use to our advantage." He jumped with preternatural grace, higher than a human could have, and grasped the top rail to pull himself over. He landed in a crouch on the other side and scanned his surroundings. "I think we're clear."

Ash took a deep breath before wrapping his hands around Lainey's waist and lifting her into the air. She pulled herself over the fence, and Andras caught her, setting her on her feet. Ash and Beck both jumped at the same time and landed on the other side together.

Something shivered under Ash's skin. Something that made him grit his teeth. "I don't think we should do this," he whispered as he looked around.

Beck glanced at him and shrugged. He was likely too desperate to get the information they needed so they could return to Faerie and save Nix. Ash was too, but they still needed to be careful. The others ignored his worry and continued across the lawn. They followed closely in Andras's footsteps, hoping to remain out of sight of the cameras. Ash grimaced, but he jogged to catch up.

They approached the red brick building, and Andras used his lockpicks to break into the servant's entrance. Ash's heart pounded in his chest as they slunk through the quiet house. Badon wouldn't be home at this time of day, and Selene was obviously in Faerie. But there were servants around, and guards. Ash strained his ears to filter through every little sound, but so far, it was quiet. Too quiet.

The house was massive and beautifully decorated. He couldn't truly take in the beauty and appreciate it, but he wondered what Andras's life had been like growing up here. He paused in a hallway when a portrait caught his eye. It was hanging in a shiny black frame, and Ash had zero doubt who it was. Andras's mom.

She was beautiful. Andras clearly got his looks from her. They shared the same pale skin, black wavy hair, and pale blue eyes. She had delicate-looking kudu horns curling from her skull, with light green bands circling the lower half. The portrait made her appear graceful and ethereal, almost angelic, yet there was a quiet strength to the tilt of her head. A quiet strength he saw in Andras as well.

Pulling himself from the portrait, he found his companions stopped farther down the hall. Andras was once again using his lockpick to unlock a door. Ash hurried forward and joined them as the door swung open.

Selene's office was tidy. A large wooden desk sat in the middle of the space with a black leather wingback chair. A wall of books took up one side of the room, and the other was mostly a giant piece of abstract art. Her desktop was empty, save for a computer screen and a small stack of papers neatly piled in the corner.

"I'll check the desk. Ash, you get the file cabinet. Lainey and Beck, check the bookshelf," Andras ordered as he made his way to the desk.

Ash swept the room with an all too observant stare one last time before heading to the file cabinet tucked in the corner. It was surprisingly unlocked, and he tugged the top drawer open. He riffled through the tabs, occasionally pulling out a sheet of paper to scan its contents. There was nothing interesting, just insurance policy documents for different people.

The second drawer was also useless. But a tab in the third drawer grabbed his interest. *Unseelie* was scrawled in a flowy script on a small tab. He pulled out the three files behind the tab, all bursting at the seams.

"I found something on Unseelie," he muttered as he walked to the desk and sat the files down.

He glanced at Andras and froze. The demon was holding an open file in his hands. The folder shook as tremors worked through his body. Ash placed a hand on his lower back and peered over his shoulder. He saw Zurie's name multiple times, as well as what appeared to be numbers to a bank account.

"Andras," Ash said quietly.

The demon looked at him, eyes shining with despair, yet his shoulders relaxed knowing they finally had answers. Pulling his phone from his pocket, he checked the screen and swallowed thickly before handing the files to Ash. "Go ahead and head out the way we came in. I'll meet you guys outside." With that, he left the office without saying anything else.

Ash looked at Lainey and Beck with raised brows, and found his expression mirrored on their faces. He shrugged and said, "Okay, let's go."

Pushing through the door, Ash scanned both directions and froze. Andras had a guard pinned against the wall, his body pressed tight to the other demon's, mouths molded together. Ash's stomach dropped so fast, he almost threw up. He couldn't tear his gaze away from the pair, even as his heart cracked and splintered, and shame crept up the back of his neck.

Lainey peered around him and gasped softly. She marched into the hall as if she was going to give Andras a piece of her mind, but Ash stopped her. Andras tugged the guard away from the wall, never breaking their kiss. His hand slipped under the guard's shirt and slid up his back. Bile climbed up Ash's throat, and he watched as Andras tugged the guard around the corner and disappeared.

Ash couldn't tear his gaze away from where they'd retreated. The image was burned into his mind. The longer he stood there, the harder it became to breathe. His chest was too tight, and it wouldn't expand enough to let air in.

"Ash," Lainey breathed. She cupped his cheek and turned his head to make him look at her. Her blue eyes shone with sadness. "We need to keep moving." Lacing their fingers together, Lainey tugged Ash down the hall, following in Beck's footsteps.

Ash wasn't sure how he got over the fence and back onto the

street, but Lainey kept hold of his hand the entire time. His mind was a strange mix of numbness and whirling chaos. Two different images played in his head, overlapping and twining together, throwing him into the past, to a place he never wanted to return.

Beck got them back to the apartment, something Ash would have to thank him for eventually. But at the moment, he was too lost. Each beat of his heart ached, a piercing throb spreading through his chest. Andras had kissed another man. They'd never had a discussion about relationships—if they were in one or wanted to be in one—Ash had just stupidly assumed. A mistake he couldn't believe he had made, not after everything that had happened before.

Ash collapsed onto the couch, not seeing or hearing Lainey and Beck move around him. A bottle of water was placed in his hands, along with a softly murmured, "Drink," from Lainey. He didn't though. He couldn't. Vaguely, he realized he was disassociating. His mind was protecting him from the pain of his past. It wasn't working very well, though. He was still hurting. So much so, that he felt like ... like a piece of him was missing.

He closed his eyes and tried to focus on anything other than Andras. But the image of Andras with the guard was playing on repeat. He listened to Lainey and Beck talking, the animosity between them gone for the time being, but he didn't hear the words they said. He kept his eyes closed. Kept pushing thoughts of Andras out of his mind as soon as they popped in. It was like a full-time job.

He had no idea how much time passed, but Lainey kept plying him with water and food that he refused to eat. If he did, he'd probably throw it all back up. When the door to the apartment opened and Andras strode in, Ash froze. His hair was mussed, like someone had been running their hands through it, and Ash had the inexplicable urge to find that guard and remove his fucking hands from his body. Followed by his head.

Andras's gaze landed on Ash, and the regret in those icy blue eyes made Ash see red. How dare he fucking act like he regretted what happened. In between the broken shards of his heart, fury grew, trying to squeeze into the cracks.

"Ash," Andras said, taking a step toward him.

Unable to listen to his voice, to hear the words come out of that perfectly kissable mouth, Ash pushed up from the couch and brushed past him, heading toward the room he'd shared with Lainey the other night.

Collapsing onto the bed, he stared at the ceiling as the past and present collided. He'd worked so hard to move on, and he thought he had. But this just proved how much he hadn't. And he hated himself for getting into this position in the first place. So many mistakes were made, and now he was dealing with the consequences.

A soft knock on the door drew his attention from the ceiling. Lainey slipped into the room and climbed onto the bed, leaning against the headboard. She patted her thighs, and Ash curled onto his side, resting his head on her lap. When her fingers trailed through his hair, untangling the blond locks, his eyes closed.

"He explained it to me," she said quietly. "Do you want to know what he said?"

Did he? What were the chances he gave Lainey some bullshit excuse? He probably needed to know, and currently, he couldn't even think about being in the same room as Andras. It hurt too much. Rubbing his chest, he nodded.

"He said he still has the security app on his phone from when he lived there. He got a notification that a guard was approaching, and when he checked, he found out it was his ex."

Ash tensed, and his heart thundered as nausea curled in his gut. His ex? He debated telling Lainey to stop, but it was too late. He needed to know now.

"Apparently, his ex only wants to move up the ladder, and he'd do anything to get to the top. That includes dating Andras and reporting everything back to Selene and their dad. Andras panicked and knew he had to do something to distract the guard so we could get out safely."

"What a fucking coincidence the guard was his ex, and he could *just so happen* to distract him with his body." The bitterness in his tone took him aback.

"Yeah," Lainey agreed. "It was a shitty move, and I agree he could have handled it differently. But …"

Ash groaned. "Of course there's a 'but' from you."

"Buut," she drawled, tugging the strands of his hair to make a point, "I think he's being honest.

"Did I ever tell you I was engaged once?" he asked.

"No." There was surprise in her tone, and it made him smile.

"Yeah, the man whore was engaged. I was nineteen, way too young to be getting married, but I was in love. Or at least I thought I was." His words were slow and quiet as he shared this story of his life. "He was six years older than me, and when he proposed, I thought there was no way I could ever be happier. The wedding was mostly planned, we were only a few months out when I returned home one day and found him in bed with someone else."

Lainey gasped softly, her fingers stilling in his hair.

"He tried to make me stay with him. He told me it was a mistake and promised it wouldn't happen again. I almost believed him. I almost stayed. Nix wouldn't let me, though. I was so pissed at him at the time, but he was obviously right."

"Ash," she whispered.

"This hurts worse," he admitted. "Like, I hear what you said, and it's probably the truth, but I swore I wouldn't let myself get caught in this position again. It's why I've never had a relationship since. I've always just messed around. Became the man whore, Nix likes to call me. It was safer." He shrugged. "I let my guard down, and I should have known better."

Lainey resumed running her fingers through his hair. "I'm sorry, Ash. I know how much this hurts. Give it some time. Be hurt and angry right now, give him hell for doing this, but give him a chance to explain. Everyone makes mistakes, right? That has to include demons too."

He thought about her words and nodded before pulling a blanket over them both. "Okay."

He sounded like a lost child, and he hated it. Scooching down in bed, Lainey held his head to her chest and continued running her fingers through his hair until he fell asleep.

"OKAY. I'll leave that decision to Ash," Lainey said as Ash sauntered into the kitchen.

"What decision am I making?" he asked. He didn't fail to notice Andras's attention on him. He'd purposely worn a pair of gray sweatpants he found in the dresser and nothing else. Pouring himself a cup of coffee, he leaned against the counter and stared at Lainey. Ignoring Andras's attention was hard. He could practically feel the demon's eyes traveling over his body, igniting heat wherever he looked.

Lainey smirked. She knew exactly what he was doing. "If we are still going to help rescue Zurie and when."

He glanced at the cereal boxes on the counter, trying to decide what he wanted to eat for breakfast. He laughed as he read the names. *Cursed Omens.* Basically, hell's version of Lucky Charms, complete with evil eye, skull, pentagram, pitchfork, and ouroboros marshmallows. And *Evil-O's.* Clever. "The choice is yours, little half-breed. Nix is your mate."

She gave him a knowing stare with a small smirk before turning to Andras. "We'll get ready and leave. I don't want to waste any more time. Who's waking up Beck?"

Ash cackled and rubbed his hands together. "Leave that to me."

ASH

IT WAS SO HARD IGNORING ANDRAS. ASH WANTED nothing more than to talk to him, look at him, touch him. But every time he thought about it, he remembered the sharp sting of betrayal and the image of Andras with another man burned into his mind. The pain was too fresh, too close to the surface, for him to even think about talking to the demon. Adding that to his past trauma, Ash was a hot mess.

Still, he missed talking to him. In their short time knowing each other, Andras had become a pillar, someone he could talk to about things he never shared with anyone. Not even Nix. It had been too easy to let himself get lost in the demon. He'd fallen too hard, too fast, and now he was paying the price.

"How long will it take us to get to Selene's torture mountain?" Lainey asked from the seat next to Ash in the back of the car.

It turned out, Selene had some kind of jail-slash-torture chamber in the mountains, and that was where she was keeping Zurie. Because what woman doesn't have one of those?

"About three hours, then we'll have to ditch the car and go on foot from there," Andras said from the driver's seat.

They were driving in some kind of sedan that reminded Ash

of a Honda Accord. Ash sighed and set the papers he was holding in his lap. They were from the file he'd found in Selene's office, the ones marked *Unseelie,* but he couldn't focus enough to go through them. He'd already read the same page three times and had no idea what it said.

Lainey glanced at him with a raised brow, but he shook his head and turned his attention to the window. The landscape blurred by. They'd long since left the city behind and were now traveling through farmland. It was remarkably similar to the human realm, only slightly darker, and with stranger farm equipment. Ash briefly wondered how the crops fared so well without the full force of the sun, but he didn't really care enough to continue with that train of thought.

"So ..." Beck began from the front passenger seat. "When we ditch the car, we're just going backpacking or something?"

"Basically," Andras replied.

"With what supplies?" Beck asked.

"I loaded the trunk last night with everything we'll need."

Beck snorted. "Awfully brave of you to think we'd agree before we even discussed it."

"Wouldn't matter. I'd be making this trip anyway, with or without your help." Andras's voice was quiet and missing the thoughtfulness that made him ... well, Andras.

They traveled the rest of the way in silence, much to Ash's relief. He tried multiple times to read through the documents, but it was useless. He couldn't focus on anything but the turmoil inside him and the demon in the driver's seat. When Andras finally pulled the car to the side of the road, Ash was more than ready to get out of the confining space. It was becoming harder and harder to keep his eyes on the landscape and not on the profile of the demon he still found so attractive.

"This is where we leave the car." Andras turned off the engine and stepped outside.

In the distance, Ash could just make out the mountains on the horizon. It would be a long walk.

"There has to be an easier way to get there," Beck said as he eyed the mountains as well. "How does she get her prisoners there?"

"Through the main entrance, which is warded, guarded, and spelled." Andras popped the trunk and pulled out a bag. "We would never make it through. This is our best chance at sneaking in. It's the closest I can get us."

Beck sighed dramatically but shouldered the bag Andras handed him.

"You didn't complain this much when we trekked through Faerie," Lainey observed. She also took the bag Andras handed her.

"I'm familiar with Faerie. Who the fuck knows what we'll encounter on the way to this mountain?"

"I know what we'll encounter. We'll be fine," Andras said quietly and held out a larger bag to Ash.

Ash still refused to look into his eyes. He knew as soon as he did, he'd be lost. So he kept his gaze on the ground as he took the bag. His fingers brushed Andras's, and the demon sucked in a breath at the contact. It made Ash's chest ache.

Without waiting for anyone else, Ash turned around and made for the mountain in the distance. The craggy ground was spider-webbed with cracks that wove through stray tufts of dry grass. An occasional dead tree reached bare limbs to the sky, interrupting the never-ending barren landscape. Add some fire and lava and this would have been exactly how Ash had pictured Hel.

The only way he could track the time was by the position of the sun. The light it put off was the same from dawn to dusk, dim and orange. He estimated they'd walked for a couple of hours before Andras called for a stop to eat lunch.

"Oh thank god, I'm starving," Lainey groaned as she plopped down onto the ground, uncaring about getting dirty.

"The food is in your bag, Ash." Andras's tone was soft, yet

there was an undercurrent of pain lacing his words, a slight tremor to his voice as he said Ash's name.

Just hearing his name on Andras's tongue was torture. He grit his teeth and forced his attention to his bag as he let it drop to the ground. The food consisted of pre-packed bags of protein bars, nuts, and some kind of jerky. He wasn't about to ask what animal it came from. He passed a bag to everyone, then sat and opened his own. It was bland and not really filling, but it would do.

"I'm still hungry," Lainey said quietly as she rubbed her belly.

Andras tossed her his jerky, and she gave him a grateful smile before tearing into it. Ash had to turn away. Not only was he happy to see Lainey eating, despite the meager provision it was, he didn't want anyone to see what Andras's actions did to him. Through all of this, Andras had taken extra care with Lainey. Her bag was lighter than the others, and Ash knew it contained extra clothing the rest of them didn't have. He'd kept close to her, making sure she was safe and as comfortable as could be during this trek. It meant the world to him that Andras would take such good care of his best friend solely because he knew she was important to him.

After they'd eaten their lunch, Andras helped Lainey to her feet, and they all set off again. They'd only been walking for an hour or so before Lainey sidled up next to Ash.

"Hey," she said quietly. She peered behind them, where Beck and Andras were following along at a distance. "Do you want to talk about anything?"

"Not particularly," he said.

"Let me rephrase that." She bumped him with her shoulder. "Let's talk."

He gave a grudging nod as she beamed up at him.

Her smile quickly faded though. "It hurts, doesn't it? The betrayal?" The pain was evident in her quiet tone. "Even after you learn the reason behind it. It's hard to separate the truth from your emotions. Logically, I know none of this is Phoenix's fault, but my heart has a hard time understanding that. It just feels the pain, and it ... *sucks.*"

"I'm having a hard time separating my past from the present," Ash admitted. "I got used to the flings and playing around. I swore I would never get attached again. But this ..." He trailed off, unable to find the words he was searching for.

"It's different?"

"It's very different. I don't know how to explain what it is I feel. 'Connection' doesn't seem like a strong enough word, but 'bond' is too strong. Whatever it is, it's more than I've ever experienced, and I don't like the vulnerability. What he did reminded me of how much I could get hurt. Again."

"You were never at risk of getting hurt before because you never let yourself care." She nodded her head in understanding.

Lainey hit the nail on the head. He really wasn't angry with Andras anymore. He understood the reasons behind his actions, but the realization of what his actions had done to him? The reminder of that pain? That was absolutely terrifying.

"I've never given someone so much power over me since that first relationship." He ran his hands through his hair and sighed heavily. "I don't know how to come to terms with the fact that someone has the ability to utterly destroy me. It makes me want to shut him out and walk away, no matter how much it hurts. It's better than the risk of him hurting me even more."

Lainey hummed. "But is that really true? That you've never given someone power over you since then? What about with me? I could hurt you just as much as Andras has. Maybe in a different way, but the possibility of hurt is still there."

He'd never really thought of it that way. His relationship with Lainey was different but no less important to him. He *had* given her the power to hurt him just by letting her into his life, his heart. Why was it so different with Andras? Why could he let himself risk being hurt by his friends? Was it because of the possibility of what Andras could become? Someone more than a friend, more than family. Someone who was the other piece of his soul. His other half.

Lainey continued, "What's the saying, 'it's better to have loved and lost than to have never loved at all'? I don't know how true that is, but I can tell you, my memories of Nix are what's keeping me going. The good times we had before everything went to shit. They are the reason I keep fighting, keep pushing forward. Because I know what I had was worth it, and I'm not about to lose it. The risk I took in letting Phoenix in, it was all worth it, even with me traipsing through the demon realm currently."

Ash looked at his friend. She'd grown so much since he'd met her. She was still scrappy, still fierce, but there was something more to her now.

"I know you keep saying you can't be a queen and that you don't know what you're doing, but I have to disagree." He kicked a rock in his path, sending it skittering over the ground. "I've always believed in you, Lainey, but since you've returned to Faerie, you've been different. More mature, more queen-like."

She shrugged. "Yeah, well, I've had a lot of time to think about everything. Coming so close to losing it all—Nix, the villagers, the orphanage—it's made me realize how much I really want it and how much I really want to help bring Unseelie back to its former glory."

"I've said it before, and I'll say it again. You're going to be great, Lainey."

She said nothing, but he could have sworn he saw a small smile on her lips before she turned away.

THE NEXT NIGHT, Lainey groaned as she sat on the ground around the small fire Andras had started. "I really didn't want to spend another night out in the open," she complained.

Ash agreed. The night before, their first night spent outdoors in the demon realm, had been unsettling to say the least. Once the sun fell below the horizon, darkness encompassed everything. Without a moon to light the night sky, it was impossible to see more than two feet in front of them. The darkness in Hel was deeper, the shadows impenetrable. Even the stars were afraid to shine too brightly. They hung dimly in the vast black sky, barely shedding their light into the universe.

"We'll have one more before we reach the mountains," Andras replied quietly.

The demon had said little since they'd started this venture. Ash caught him staring often though, and a few times, he'd looked as if he were about to speak but changed his mind.

Ash sat next to Lainey in the circle of firelight and passed out the bags of food. He was really sick of protein bars and jerky.

"I'd kill for a cheeseburger right about now," Beck said as he stared at his food with longing.

"And a chocolate milkshake," Lainey added wistfully.

Ash snorted. "I'd be happy with a fucking veggie burger at this point."

Beck fake gagged. "I don't think I'm that desperate yet."

Ash glanced at Andras out of the corner of his eye and wished he hadn't. He was sitting a little way apart from the rest of them, eating his food in silence. But occasionally, he'd look longingly at the group, almost as if he wished he belonged with them. Ash wanted him to belong with them. With *him*.

He was about to open his mouth to ask Andras to sit with them when a howl cut through the night, deep and menacing, and ending on a low growl. An answering howl followed, and the hair on Ash's arms stood on end.

Andras stood immediately, his icy eyes glowing animalistically in the firelight. A faint blue light wreathed his hands and quickly climbed up his arms to his shoulders.

"What was that?" Lainey asked with a tremor in her voice.

Ash and Beck stood, and he could sense Beck gathering his magic at the same time he did. He pulled Lainey to her feet and kept a hand wrapped tightly around her upper arm.

"Hellhounds," Andras replied quietly. He spun in a slow circle, his icy eyes scanning the darkness surrounding them. "I'd hoped we would get through this without encountering them. They are one of the fiercest creatures in Hel. Pack animals, similar to wolves, only meaner. More aggressive."

"Do we run or fight?" Beck asked, his own gaze searching the darkness for any sign of the creatures.

"Don't run," Andras replied sharply. "You'll never make it if you do. Stay in the light of the fire. They'll hesitate to enter it, but it won't stop them forever."

"How do we fight them?" Lainey asked. The small hairs that had escaped her braid lifted from her face and blew in a breeze that hadn't blown all day or night.

Ash peered into the darkness as he waited for Andras's response. He couldn't see anything past the ring of light cast by the fire. It was like the world ended outside their circle of safety. Trepidation stirred inside him at the realization that they were going into this blind, literally and figuratively.

"Fire won't work against them. The only thing that kills a hellhound is iron. Your best bet is to use your magic to trap them, then a dagger in the skull to kill them. They run in the shadows, using magic to disappear from one place and then appear in another." Andras ceased turning and settled into a low stance. "And whatever you do, avoid their claws. They burn hotter and faster than fire."

Ash squinted into the distance over Andras's shoulder. Four pairs of glowing red eyes materialized, low to the ground and quickly moving closer. He pulled Lainey behind him, and she huffed before stepping back to his side. Of course she would be difficult at this moment.

"I think there are only four," Andras muttered. "We may have just gotten lucky."

Beck snorted and fell into a fighting stance. "You call that lucky? Those things are massive."

As the creatures prowled closer, Ash could make out more of

their features, and Beck wasn't wrong. They were absolutely mammoth. He could barely make out their black furry bodies in the darkness, but the occasional glint on their fur from the stars above emphasized their size and strength. Each was easily as large as a lion.

Their red eyes glowed in enormous heads, mouths were filled with flesh-shredding teeth, and smoke curled from the ground under massive paws tipped with claws as long as Ash's hand.

"Holy fuck," Lainey breathed as she shifted on her feet.

Ash handed her a dagger. "Please be careful, Lainey," he said, resigned. He would never be able to keep her from jumping into the fray.

She didn't have time to respond before the first hellhound pounced.

ASH

ONE SECOND, THE HELLHOUND WAS SEVEN FEET AWAY; the next, it was right outside the circle of light cast by the fire. He couldn't help it—he jumped. He'd never faced anything so big before, and staring this thing down was unnerving.

"Remember," Andras growled, "avoid those claws." He didn't wait for a response before launching himself at the hellhound.

He rushed to the edge of the circle of light and flung his hands forward, shards of ice shooting straight for the hound. The beast dodged the attack with preternatural speed and intelligence. Andras's momentum propelled him forward, past the light and into the darkness with the beasts.

Ash didn't hesitate. He ran past Beck, whose magic was ramping up, and crossed over the dividing line between light and dark. A hellhound appeared in front of him as soon as his feet hit the ground outside the firelight.

He directed roots to wrap around the creature, caging it and keeping it from attacking him. As he readied his dagger, the fucking thing disappeared. He jerked to a halt, arm raised, dagger poised and ready. He looked around wildly. Where had the fucker gone? A scream tore through the night, and his blood ran cold.

Spinning on his heel, he saw Lainey on the ground. Her eyes

were wide and her chest heaving. The dagger he'd given her had fallen from her fingers. Before he could get to her, she jumped up, grabbing her dagger at the same time.

"I *hate* dogs," she spat as she threw her hands forward, and the hellhound froze in place.

She was fast as she shot forward and shoved her dagger into the beast's eye before it could disappear. The creature slumped, unable to hit the ground because of her magic, but as soon as she pulled that back into herself, it collapsed in a heap.

Pride soared through Ash as he watched her take out the hellhound. "That's my girl," he yelled with a fist pump in the air.

He shot a glance at Beck. He was working on taking out his own hellhound, and a quick check on Andras showed him doing the same. Ash was closer to Beck, so he jumped into action. Between the two of them, they were able to destroy the beast in seconds. When Ash turned back to Andras, he was gone, and there was a dead hellhound on the ground.

"No!" Lainey's scream pierced the night.

Ash whipped around in time to watch Lainey fall to the ground, shoved out of the way of another hellhound by Andras. Time seemed to slow down as a massive paw swiped out and connected with Andras's chest. He fell to the ground, grunting and holding the wound. Ash's stomach dropped watching the demon hunch over in pain. Smoke curled between his fingers, and the smell of burning skin drifted through the air.

The hellhound that had clawed him was poised, ready to pounce, and Andras was not prepared to fight it. Ash watched the beast close in, heart thundering, and he knew he had to stop it. He raised a hand, and a twisting branch shot out of his palm. It lanced the hellhound in the side, and the creature stumbled. Unfortunately, that didn't stop it from advancing. The branch was a mere thorn in its side.

Ash pushed down his paralyzing fear and charged the beast. Its teeth were inches from Andras's throat when he lowered his shoulder and slammed into the creature, taking it to the ground.

He wasn't sure how he avoided the claws or teeth, but his dagger found its place: buried in the hellhound's skull.

He lay atop the beast as its heartbeat slowed, then stopped. Silence once again surrounded their camp, aside from everyone's heavy breathing. He wasn't sure he could make himself move. He was terrified of what he would find. Was Andras okay? How badly was he injured?

A small groan propelled him into action. He pushed off the dead hellhound and stood, gaze homing in on Andras. The demon was on his knees, both of his hands still pressed to his chest. His shoulders rose and fell with the small, panting breaths he was taking. Ash rushed to his side and placed a hand on his shoulder. A shock rippled through him. It was the first time he'd touched Andras in days.

"Get him into the light," Lainey said, glancing around nervously.

"Should we do something about these bodies? Will they draw the attention of other monsters?" Beck nudged the hellhound they'd killed with the toe of his boot.

Ash paid Beck's question no mind. He only had thoughts for Andras. He helped the demon stand, letting him lean on his shoulder as they limped their way into the circle of light.

"Give them ... a few ... minutes," Andras panted as he sat next to the fire "They'll burn up ... on their own."

Ash clenched his jaw. Andras was paler than usual, which was a feat in and of itself, and sweat beaded on his brow. "Lainey, get the first aid kit out of Beck's bag." Ash knelt in front of his demon, and his hands hovered in front of Andras's chest. "Is this the only injury?"

Andras nodded. "Got me with his claws." He attempted to look down at the wound but grunted as the movement pulled the skin and muscles of his chest.

"Sit still," Ash said quietly.

He pulled Andras's knife from the sheath at his waist, since Ash had left his in the hellhound's skull. As gently as he could, he used it to cut Andras's shirt away. He tried to keep his hands from shaking, but he wasn't sure he was successful. Seeing Andras hurt and in pain cut through him like a blade. And the reason he was hurt? He'd saved Lainey's life.

"Holy fucking hell," Andras groaned. "That stings."

As Ash pulled the pieces of fabric away, he cringed. "That looks like it more than stings."

Four angry red claw marks slashed across Andras's chest, from his left shoulder to his right pec. Only one slash was deep, but it was the edges, burned black and the skin crispy, that made Ash swallow. This was ripe for infection, and they had no one with them who possessed healing magic.

"That bad, huh?" Andras attempted to joke through gritted teeth.

Ash finally met the demon's stare. For the first time in days, he peered into those icy blue eyes. But instead of the attraction he was used to, he only felt fear. He swallowed again and tried to school his features. It must not have worked.

Andras grimaced. "Your face says it all."

"What's wrong with my face?" he asked, attempting to make light of the situation. He expected Andras to continue with the joking to keep his mind off of the pain.

He didn't expect the yearning in his voice when Andras quietly said, "Nothing."

Lainey handed Ash the first aid kit, and he gratefully took it, not wanting to go down that road yet. He busied himself with cleaning, stitching, and bandaging Andras's wounds. There was no way they wouldn't scar. Even with Andras's accelerated healing, this wound was too severe to heal cleanly. Not to mention, his boy scout sewing skills were less than stellar.

He helped Andras lay on the ground, wincing each time the demon grunted from the pain. "Rest," he whispered. "Let your magic do its thing. I'll keep watch."

Andras's eyes closed immediately, too exhausted to fight it.

Ash reached out and brushed a curl from Andras's forehead, yearning burning deep within him.

Ash couldn't have been more relieved to reach the base of the mountains. They hadn't encountered any more hellhounds, but he hadn't been able to let his guard down since the attack. Inside, he was a knotted ball of emotions—worry, fear, anxiety—that wouldn't stop churning in his gut. He was edgy and exhausted, and he was about to take it out on Beck.

"I'm just saying, it would be safer if you stayed down here," Beck argued. "Not to mention, this mountain looks impossible to climb. We'd just have to worry about you falling to your death."

Lainey glared at Beck, her hands on her hips. Maybe Ash wouldn't have to take it out on him. Lainey was about to do it herself.

"Excuse me?" Her brows raised to her hairline, and a dangerous light burned in her stormy blue eyes.

"If you get hurt, my dad and Phoenix will both kill me. Just do us all a favor and stay here."

Lainey's mouth worked on a response, but nothing came out. She spluttered indignantly, cheeks turning red.

"You agree. Good." Beck turned his back to her, and Ash whistled through his teeth.

"You mother fucking, murdering, cock sucking, arrogant asshole!" Lainey whipped out her arm, and a blast of air hit Beck in the back, knocking him to his knees.

Beck pushed to his feet and whirled around, brows drawn down and jaw clenched.

"What's wrong with cock sucking?" Andras mumbled quietly to himself.

Ash choked on the mouthful of water he'd just taken. His gaze shot to Andras, and he found the demon leaning against a scraggly tree, watching the exchange between Lainey and Beck with amusement. He was sexy as hell, with his hands shoved in his pockets and Lainey's wind tugging his curls this way and that around his horns.

"Never use your magic on me again, princess," Beck growled. He took one menacing step toward Lainey and froze.

Literally.

Andras had pushed off the tree, and his eyes glowed with feral intent. A sheet of ice coated the ground under Beck, freezing his feet in place.

"Do not threaten her," Andras said darkly. "You guys can argue all you want, but you will not threaten her."

Ash sighed heavily. "All of you guys, just stop." He ran a hand down his face, trying to scrub away his frustration. "I'm tired and hungry, and if I hear you guys bicker one more time, I'll gag all of you."

Andras stared at him, and his eyes darkened with desire. Ash turned away. Fuck. That was not what he'd been going for, but now he couldn't get the image out of his mind. Andras gagged and bound, completely at his mercy. He barely bit back a groan as he shoved that thought aside.

He hadn't talked to Andras since the attack two nights ago. Lainey had been caring for his wounds because Ash couldn't bring himself to get that close to him without succumbing to his desires. He'd already forgiven Andras, but he couldn't figure out what he wanted to say to him. He needed Andras to know about his past, but that kind of trust was something he didn't take lightly, and Andras's actions had really screwed with his head. And heart.

Getting his desire under control, Ash turned back to the group. "Lainey's going with us, so drop it, Beck. Do you really think she'd be any safer alone, waiting for us here?" He didn't wait for a response. Instead, he turned his attention to the mountain and changed the subject to more pressing matters. "How the fuck do we climb that?"

The rocky face of the slope looked impossible to climb. The

boulders dotting the ground were the only things marring the smooth, almost reflective surface. Ash could picture them trying to climb only to slide back to the bottom, cutting themselves on the small cracks that looked like broken glass.

"We're going to need your and Beck's magic to create some kind of foothold for us." Andras glanced between them.

"You're fucking kidding me," Beck said as he studied the mountain, his gaze traveling up, and up, and up. "Even with both of us, we'll tire out long before we reach the top."

"We don't need to reach the top. The cave is about midway up." Andras pointed to a darker patch of black halfway to the top.

That was still an enormous distance. It exhausted Ash just thinking about it. "When we reach the cave, Beck and I will be useless. We'll be too drained to be of any help. If we have to fight, it will just be you and Lainey." He didn't like that at all.

"We'll manage," Andras replied.

For once, his cocky attitude did nothing for Ash. "I'm not willing to risk Lainey's life like that."

"It's my life to risk." Lainey glared at him. "God, you're all possessive alphaholes. I can make my own decisions. If this is our best chance at saving Nix, I'm doing it. Nothing is too risky for that."

"Alphaholes?" Beck asked with confusion.

Ash sighed. "You read too many books, Lainey."

She quirked a brow at him, hands on her hips.

"Fine, you're right," he conceded. "It's your choice. But please, for my sanity, be careful."

Lainey beamed at him, and he shook his head with a rueful grin.

"All right," Andras said, approaching the base of the mountain. "This is probably the best path up. I'd imagine using vines will give us the most foot- and hand-holds."

With sigh and a mental pep talk, Ash used his magic to reach deep underground and grasp any plant life living there into a set of steps made from roots and vines. They burst through the glassy black surface, rock shattering and flying everywhere. The sound echoed around them, and he winced.

"Well, that will certainly alert everyone to our presence," Beck said.

Lainey reached out a hand, and an invisible shield fell over the makeshift steps, blocking any sound from escaping.

"That will drain you, Lainey. You can't keep that up the whole way," Ash said as he thought through various options.

She shrugged. "It actually takes very little magic. I think I'll be okay."

He studied her. She was desperate to find answers and save her mate. How much would she push herself in the process? He'd have to keep a close eye on her as they climbed.

Relenting, he said, "Fine. Let's get this over with, then."

Ash

Only two people standing next to each other could fit into the cave entrance. Ash and Beck, panting heavily, leaned against either side. A stitch had formed in his side about halfway up. Each inhale and exhale cut through his chest as if he were breathing glass, and he wouldn't have been surprised to find out his lungs were bleeding. He'd never been so drained of his magic in his life and it was absolutely crippling.

"Holy ... fuck," Beck breathed harshly. "That was ... unpleasant."

Ash couldn't even muster a grunt of agreement. Lainey's breathing was slightly elevated, but he couldn't tell if that was from using her magic or physical exertion from climbing the vine stairs up the mountain. Andras looked as if he was about to ask Ash if he was all right. Concern shone in his icy gaze, but he changed his mind and spun away.

A small ball of glowing blue light appeared over Andras's shoulder as he peered into the cave. "This should lead us to an opening in the main structure of this ... facility. From there, the cells are toward the back of the building."

"How do you know all of this?" Lainey asked cautiously as she peered over Andras's shoulder.

"Blueprints I found in the files on this place."

"Awfully convenient," she said.

Andras gave her a pleading look, begging her to trust him. Ash did. Against his better judgment, he would always trust this demon. He'd saved Lainey's life. He'd taken care of her during this trek. Ash just hoped his trust wouldn't lead him to heartbreak.

Ash pushed off the wall, taking a deep breath and fighting the cough that itched in his lungs. "Okay, let's go." His legs were embarrassingly shaky as he made his way down the tunnel with Andras at his side.

Lainey shouldered her way between them, forcing Ash to fall behind. "You shouldn't be leading this, Ash. Stay behind us."

"Not a chance, cupcake," he rasped.

"You are in no condition to be in the front." She gave him a gentle shove, and he stumbled. With one lifted brow, she made her point. "See?"

He grumbled but complied. She was right, unfortunately. He just had to trust that Andras would keep her safe.

When they came to the end of the tunnel, a small crack appeared before them. Andras let his magic wink out, and the light from the other side spilled into the opening. Andras peered through the crack and stepped inside. Ash could see him check both ways before waving for the rest of them to follow.

Ash's first impression was of a darker version of a sterile medical facility. Instead of the all-white walls, floors, and ceiling, everything was the same shiny black stone as the peak they had just climbed. This entire facility had been carved straight into the mountain. Electric lights lined the ceiling and cast a yellowish glow over the dark hallway, reminding Ash again of the similarities between Hel and the human realm. Although, instead of the lemony disinfectant smell of a hospital, this place smelled like stale air.

They made their way through the winding labyrinth, passing doors carved into the stone walls and generic-looking office paintings. It was quiet. Too quiet. They made it through the halls and stopped in front of a door labeled "authorized personnel only."

"This has been way too easy," Beck muttered, voicing Ash's concern.

"Keep your eyes open," Andras muttered as he pressed his hand to the pad next to the door. Blue light flared, and frost spread over the panel, causing it to spark and smoke.

Ash braced himself for an alarm, but none sounded. He looked around in confusion. This was all wrong. They were, for sure, being set up. He almost said they should turn around, but they'd come this far, and he knew Andras wouldn't leave without his twin. Doubt about Andras's trustworthiness briefly rose to the surface, but he quashed it, not wanting to fall down that rabbit hole again.

The heavy stone door swung open, and they slowly entered. Disgust and dread curled in his gut. Row upon row of cells greeted them. No, not cells. They were *cages*. Most were empty, but a few held what Ash assumed to be demons, or even fae. It was hard to tell. They were dressed in rags, if they were dressed at all, and so curled in on themselves, he couldn't tell their age or the state of their well-being.

"What the fuck is Selene doing here?" Ash murmured as they made their way down the middle row.

Lainey stopped in front of a cage, arms wrapped around her middle as she stared inside in horror. The occupant was female, and Ash could only tell because she didn't have any clothes on. Her body was bruised and battered, scars and burns covering her flesh. Her matted hair was a fiery red, but there were clearly no horns protruding from her head.

"Fae," Lainey breathed. She whipped around to look at Ash. "She's fae. Ash, we have to do something." Her blue eyes shone with tears.

Regret and disgust rose within him. "There's nothing we can do right now, Lainey. We need to find Zurie and get out of here.

Once we get everything settled in Faerie, we can figure out a way to save them."

Her lower lip wobbled. "What if it's too late by then?"

"Then we'll stop whatever it is Selene is doing so no more fae or demons get hurt by her again."

She looked like she was about to argue, but a soft gasp farther down the row drew their attention. Andras was on his knees in front of a cage, his magic glowing as his hands grasped the metal bars. Ash and Lainey hurried forward, watching as the ice crept up the cage, covering it completely.

Andras stood and kicked out his booted foot, connecting with the bars and sending them shattering in shards of frozen metal. Inside was a woman wearing a ragged hospital gown, stained and torn. Her skin was a ghostly shade of gray. Small white horns protruded from her short, matted black hair—a color of horn Ash hadn't seen on any of the demons he'd encountered so far.

Andras was shaking as he reached a hand out to his sister. Ash knelt next to him, lending him silent support. As soon as Andras's fingers brushed her forehead, her eyes fluttered open. Her irises were eerily white, rimmed in a blue so dark, it was almost purple.

She sucked in a shocked breath, the sound rattling in her chest. "Dras?" she croaked.

Tears spilled over Andras's eyes as he cupped her cheek. "I'm here, Zurie. We're getting you out." His voice cracked and he swallowed thickly.

Her eerie eyes slid to Ash and widened further. "You found your fox," she whispered before looking back at her brother.

Startled, Ash glanced at Andras. His jaw was clenched, but he reached out to pick up his sister. As they stood, shouting sounded from the end of the aisle.

"Uh, guys?" Beck said, worry painting his voice. "We have a problem."

Ash glanced down the aisle to find at least ten demons advancing on them.

"Fuck," Andras cursed. He looked at Ash, icy eyes pleading. "Take her. Get her out of here. Lainey and I will make sure you get out."

Ash wanted to argue. It went against every one of his instincts to leave Lainey behind. But he knew he'd be useless in a magic fight. His was still just a gently pulsing ember in his core. He was drained. He grabbed Lainey on either side of her head, pulling her in.

Resting his forehead against hers, he quickly said, "Be. Careful." He kissed the top of her head and turned back to Andras.

"Ash will make sure you're safe," he said gently to his sister.

She nodded and wrapped her arms around Ash's neck as he took her from Andras.

"Make sure she makes it out of here alive," Ash said to Andras, nodding his head in Lainey's direction. "Make sure *you* make it out of here alive."

Andras opened his mouth to reply, eyes burning with emotion, but grimaced instead and closed his mouth. Reluctantly, Ash turned his back to Andras and Lainey, and followed Beck the opposite way, in the direction they'd originally come from.

"Do you remember how to get out of here?" he asked Beck.

"I hope so," Beck replied.

Zurie shifted slightly in Ash's arms. She was so tiny—smaller than Lainey—and obviously malnourished. Her bones protruded from her skin grotesquely. But her voice, although hoarse, was strong. "I can get us out of here."

She gave them quiet directions, different from the way they came in. They passed different artwork and doorways, and each second that passed, Ash's tension grew.

"I have a bad feeling," he said as he rolled his shoulders as best he could with Zurie in his arms.

Her eyes remained closed, but she gave him a small smile. "You have good instincts. The next corner, there will be two demons."

"If Lainey doesn't make it out..." He trailed off, glaring at Zurie and leaving the threat hanging in the air.

Ash ignored Beck and gently laid Zurie on the blanket before covering her with his own. "Will they ..." He stopped himself, unable to voice the question.

"They'll be fine," she answered anyway. Her voice was barely a whisper as she drifted off to sleep once more.

He studied her for a second more before looking back to the mountain. Even with her assurance, nervous energy spurred him to his feet. His skin was too tight, like it was stretching uncomfortably over his bones. He needed to know Lainey was okay. And, deep down, he needed to know Andras was too.

He paced along the base of the mountain, gaze trained on the makeshift stairs. Thankfully, Beck kept his attention on their surroundings. Although, if they were attacked now, they'd all die. With how much magic they had used, he and Beck would need a deep restorative sleep and a hearty meal to build up their magic supplies again.

As the time wore on, only Zurie's words kept him from charging back into the mountain. At one point, a rumble like thunder shook the ground, sending rocks and pebbles skittering down the mountainside. Ash's heart stopped, and Beck had to talk him down to keep him from going into full blown-panic mode.

The sun was just disappearing below the horizon when Ash spotted movement on the mountain. His anxiety didn't ease until Lainey was in his arms and Andras had given him a nod.

"Are you okay?" he asked. "You're limping."

She snorted. "Yeah. Clumsy me. I rolled my ankle on the way down."

He pulled back to give her a once-over. Of course that would be how she injured herself.

"What happened?" Beck asked as he got a fire started.

"Well, they were pissed we broke in and stole one of their prisoners." Lainey limped toward the fire with Ash's help. "There were too many to fight, so we had to bring part of the mountain down to block them in the room with all the cages."

Ash stared at her. "You brought part of the mountain down?" How much magic had that taken? Looking at her closely, he could see the toll that had taken on her.

Strain bracketed her eyes and mouth, and her usual bright blue irises were dull. He helped her sit against a tree, and she sighed as pressure was taken off her ankle. Beck handed her water and some food, and she nodded at him gratefully.

"It was the only way," Andras said quietly.

He was sitting next to his sister, appearing as exhausted as Lainey. They'd both used a tremendous amount of power to pull that stunt. He stared at Ash, and that connection between them pulled taut. Ash couldn't look away. He read all the emotions in Andras's eyes. Yearning, pain, exhaustion, fear.

"Thank you for getting Zurie out," Andras said as he returned his attention to his sister. He brushed her matted hair from her face with such tenderness.

Ash's heart thumped in his chest. Seeing Andras care so deeply for someone, and wanting it to be him, was painful. He closed his eyes and leaned his head against the tree trunk.

"You're welcome," he whispered.

Lainey laid her head in Ash's lap, and it wasn't long before exhaustion claimed him.

ASH

"Let me check your wound," Lainey said to Andras as they made camp the next night.

The demon grunted but tugged his shirt over his head, and Ash's gaze latched on to the pale skin now on display. They needed to talk. Ash couldn't keep ignoring him; the desire he felt for Andras grew more each second they were apart. He watched Lainey peel back the bandage. The smaller claw marks were healing nicely. The deep one, though, was still angry looking. The blackened edges weren't healing together, and the surrounding area was red and puffy.

Lainey bit her bottom lip. "I'm not good with medical stuff, but this doesn't look good. Shouldn't it be healing by now?"

"All we can do is keep it covered until we get back to the city," Andras said, glancing down at his chest. "I'll see a healer, and it will be good as new."

Reluctantly, Lainey cleaned the wound with disinfectant, making Andras hiss through his teeth. Then she applied a new bandage. "There. You can put your shirt back on."

Andras glanced at Ash before doing as Lainey said, and Ash wanted to tell him to leave it off. Desire shone in Andras's eyes, no doubt matching Ash's own. The light of the fire danced off his horns, and Ash's fingers itched to wrap around them.

With the fire going, and meager meals passed out, they sat in silence as they ate. Ash noticed Lainey studying Beck with a troubled look. He nudged her shoulder and raised a brow, silently asking what was on her mind. Releasing a breath, Lainey turned to Beck.

"Why'd you do it?" she asked quietly, her question drawing everyone's attention.

Startled, Beck stared at her. "Do what?"

"Why did you so desperately want to break the curse that you would murder an innocent woman? You must have had a reason. Explain it to me. Because the longer I sit in your presence, the angrier I get."

Beck released a heavy breath and settled himself more comfortably on the ground. He didn't meet her eyes as he talked. "Growing up, I was always the kid whose dad caused the curse. I watched my mom struggle with losing her mate, dealing with the hate and judgment, and then having to help me process everything as well. It was ... awful." He scooped a handful of dirt into his palm and let it sift between his fingers. "I was bullied and treated like filth because of what my dad did. As I got older, I became more and more determined to find a way to break the curse that ruined my and my mom's lives. I thought ... I thought maybe if I broke it, people would change the way they thought about us."

"Did you ever once think about what your actions would do to the people in Emma's life? You may have been suffering, but your actions caused others to suffer as well. How is that right?"

Beck rubbed the back of his neck. "I honestly didn't think about it. I just wanted my family's pain to end. Do you know what it's like watching your mom suffer every day for something out of your control?"

Lainey huffed a laugh devoid of humor. "You don't want to talk to me about that. Because of the curse, the same curse you're talking about, my mother committed suicide when I was fifteen years old. So, yeah. I know exactly what it's like to watch someone you love suffer. That is no excuse, Beck."

"Yeah." Beck nodded his head, and in the firelight, Ash could see him swallow. "I was selfish, and I was only thinking about myself. My dad and I have talked about it, and I've realized I have a lot of things I need to work through. One of them is the fact that I killed your sister. I'm sorry, Lainey. I wish I could change what I did, but I can't. Now I'm just doing what I can to make it up to you. That's why I wanted to come. I know I said it was for Phoenix, but I don't even know him. I wanted to come to help you."

Lainey took a huge breath and let it out, shoulders slumping as she did so. "That's a start, I guess. I mean, I can't just forgive you. This is going to take me time to work through too."

Beck finally met her gaze. "That's fair."

Ash stood and pulled Lainey to her feet. "I want to talk to you," he said as he tugged her away from the others. Standing outside the circle of light from the fire, Ash tipped his head back to stare at the dim stars above. "How are you?"

"I'm fine."

He bumped her shoulder. "How are you really?"

"Not good," she replied quietly. "The bond is even thinner. There are times it seems like it's just one thread away from snapping. I'm so fucking scared, Ash." Her voice broke, and she rubbed her chest.

Ash wrapped his arms around her and held her tight, as if he could help hold the bond together. "Stay strong, Lainey. I know it's hard, but Nix needs you to keep pushing forward."

"What if I can't?" she whispered. "What if the darkness wins?"

"I won't let it. And I know how strong you are. There is nothing you can't do. And I will be here with you every step of the way. You can lean on me as much as you need to."

She didn't respond, but she nodded. Together, they stood

under the dark sky, and Ash lent her every bit of strength he possessed.

THE CAR WAS STILL where they'd left it, and Ash had never been more thankful for anything. They were a ragtag group crossing the desolate landscape. Zurie could only manage walking for ten minutes at a time, Lainey was limping, and Ash, Beck, and Andras's energy was quickly fading.

"That is the best thing I've seen in a really long time," Lainey moaned as the car came into sight.

With their bags in the trunk, and everyone piled into the sedan, the trip back was quiet. Lainey had long since passed out with her head on Ash's shoulder. Zurie was asleep in the front seat, and Beck's head was nodding as he tried to remain awake. Ash's eyelids felt like they weighed a ton, and each blink made it harder to open them again. But he forced himself to stay awake, to make sure Andras was doing okay in the driver's seat.

When they pulled into the parking lot, Ash had to practically carry Lainey inside, she was so tired. But once he set her down, she made a beeline for the shower. Zurie and Beck headed to their rooms to crash, leaving Ash and Andras alone in the living room. It had been a while since they'd been alone together, and butterflies suddenly swirled in his belly as they stood across from each other.

"Ash," Andras whispered. His icy eyes flared with emotion. When Ash didn't cut him off, he continued. "I don't know what to say. Sorry doesn't seem like enough for what I did." He swallowed and ran his hands through his hair. "I never wanted to hurt you, but when I saw him approaching, I panicked. The only thing I could think of to keep you safe was to distract him. I'm so sorry."

Rather than address what started all of this, Ash focused on something else. Something that had been bothering him since they rescued Zurie. "'You found your fox.'" His voice was rough, and he cleared his throat. "What did Zurie mean by that?"

Andras's breath hitched in his throat, and he rubbed his hand on the back of his neck. "When we were younger, Zurie used to have dreams, and they always ended up coming true. Eventually, she stopped dreaming and started to be able to *see* things without dreaming. But one dream she kept having. It was of a raven and a fox."

Ash wasn't breathing. He stared intently at Andras, a sensation growing in his chest. A warmth spreading outward, encompassing all of him.

"She said the raven was always nipping at the fox's ears, and the fox would swipe at the raven in response." A small smile curled his lips as he no doubt remembered the time he'd done just that, pecked at Ash's fox ears until he swatted at him. "She could never tell if the fox was friendly or a danger to the raven, but she warned me each time she had the dream. And she felt that it was imperative for me to find the fox." He paused and walked to the window, peering out at the landscape. "I saw your tattoo when we sparred, but I never thought anything of it. Not until you told me you could shift into a fox. I knew then that Zurie's dreams had once again come true, and somehow, instinctively, I knew you weren't a danger to me."

He turned to Ash again, his eyes open and vulnerable. Ash took one step forward before stopping himself. He wanted to go to Andras, to tell him everything was okay. But first, he had to make sure Andras understood.

"It hurt, what you did. It hurt a lot." Ash watched a shudder work through Andras, and he clenched his fists to keep himself from moving forward. "I was engaged once, when I was younger. Too young, really. When the wedding was only a few months away, I walked in on him in bed with another man. I swore to myself I'd never end up in a position where that could happen again, where I could get hurt like that again. Then seeing you ..." Ash trailed off, swallowing thickly. "It brought back all those emotions. It blurred the lines between then and now."

"Fuck," Andras said, his voice hoarse with emotion. He stepped closer but hesitated when he reached out to touch Ash. "I'm sorry. I never should have done that, and I have regretted it every second of every day. Knowing I hurt you has been a constant weight on my shoulders. I'll do anything in my power to make it up to you and earn your forgiveness, even if I don't deserve it. I'm so sorry, Ash."

Ash swallowed the lump that had formed in his throat. He reached out and wrapped one of Andras's curls around his finger. "Fuck, Andras," he whispered. "You're already forgiven."

Andras's eyes gleamed with unshed tears, and his hands shook as he brought them to either side of Ash's face. All of Ash's exhaustion evaporated as their lips met. It started gentle and sweet. But when Ash wrapped his arms around Andras and pulled him close, a moan escaped the back of his throat. It felt too good to have his demon back in his arms.

The sound snapped something in Andras. He roughly pushed Ash against the wall and slid his hands under Ash's shirt. His skin burned where Andras's fingers touched, and his desire grew, heating him from the inside out.

Andras pulled away, only to bite the side of Ash's neck. "Fuck, I missed this," Andras groaned, pressing his hips against Ash's. "I missed *you*."

"Andras, I need—"

A startled gasp pulled them apart. Zurie leaned against the wall in the hallway, cheeks burning red, and a hand over her mouth.

"Oh! Oh my. I'm so sorry! I didn't mean ... um ... carry on!" She gave them an awkward little wave, spun on her heel, and disappeared down the hall.

Andras huffed a laugh and let his head fall forward onto Ash's shoulder. "Fuck, that couldn't have been more poorly timed."

Ash groaned and his head thumped back on the wall. The

exhaustion that had been shoved to the back of his mind amid the rush of adrenaline came barreling forward again. He yawned; his jaw cracked and tears sprang to his eyes at the intensity of it.

Andras pushed away and nodded. "Yeah, we probably should get some rest. And I need to check on Zurie." Before he walked away, he looked at Ash, his expression turning serious. "I'm so sor—"

Ash cut him off with a kiss. "Don't," he said when he pulled away. "You already said it. I already forgave you. Let's just move forward."

They parted ways in the hallway, Andras heading toward Zurie's room, and Ash heading toward Lainey's. He opened the door and found her already in bed. He thought she was asleep, but she cracked one eye open and smiled.

"Did you get lucky?" she asked with a snicker.

He groaned and adjusted himself, trying to hide the evidence of his arousal. Climbing onto her bed, he flopped down, exhaling in ecstasy as the feather mattress enveloped him. "Oh, this is heaven," he murmured.

"A little bit of heaven in hell," she said as she curled next to him and laid her head on his shoulder. "Ash?" she asked after a beat of silence.

"Hmm?"

"Why didn't you tell me you're gay?"

"What?" He choked out a laugh.

"I mean, when we first met, you flirted with me, so I always just assumed you were straight."

"Lainey, you're beautiful. I'd be crazy not to flirt with you. Plus, I quickly realized how much it got under Nix's skin, and it became a fun game for me. See how far I could push him until he snapped."

"But—"

"I'm bi, Lainey. Most fae are, actually." She lifted her head from his shoulder, but he was too tired to open his eyes.

"Really?" she asked.

"Mhmm. Fae are creatures of pleasure. It doesn't matter what form that pleasure comes in. In Faerie, there is no stigma, we love who we love. End of story."

"Oh."

He could practically hear the wheels turning in her head. "Nix, on the other hand, is one hundred percent straight. That guy is too … I don't know … unable to be bi? That doesn't sound like a proper sentence, but I don't know how else to explain it." He snorted as he pictured Nix trying to flirt with a guy. It was too absurd. "And Lainey? I didn't tell you because I honestly didn't think about it. Not because I didn't want you to know or worried about what you'd think."

She snuggled closer and sighed. "Good. Because it doesn't matter to me."

He smiled. "I know."

WHEN ASH WOKE, he felt better than he had in weeks. While his magic wasn't completely full—he needed a good, solid meal for that—the deep, restorative sleep he'd just woken from had done wonders. Stretching his arms overhead, he glanced at Lainey and found her still sound asleep.

As quietly as he could, he crawled out of bed and padded barefoot to the kitchen, following the scent of fresh coffee and bacon. The sight that greeted him made him glad no one else was there.

Andras stood in front of the stove wearing nothing but low-slung, gray sweatpants. Fucking gray sweatpants. Ash crossed the kitchen and wrapped his arms around Andras's waist, dropping a kiss to his shoulder. Andras's skin against his own made his heart flutter in his chest. After so long apart, it was like the first time all over again.

"Good morning," he murmured against Andras's neck. He

craned his head over Andras's shoulder and inhaled. "Are you making me breakfast?"

Andras hummed and wiggled his ass against Ash's growing erection. "I'm making breakfast for everyone, and you would be included in that group, so … yes. I'm making breakfast for you."

He slid his hands lower over Andras's bare abdomen and slipped his fingers under the waistband of his pants. Andras sucked in a breath, and Ash nipped the lobe of his ear, growling, "Bacon is my second favorite breakfast food."

"What's the first?" There was no denying the breathlessness of his question.

Before Ash could slip his hands farther south, an irritated huff stopped him in his tracks.

"I'm sure that is some kind of health code violation."

Ash whirled around at the light and breezy voice. Zurie stood in the doorway, her black hair brushed and clean, falling to her chin in a sleek bob. She looked so much better than she had last night. Still bone thin, but the weariness was gone from her eerie white eyes.

"Zurie," Andras said, stepping around Ash. "I didn't get a chance to really introduce you guys. This is—"

"Ash, I know." She placed her hands on her hips and approached him. The top of her head barely reached his pecs. She stared up at him with her milky eyes, studying him closely. "Just know, if you hurt my brother, I will make your life a living hell."

Ash smirked. She was fiery. Opposite of Andras's quiet demeanor.

"Zurie," Andras admonished, but the smile in his voice was clear.

"What? It's true." She shrugged her shoulders and rolled her eyes at her twin.

"Is that bacon burning?" Beck appeared in the doorway to the kitchen, a frown on his face as he sniffed the air.

"Shit." Andras hurried back to the stove and lifted the skillet off of the flames. "Eh, just a little crunchy."

As they settled around the small table to eat, Lainey limped in. Her face was drawn and pale, and her eyes were glazed and filled with unshed tears. Her gaze immediately found Ash's, and dread formed in his stomach like a lead ball. He was very glad he hadn't eaten anything yet.

"Lainey? Are you okay?" He stood, rushing around the table to reach for her and grasping her shoulders tightly.

The levity in the room dropped away as everyone took in Lainey's appearance and Ash's concerned tone.

Lainey shook her head. "It's gone," she whispered hoarsely. "The bond. It's gone."

End.
For now.

Acknowledgments

As always, this book wouldn't have been possible without the support of my husband. Thank you for being my Nix, Ash, and Andras all rolled into one.

To my publisher, Midnight Tide Publishing, thank you for taking the chance on this series. I am where I am today because of this family I have found in you.

To the reader. I keep showing up everyday because of you. Thank you.

About the Author

Whitney L. Spradling is a full time Occupational Therapist and autism mama, who has had a dream to write and publish a novel since she was a little girl. She lives outside of Cincinnati with her husband, son, and two cats. When she is not writing she can be found in her craft room making custom tumblers, or curled up with a good book and a cup of coffee (or glass of wine).

Sneak Peek

Continue reading for a sneak peek of Of Embers and Rising.

Lainey

IT WAS GONE. THE CONNECTION TO NIX, THE LINE THAT ran between them, was just ... *gone*. There was nothing inside of her except roaring, vast emptiness. That place where Nix should have been was hollow, and she was so cold inside. Her whole body trembled. She was on the verge of collapsing.

Ash gaped at her. "What do you mean 'it's gone'?"

She couldn't form any more words. It was like everything inside had frozen and there was nothing left of her. She placed her hand on her chest, and her fingers contracted, digging into the flesh. If she could just reach inside herself, maybe she could find a bit of the bond still floating there. A thread, a small string. Anything to grasp and cling to.

She pushed harder, her nails scraping even through the fabric of the shirt she wore. Ash grabbed her hand and pulled it away, holding it in his.

"Lainey, talk to me. The bond is gone?"

"What does that mean?" Beck asked, coming to stand next to them.

She had no idea. It was getting harder and harder to breathe. Her lungs didn't want to expand, her ribcage was a cage, caging her lungs in, refusing to let them do their job.

"Shit, Lainey, you need to breathe." Ash grabbed her face and made her look at him. She distantly noticed his green eyes swimming with concern. The darkness was closing in though, creeping into her vision and swallowing everything in its path.

"Phoenix lives."

Those two words, spoken in a high voice that rang like bells, halted the darkness. Zurie's tiny frame came into view as she pushed Ash out of the way. Her chin-length black hair gleamed as she tilted her head to the side. Those eerie white eyes focused on Lainey, and Lainey shivered even through the haze.

"He's alive," Zurie repeated. She placed a small hand on Lainey's chest, right over the raging emptiness inside of her. "The demon has consumed the bond." Her eyes narrowed, and she peered at Lainey's chest as if she could see all the way through to where the bond was supposed to be. "This is dangerous. Very dangerous."

"Would someone please explain to me what is happening?" Ash was on the verge of hysteria, Lainey could hear it in his voice.

Zurie tugged Lainey to the kitchen table and gently pushed her into a chair. Her legs gave out, and she collapsed numbly.

"The demon in possession of Phoenix has consumed the bond," Zurie explained patiently. "He is still alive, but the demon will have even more power and control over him. The bond was the one connection Phoenix would have had to himself. His other half. It was his tether. With it gone, there will be nothing for him to use to fight against the demon."

Lainey closed her eyes tightly against the fear Zurie's words created. "We're too late," she whispered.

"Not too late," Zurie said quietly and placed a hand on Lainey's shoulder. "We can still save him. But he isn't the only one in danger now. Do you feel the darkness, Lainey? The darkness inside of you?"

The bubble of hope her first words had created popped as she asked Lainey about the darkness. The darkness that had been spreading within for a while now. She swallowed. "Yes," she whispered. "What is it?"

"I guess the best way to describe it would be an infection. That first bite the demon took out of your bond with Phoenix would have infected you with his evil. It remained limited by the bond, but with the bond gone, it now has free rein over you."

No one at the table made a sound. Ash was tense, his chest heaving. He looked like he was ready to fight someone, but there was no one here to fight.

"What's going to happen to me?" Her voice trembled, and she realized it wasn't just her voice. Her whole body shook.

Ash walked over and wrapped his arms around her, trying to hold her together. She inhaled his earthy scent, the one that usually calmed her. It did nothing to help this time.

"Eventually, it will take over your mind. Essentially turning you into a demon. And not your friendly neighborhood demon, like Dras and I. You will become a slave to the whims of the one possessing Phoenix, and I imagine those whims are not so altruistic."

All the breath left her lungs as she exhaled. Nausea churned in her gut, and she was seconds away from getting sick. The trembling increased, and Ash squeezed her tighter.

"How long?" he asked. It was the most somber she'd ever heard him, and it scared her even more.

"I don't know," Zurie answered. "I haven't seen anything to give me any indication. I would imagine the stronger she is, the longer it will take."

Strong. Could she be strong enough for this? She'd have to be.

"How do we stop it?" Beck surprised her with his question. He actually sounded like he cared.

"Killing the demon who has possession of Phoenix. Which will also save Phoenix." Zurie's white-eyed gaze traveled over the group.

Lainey sat up straighter. This was something she could focus on.

Saving Nix had always been her goal. If she killed herself in the process, at least he would live. That's what she'd been telling herself this whole time. Having something to focus on, something so important to her, made it easier to push aside the fear of what was happening to her.

"How do we save Nix?" She stared intently at Zurie.

The little demon smiled, and it was a chilling smile. She turned her gaze on her brother.

"We'll need to visit an old friend."

THAT OLD FRIEND turned out to be an angel. Literally.

Lainey watched Andras pace the length of the living room, and her leg bounced uncontrollably, shaking the vase of flowers on the coffee table.

"Another fucking realm," she grumbled. "Another trek across ... whatever the fuck separates realms." And by Andras's reaction, it wasn't a pleasant option.

"Andras?" Ash asked. He sat next to Lainey, his hand on her leg doing nothing to stop the shaking.

"Another way, Zurie. Give us another way." Andras stopped his pacing long enough to pierce his sister with his stare.

"It's the only way, Dras," Zurie said for the hundredth time.

Andras groaned and threw his hands up in the air, resuming his pacing.

"You know getting rid of a demon like the one possessing Phoenix requires celestial help." Zurie sat in an armchair, munching on something that reminded Lainey of pretzels.

"It's too fucking dangerous!" Andras shouted.

"What kind of demon is possessing Nix? And how do you know?" Ash asked, his never-ending patience wearing thin, if the strain in his voice was any indication.

Zurie smiled at him and tapped her temple. "I see things, remember?"

Her white eyes seemed to glow, and both Ash and Lainey shivered. Zurie saw their reaction and cackled.

"As for what kind of demon, there is only one capable of infecting others with that kind of darkness. Balam."

"Oh, fuck," Andras cursed.

"Who's Balam?" Beck asked. He'd been staring out the window, listening to everyone bicker but mostly keeping to himself.

"A fucking monster," Andras said and finally sat in the chair opposite his twin. He gave Ash a resigned expression. "And if he's the one who's possessed Phoenix, then celestial intervention is our only hope."

Lainey groaned and let her head fall back to rest on the couch. "So, to the angel realm we go?"

"It appears so," Andras said with a grimace.

"How do we get there? And is it safe for you?" Ash asked, leaning forward.

"Safe enough. And there is a portal, similar to the gate trees in Faerie. The only problem is, it's in the government building. We'd have to sneak in."

"Which won't be a problem with me," Zurie chimed in with a smile.

Andras shook his head. "No. You're not going."

She snorted, and even that sounded delicate coming from her. "You'll never make it without me, and you know that."

"Zurie ..."

"Andras ..."

They stared each other down. Lainey would have found it amusing if her life and Nix's hadn't been on the line. Even so, she wasn't surprised when Andras cursed and rubbed his hand down his face. Zurie was a force to be reckoned with.

"It's settled, then." Zurie stood and gave Lainey a bright smile. "We'll leave this evening. Sneaking into the government building will be easier at night. By this time tomorrow, we'll be in Celesita."

"Saints preserve us," Andras muttered.

Zurie snorted. "You do remember you're a demon, right? We don't have saints."

Ash turned to face Lainey. "You're sure about this?"

She shrugged. "It doesn't sound like we have much of a choice. And for Nix, I'd do anything." She rubbed the achingly empty spot in her chest. "I've already gone to hell for him. How bad can heaven be?"

Of Embers and Rising.
Coming July 17, 2024

More By Midnight Tide Publishing

See the full catalog at:

www.midnighttidepublishing.com

***

Through the Wicked Wood by Kristen R. Moore

"What is more fearsome? The monster that stands before you? Or the one that lives within you."

Elora Leigh is in hiding.

As an Enchantress, she has spent the last several years running not only from a king that hunts magick, but from the guilt and grief of losing her mother.

Content in her solitude, Elora's life among the trees is disrupted when she crosses paths with the most unlikely of allies.

A thief determined to keep his village afloat, Sorin will do whatever it takes to provide for his people, especially now that the lands have been hit by Mother Gaia's fury. Fishing has ceased, crops won't grow, and the animals they've relied on for food have mostly disappeared leaving him desperate for a change.

When Elora and Sorin discover a common thirst for justice in the Kingdom of Valebridge, they set out on a journey to fend for those who cannot fend for themselves and take back power from the corrupt king.

But the deeper they go through the Wicked Woods, the more Elora realizes those she thought she could trust may not be who she thinks they are.

Family secrets, ancient magick, a kindling romance, and tangles of lies begin to reveal themselves. Elora must make a decision; trust this stranger to help defeat those harnessing magick in the Kingdom, or let the demons of her past push her back into hiding and away from who she was born to be.

Through the Wicked Wood is an adult fantasy romance and intended for readers over 18 years of age. Please check content warnings as some material may be sensitive for some readers.

***

Of Love & Ruin by Lou Wilham and Christis Christie

Sometimes, love comes along at exactly the wrong time.

For over a hundred years, life for Ander and Mab has been a series of parties and adventures spanning the world over. Once the two finally decide to settle in Miami to open a nightclub, the last thing Ander expects is for the love spell he cast over a century ago to come back and bite him.

The Fates seem to have a sense of humor when they lead Maximus Schields, son of Ander's nemesis, through the club doors. Max, who is beautiful. Sweet. Kind. And part of an ongoing investigation concerning missing young women that leads the Sanctum directly to Ander.

As the tangled web of Miami's underground draws tighter, Ander will be forced to face demons from his past in order to protect what he cares